D0583291

THE
SUPERMAN
PROJECT

Also by A. E. Roman

Chinatown Angel

THE
SUPERMAN
PROJECT

A Chico Santana Mystery

A. E. ROMAN

A THOMAS DUNNE BOOK

Minotaur Books ❧ New York

A THOMAS DUNNE BOOK FOR MINOTAUR BOOKS.
An imprint of St. Martin's Publishing Group.

THE SUPERMAN PROJECT. Copyright © 2010 by A. E. Roman. All rights reserved. Printed in the United States of America. For information, address St. Martin's Press, 175 Fifth Avenue, New York, N.Y. 10010.

www.thomasdunnebooks.com
www.minotaurbooks.com

Library of Congress Cataloging-in-Publication Data

Roman, A. E. (Alex Echevarria)
   The superman project : a Chico Santana mystery / A.E. Roman. — 1st ed.
       p. cm.
   ISBN 978-0-312-37501-0
   1. Private investigators—New York (State)—New York—Fiction.
2. Hispanic Americans—Fiction.   3. Murder—Investigation—
Fiction.   4. New York (N.Y.)—Fiction.   I. Title.
   PS3618.O566S87   2010
   813'.6—dc22

                                                      2010012866

First Edition: August 2010

10 9 8 7 6 5 4 3 2 1

This book is for Armando Echevarria.

Inside of me there are two dogs.
One of the dogs is mean and evil. The other dog is good.
The mean dog fights the good dog all the time.

—Native American saying

If you meet the Buddha on the road, kill him.

—Zen saying

THE
SUPERMAN
PROJECT

ONE

This story begins like many stories do, with a knock and a murder. The alarm went off, one of the most hateful screeching sounds in the world, and I woke up in my office in a foul mood, sprawled on my tattered couch, fully dressed, still wearing my Rockports, gasping for breath, soaked with sweat, head pounding, nauseous, stabbing pains in my side. I stood up in terror. Thank God it was only a screwed-up nightmare! It was morning in sweltering New York City. My Hamlet coffee cup was empty and waiting for Bustelo. Ruben Blades was singing "Don't Double-Cross the Ones You Love" on my little black radio. I looked out the window across the Bronx, a lone roach crawling up the wall. I heard a police siren outside my window and voices in my hall.

I was alone except for my Chihuahua, Boo, big head, big ears, big eyes, nervous, trembling, planted like a Sphinx before me and looking up with visions of turkey slices dancing in his eyes. Then he started barking like mad at the knock on the office door and I prayed it wasn't the landlord looking for rent money. I went and opened it and caught my first glimpse of Pablo Sanchez.

Pablo Sanchez was short, curly-haired, worried-looking, pale, and fat—about 250 soft pounds of fat. He stood sweating and gasping in my doorway like uncooked dough wrapped in dark blue shorts and a red T-shirt with the comic-book hero Superman flying across his chest, a black bag marked *Cosmo Comics* slung across his shoulder, and orange Doritos dust on his collar. He had lively brown eyes and not one hair on his face. On the phone, he had said he was eighteen years old, but he looked about fifteen.

"This is my mother," Pablo said in a soft voice not in keeping with his size, and pointed at the short and bony woman with him. She was wearing an old "Obama for President" campaign button, smoking a cigarette, and tottering on a steel cane. She was also wearing dark blue shorts and a T-shirt. Maybe there was a mother-son sale at Macy's.

"Esther Sanchez," the old woman said, blew smoke, and put out her skeletal, pale hand. I shook it. Esther Sanchez had white hair and a strong handshake.

Pablo and his mother hobbled into my small office, and I closed the door.

My office on 149th was hot and bewitched. I leaned my head on my hands to ease my throbbing head. I had only two hours of sleep in me. My hands were shaking like Shakira at a hula-hoop convention. I needed coffee. I was up to about three pots a day. I needed those pots to wash down the ten chocolate bars I was using to keep my strength up since I stopped smoking and drinking—again.

The room was still damp and alive with the scent of coffee grounds and perfume.

The girl from the Starbucks where I had gone after bowling

at Harlem Lanes last night was gone. Great lips, thick, big hips, and big dark lovely legs, sure. But it was the way she whispered with a smoky voice, "Sir, we'll be closing in fifteen minutes," that really got me going. But she was not Ramona.

So what?

Marriage. Ten years. Divorce papers waiting to be signed, heavy on my desk beside my Zippo lighter and a postage-stamp-sized black-and-white TV. Ramona on my mind. Her second book, *The Detective*, was out. She was thriving without me. I considered stalking Ramona for about a minute, but I've never been that kind of guy. I wouldn't know what to wear.

The divorce papers sat beside an address I had for my mother (yeah, she was still alive) and a yellow Post-it reminding me to go see Willow Mankiller Johnson in Parkchester.

I thought about the sixth commandment: Thou shalt not kill, and the nightmare, a mixture of my father's murder and the murder that I had committed on the Kirk Atlas case (self-defense, Santana, not murder, self-defense). The details don't matter, the nightmares did. They came back. Again and again. Every time I closed my eyes at night or at noon. They came back. The gunshot, the ears ringing, the blood and bone, the body slack and slumping, the skull fragments in a pool of red. They came back. I wanted to forget. I couldn't. I was marked and there was nothing I could do about it and now . . .

Pablo looked around and said, "I like your office."

Esther Sanchez looked around at my unpacked cardboard boxes, dirty dishes, scattered shirts and socks, with a scowl and said, "It's not very neat or comfortable in here. Is this where you live? This is how you do business, *muchacho*?"

"Ma!"

"I make noise when I eat spaghetti, too," I said, rubbing my temples. "I'm an acquired taste."

She looked me up and down. "Are you smarter than the average private investigator, Mr. Santana?"

"No," I said. "But I'm taller."

"Cigarette?"

"No thanks. I quit."

"Too bad," she said, lighting up again and coughing a bit. "They're delicious."

"And good for you, too," I said.

Mrs. Sanchez eased out of her coughing fit.

"Jesus! Your office is hotter than a cave in Bonao. You ever hear of air-conditioning?"

I nodded. "World peace. Air conditioner. It's on my to-do list."

Apparently, Boo didn't like the looks of Pablo and Esther Sanchez, and seeing that his order of turkey slices would be late, returned to his corner, sipped some water out of his silver bowl, and went back to sleep near the open window to wait on cool August breezes that would never come.

I sat on the new swivel chair that Officer Samantha Rodriguez bought me as a gift.

"How did you know where to find me?" I asked Pablo.

Pablo looked at his mother.

"Joey," said Pablo, out of breath. "He saw your ad. Chico Santana and Company."

Yeah. I had an ad. I had a bunch of ads in the newspapers, *The Village Voice, El Diario, New York Amsterdam News*, and on Bronxnet TV, and still I was stone-cold broke.

I was over seven months into renting my own office and the 1972 Charger with the white racing stripes and the sea-blue paint job had broken down (again). It was in the shop on River Avenue for a total overhaul, body work, and a new engine. Nothing serious. It was my father's car. Vintage, my ass.

Sure, I'd had a couple of low-paying gigs since I opened the joint, mostly for kids taken in custody battles, by mothers and fathers who refused to negotiate or be reasonable, all returned safely, thank God, not a punch thrown, not a knife pulled, not a shot fired.

Sure, I got some bites on cheating husbands. But no thanks.

Hiding in closets with a digital camera ain't my idea of honest work. It's more of a hobby.

Sentimental reasons were putting me in the poorhouse.

And then it was either give up the basement apartment in Pelham Bay or give up the office on 149th Street. So, goodbye basement apartment. The office had become my home. I didn't entertain much anyway.

Troubles, I had troubles.

"Are you Dominican, Chico?" asked Esther Sanchez.

Here we go again. Why did people always wanna know my lineage, as if I were some kind of rare show dog or something, as if it made any difference to the case? "No, I'm not Dominican," I said.

"Where are your people from?" asked Mrs. Sanchez.

"Puerto Rico."

"You look more Dominican than we do," said Pablo and cocked his pale head.

"Everybody's got a cross to bear," I said.

"Dominicans and Puerto Ricans are cousins. Same face, same race," said Mrs. Sanchez.

I didn't want to tell her that her face, while Dominican, was pale as flour, and looked nothing like mine. But that would spoil the rhyme. And I'm a sucker for rhyme. "Same face, same race. Yes, ma'am."

"*Hablas español?*"

"Not really," I said. "My parents . . . I never learned."

"*Que vaina.*"

"What do you need from me?"

Mrs. Sanchez looked questioningly at Pablo.

"You got the clipping I pushed under your door yesterday?" he asked. "The one about Joey?"

"Yeah."

I picked up the newspaper clipping that Pablo Sanchez had slipped under my door the day before and glanced at it again. I read:

5

Law enforcement sources said Ms. Gabby Gupta, an artist from Williamsburg, Brooklyn, 37, went missing shortly before midnight two weeks ago. Police are still searching for her husband Joseph Valentin, 33, in connection with her disappearance. "We believe that Joseph Valentin has information as to his wife's whereabouts," said Detective Margarita De La Cruz. "Anyone with information about Ms. Gupta or Mr. Valentin is being asked to contact authorities."

The article also said that Gabby Gupta had been missing sixteen days and there was no body or blood but there were problems in the marriage—infidelity and domestic violence—and the police were called out three times before Gabby Gupta disappeared. Joseph Valentin never reported his wife missing, assuming, he said, she had packed a bag and run away, as she had threatened to do.

In the fireplace of the apartment Gabby Gupta and Joseph Valentin shared in Williamsburg, the police found unusually large piles of ashes, mementos and photographs Joseph Valentin claimed that Gabby Gupta must have burned. The police also found a one-way ticket to India, purchased by Joseph Valentin (who was reportedly thinking of divorce).

Shortly after the police swooped in again, Joseph Valentin vanished. Police found his car abandoned on Brook Avenue in the Bronx.

I threw down the clipping.

Joseph "Joey" Valentin had been a member of my childhood gang—*The Dirty Dozen*. The Dirty Dozen, Nicky, Rob, Gabriel, Leroy, Bryan, Tito, Fitzroy, Michael, Terry, Albert, Joey, and me. First that trouble with Albert on the Kirk Atlas case and now Joey Valentin was a wanted man. Joey Valentin was an artist. At least he was when I knew him as a kid. He was the best artist at St. Mary's Home for Boys. Before I met Joey, I thought Goya was just a can of beans.

Joey was tall, dark, muscular, almost pretty with dark eyes and black hair that he wore long.

He was known as "Conan" or "El Indio" on the street. His father was black as coal, mother white as milk, both Puerto Rican. Joey came out looking like an Indian. He looked like one of those Indians from the cowboy pictures or one of those Tainos that I heard and read about (at the Schomburg library with Ramona) being enslaved or wiped out and replaced with Africans by Christopher Columbus and his gang when they landed in Puerto Rico in 1493.

Some dudes who were strange to Brook Avenue and Joey let the pretty face and the long hair catch 'em off guard. They learned quick. Joey was not only muscular from lifting weights; he was the kinda kid that would iron his shoelaces and creases into his jeans and he was also the best of us at the roundhouse and the flying kick.

Joey had the largest comic-book collection at St. Mary's. Boxes in the hundreds. He had once tried to run away when he was eight, to Hollywood. Joey's father, an American Marine, got back from overseas after serving in Panama and went to prison for killing his mother's lover (who happened to be a cop) upon return. After his father went to prison, Joey had run away to live with Lou Ferrigno, who played The Incredible Hulk on TV.

He didn't make it.

He got sent to St. Mary's Home for Boys instead.

But while I was still drawing *Hong Kong Phooey*, Joey moved on to reproducing Goya (war, clowns, witches, angels) in pencil so close to the real thing that Father Gregory dubbed him The South Bronx Master. Joey never let any of that go to his head.

Joey was one of those down-to-earth, open and friendly cats, funny too, always smiling and telling jokes and calling everybody pal and sweetheart and *amor* no matter what the color, the age, or the size. He was physically big and wild and unpredictable. Generous and kind, too. He was one of those guys you couldn't help wanting to be around when you met him in the yard or the classroom or the cafeteria or the street. Always grinning, like he knew where the next good time was and how you could get the dollars to pay for it. He made money selling his drawings and designs to auto repair shops before I had ever earned my first dime and he often paid for the whole gang of us to go to the Metropolitan Museum, the Museum of Modern Art, or Ringling Brothers and Barnum & Bailey circus. He was also a good dresser, wearing immaculate clothes when I was still waiting for my Lee jeans to come back in style. Sister Irene once said that Joey Valentin was like walking sunshine. He had that kinda energy. Man, it was true. The girls loved Joey. The guys loved Joey. Grown-ups, kids, hustlers, cops, teachers, beggars, priests, pimps, social workers, prostitutes, undertakers, and dentists, everybody loved Joey.

I didn't know who that Joseph Valentin from the newspaper clipping was. That wasn't the Joey I knew. And when I first read the newspaper clipping announcing that Joey might have made his wife disappear, my heart sank a little. And all night long I had those nightmares of shootings, and I had woken up in such terror because it felt like the world had a little less sunshine in it. One less *Hola, pal,* in it, and that was too much.

I wasn't sure if Joey had disappeared his wife like the paper was saying. But you never know. People change. I've seen it. And if Joey did something to his wife, I wanted nothing to do with him.

Pablo said, "Joey told me about you, Mr. Santana. Said you were a cartoonist."

"That was a long time ago. And call me Chico."

"Joey is not guilty," said Mrs. Sanchez, sitting on my broken-down couch with great difficulty. "I don't believe it. And I've lived long enough to see many things. Mothers drown their children every day. So I know what people are capable of."

She glanced at her son.

"How did you two know Joey?" I asked.

"We worked together," Pablo said. "At the Project. There was talk that Joey was going to be made president and now he's on the run. That's not a coincidence."

"President of what?"

"TSP," said Pablo. "The Superman Project. It's a spiritual program."

"A *spiritual* program?" I repeated. "Like ghosts?"

"No," said Esther Sanchez. "Not like ghosts."

"My loyalty is to Joey," said Pablo.

"The secrets I know about TSP," said Esther Sanchez, nodding and glancing at me. "I could take that place apart brick by brick. Why would Joey hurt his wife Gabby? Why now? He had so much going."

"He didn't do anything wrong, Chico," Pablo whined. "Gabby ran off. Some members at TSP jumped to conclusions, panicked, and called the cops. Joey was suspended from TSP and when the police came for him, he bounced. Guilty. All they need is a body. That's probably what the cops are thinking. Case closed. Bullcrap! Joey is an artist."

"What do you do at this Superman Project, Pablo?" I asked.

"I'm an engineer," Pablo said and took a deep breath as if fighting for air.

"Pablo!" Mrs. Sanchez scolded.

"Well," Pablo said, and gave his mother a look. Esther Sanchez shook her gray head, sucked her teeth, and looked away at Boo, who was snoring.

"I'm in maintenance, right now," said Pablo.

"He's a janitor," said Mrs. Sanchez, turning back to us.

"I maintain the building, Ma."

"*Caramba!* Janitor is a perfectly good word," Mrs. Sanchez said. "He makes a good salary. I was head of housekeeping at the program and then personal secretary to the president Father Ravi until I retired because of my heart condition. Honest work is nothing to be ashamed of."

"I'm not ashamed, Ma."

9

Pablo turned to me. "I'm not a member of TSP. I'm a janitor but it's temporary. I write graphic novels."

"Comic books!" yelled Mrs. Sanchez.

"How long have you been in maintenance at this TSP?" I asked.

"A little over a year," said Pablo, "since I graduated high school." He went into his pocket and pulled out an asthma pump and something fell out on the dusty wood floor with a clack. I looked down and saw that it was a Superman—

"Doll!" said Mrs. Sanchez and shook her head in disgust. "His doll."

"Not doll, Ma!" Blushing red, Pablo picked up the pocket-sized Superman. "Action figure."

"They look like dolls to me," said Mrs. Sanchez. "It's those dolls that keep you single."

"Well," Pablo said, pocketing his doll. "We're not here to talk about my doll—I mean action figures. We're here to talk about helping Joey."

"Good idea," I said, searching the desk drawer for my Timex watch and spotting my father's old baseball signed by Roberto Clemente. I was seriously considering putting that baseball up for sale to some collector.

"Do either of you know where Joey is now?" I continued.

"We don't know," Pablo said. "Nobody knows. He calls on disposable phones, makes a request, and moves on."

"Can you tell me where you saw him last?"

"Joey is a wanted man," said Esther Sanchez. "Innocent. And a friend. Even if we knew where he was we wouldn't tell you. What kind of people do you think we are?"

"Sorry," I said, flipping on the coffeemaker I kept on my desk. "I haven't had my Café Bustelo yet."

"There are those of us," Pablo said and glanced at his mother, "who understand that one of the greatest values is the love of a friend. When someone tries to destroy a friend and we're forced to say goodbye to what was good and strong, we have to do something. After almost a year of solid friendship, I know this, Joey did not do anything to his wife Gabby."

"Right," I said. "I'm sorry, folks. Don't mean to be rude. But we need to get to the point here. How do you think I can—"

Before I could finish, Mrs. Sanchez grabbed her cane, stood up with great difficulty, and said, "You, Chico Santana, will help Joey and find his wife Gabby Gupta. I don't agree with my son that Gabby just ran away. I think there is a conspiracy against Joey. I believe people are capable of almost any kind of evil. We need you to find Gabby for Joey so we can all get on with our lives."

"Why do you think this is happening to Joey? If what you say is true and his wife didn't just run off and he's innocent of any wrongdoing?"

"I think they just want him gone, *hijo*," said Esther Sanchez.

"Who?" I asked.

"We don't know," said Pablo. "But if it takes weeks, months, years, with or without you, Chico, I'm going to find Gabby Gupta."

"Before we agree to anything," I said, "do you want to know how much I charge?"

"Charge?" Mrs. Sanchez laughed.

"Chico," said Pablo, as if he weren't just some snot-nosed eighteen-year-old kid, "there comes a day when every man finds what he is looking for. Lucky is the man who has eyes to see it. This may be your day."

"I'm gonna be late for church. Pablo!" With that, Mrs. Sanchez signaled Pablo to follow and left my office.

Pablo Sanchez stepped to the door. "Sorry about that. I have to humor her. Church is very important to her now. She's not so old but she's sick. She almost died of a heart attack last year, that's why she's so skinny now. She—"

"Pablo!" yelled a voice from the hall.

Pablo watched the door.

"No problem, man. I understand," I said.

"Thank you."

Pablo went into the black bag marked *Cosmo Comics* slung across his shoulder and pulled out a wedding photo. In the photo, Joey was still tall, muscular, dark, cheerful, with long black glossy hair. He wore white linen pants and a white jacket with a red turban. His cheerful bride Gabby was also wearing white linen. She was tall, pretty and shapely, an Indian girl (not native American but Indian-Indian, Asian Indian). They were smiling on the deck of the Staten Island Ferry.

"Where'd you get this?" I asked.

"Joey gave it to me."

"So he didn't just call you," I said. "You met up with him."

Pablo Sanchez was lying to me to protect the whereabouts of Joey Valentin.

"Pablo!" the voice yelled again.

"Sorry," Pablo said to me and turned to the door again. "Coming, Ma! Excuse me, Chico. I'll tell you more tomorrow."

"Tomorrow?" I said. "We should talk about my fee first."

"Well," Pablo said, "I thought maybe, since you knew Joey, grew up with Joey, maybe you believed in something bigger than yourself."

"Sure," I said. "I believe in one day being able to afford cable television. Other than that, the list is pretty slim. I can't afford to help you pro bono. I need money, or I'm outta business."

Pablo spotted my father's old baseball.

"That's signed by New York Yankee Roberto Clemente," I said. He picked it up.

"Roberto Clemente wasn't a Yankee," he said. "He was a Pittsburgh Pirate."

Roberto Clemente wasn't a Yankee?

"Pablo!"

"I gotta go," Pablo said, almost terrified. He put down the baseball and handed me a big fat book and said, "See you tomorrow! And don't worry about money, Chico. I'll get you something better than money," and rushed out of my office.

Better than money?

Pablo reminded me of some fairy-tale innocent trapped in a dungeon, awaiting rescue. A guy who wouldn't steal a loaf of bread if he was starving. I looked at the big fat jacket blurb on the book *Wrestling with The Superman* by Father Ravi.

Shatter your Idols
You have the POWER to perfect yourself
Male or Female
You are THE SUPERMAN

Pablo Sanchez really was something. Not a sucker, not exactly. He was just one of those guys who felt responsible for everyone and everything. Not me, boy, not anymore, I thought as I grabbed Boo, a plastic bag, and his leash and turned off the lights, locked my office door, and headed outside for a walk and then a class trip to see Willow Mankiller Johnson in Parkchester about a favor.

But if I was so much smoother than Pablo Sanchez, why was I popping four aspirin and taking that autographed Yankee baseball and that stupid book with me?

Oh, yeah, I thought, jogging behind Boo down the stairs, half asleep, head still pounding, going to buy a hot dog with mustard, ketchup, and sauerkraut at the local rat dog sellers, that strange rip in my lower gut, feeling heat-sick. No matter what, this day was gonna be special. If I was wise, like Boo earlier, I woulda just gone back to sleep.

Why am I not wise?

TWO

It was 1:00 P.M. in Parkchester and the air conditioner was on full blast. I had jumped on the Downtown 2 train on 149th to 125th Street where I jumped on the Uptown 5 train until we came up out of the underground tunnel at Whitlock, rising up across the familiar Bronx River and the sprawling tenements of the Bronx to the Parkchester stop.

As soon as I got to the apartment, Willow turned up the AC, handed me an ice-cold Malta—my weakness—one of many—hinted at what she wanted, and left the room. I slammed back my Malta, which Nicky called Porto Reecan soda and Officer Samantha Rodriguez compared, not without disgust, to drinking milk mixed with Pepsi.

To each his own.

The two-hour snooze I got last night, the coffee, and the Malta failed me. I fell asleep and the nightmare came back and when I awoke I knew the answer to Willow's question.

I can't do it. I can't do it and I won't. Not for Nicky Brown, who called from Atlanta and suggested that Willow give me a ring. Thanks, Nicky. Not for Willow Johnson, who I hardly knew except for one case.

I admit it, Willow's new place was real nice. Willow's grandfather, Kenneth Johnson, lived seventy-five years, working as a bus driver in the Bronx for twenty of those years, burying his wife a year before his seventy-fourth and then dropping suddenly, leaving his kin his only worldly possession—a co-op apartment in Parkchester.

The living room was filled with windows and sunlight, freshly painted walls and freshly polished floors, and Gaudi prints. There was a giant TV. No trash, no dirty dishes, no mice, no cockroaches. Not bad. A kitchen table in the corner held books and dictionaries for Italian, French, and Spanish. I looked up and saw these things hanging on the walls, like giant spiderwebs attached to long white feathers—*dreamcatchers*.

I jumped up, walked to the window, and looked out at Parkchester trees beaten down by the hot summer sun. I heard voices coming from the next room. They grew louder. Three voices laughing, when there should only have been two. Willow and her niece, Max. The third voice? I wasn't sure. Then I heard, "Aye, *nena!*" and laughter and then I smelled something cooking.

I sniffed at the air.

Lotions and potions.

Perfumes and bath powders.

Mascara?

Sofrito!

And I knew.

Mimi!

Mimi, fifty-three years young, and my father had grown up together dirt poor, without shoes or indoor plumbing or much to eat, in the small town of Carolina, Puerto Rico. Mimi's husband Esteban, my father's best friend and motorcycling buddy, grew up with them and became a civil rights lawyer in the Bronx.

When my father was murdered, Esteban searched for his killer for over two years. He couldn't sleep, took to drinking and walking after midnight all over New York, from the Bronx to Brooklyn—returning days later hurt, tired, and filthy. Finally, Esteban never came back. He had called Mimi, who worked to put him through law school, "my little *jibara*," my little peasant, and he loved her and kissed her as much as my own father loved and kissed my mother.

Mimi and I have some kind of unspoken agreement, a contract. She never talks about my mother and father and I never talk about her Esteban.

And when money was tight all over and Mimi's investment company lost her entire life's savings in bad real estate investments and she needed cash to keep her apartment and her Cuchifrito restaurant on Brook Avenue open, I gave. I gave everything I had saved away from the Kirk Atlas case, and the new stuff hadn't exactly been bouncing in.

And now, what was Mimi doing there? Were she and Willow in cahoots? And what the hell is cahoot? And how long was I asleep? It made no never mind.

"I won't," I muttered. Why does it always have to be me? I gotta get outta here. Escape, Chico! Make haste, son, escape!

I turned and headed for the front door. I was running back to 149th Street. Move now, explain later, amigo.

Someone entered the room. I turned and saw a kid standing before the swinging kitchen door, looking up at me all innocent and curious. She was eight years old and small for her age, a chubby black girl in pigtails, thick lips and glasses with silly black frames, wearing orange shorts and a striped shirt. She was also wearing a red bath towel tied around her neck like a cape—probably because she had overheard me mention The Superman Project to Willow. She called herself Super Max and was also holding a cardboard box. Willow had introduced her as her niece, Max, short for Maxine, which she hated being called. Maxine, she said, was a sissy's name.

"Mornin', sir," said Max, and beamed a charmer's smile at me.

Sir? Did this kid just call me sir?

"You fell asleep, sir."

"Very perceptive," I said. "You're a regular Sherlock Holmes. What's in the box?"

"Gizmo. Wanna see?"

"Sure."

Max approached with her box. Inside was a black kitten, minus a foot.

"What happened to its foot?"

"I saw these kids back home in Detroit," Max said. "Carrying a box, yelling, 'Cat for sale! Cat for sale!' I looked into the box and saw these big blue eyes lookin' up at me. He looked as if he was smiling at me. The bad boys told me how the mother cat had chewed off his leg. They were going to take him to the ASPCA and have him put to sleep if they couldn't sell him. I paid them two dollars, all my money in the world, and brought him home."

I looked in the box again. Gizmo was full of life—scratching, swiping, jumping, meowing.

"He's a good cat," Max said. "He's not any trouble. He doesn't miss his foot. I think it bothers other people more than it bothers him. He's a happy kitty. They were gonna put him to sleep, just because he wasn't like the other cats. Can you imagine that, sir? That's not right, don't you think?"

"Not at all," I said. "And stop calling me sir. At ease, soldier."

Max gave me a confused look, said "Huh?" and cracked up laughing for no apparent reason. Kids can be goofy like that.

The kitchen door swung open again and Willow Mankiller Johnson came in, walking tall with that reddish brown skin of hers and those impossibly dark Cherokee eyes and that long, thick black braid perched on her shoulder like a snake.

"*Mire, mire,* Yankee!" Willow said, holding a second bottle of ice-cold Malta. "Look who's awake!"

She was like a giant black swan. An Indian arrowhead hung from a black leather cord around her long neck. She wore cut-off blue jeans, daisy dukes and a peasant blouse, a tattoo on her upper arm, a dreamcatcher. She had bare feet and legs that went on for miles.

Someone cleared her throat.

I turned my head and saw that Max was watching me stare at Willow's legs, and she smiled as though she had caught me with a blackbird in my mouth.

"What're you lookin' at?" I said.

"Nothin'," Max said and smiled even wider.

Kids!

"What time is it?" I asked, taking the second Malta from Willow, looking around uneasily.

"Max," Willow said, ignoring my question. "Bring Mimi's flan for Uncle Chico."

Uncle Chico? *Que hablas,* Willis? I ain't nobody's Uncle Chico.

"Okay!" Max yelled gleefully and ran from the room.

"Mimi's here," said Willow.

"I heard," I said. "What's she doing in the kitchen?"

"Making *pasteles.*"

I could always count on Mimi. She had gotten a bit nutty when I opened my office on 149th Street. She started to drop by, unannounced, to clean it, no matter how much I objected. One time she faked an attack and actually threw herself down on the floor, clutching her breast, so that she could look under my desk and see if there were any dust balls. "All better," she said as I helped her up.

Thanks for stopping by, Mimi. Really. Now drop the Pine-Sol and step away from the file cabinet.

God bless her.

Pasteles. Plantains, basil, sofrito. I loved *pasteles* and Mimi knew it. Malta, flan, *pasteles.* Willow was playing hardball and Mimi was in on it! They were even letting me eat dessert before the main course to get what they wanted! Brother, that's just evil!

It's a conspiracy. Get out, Chico! Now!

"What do you think of Max, so far?" Willow asked.

"Seems like a nice kid," I said. "Why'd your sister send her to you?"

"It was me or a foster home."

"Where's her father?"

"Dead. He was shot in the fine city of Detroit while going to work. Nobody caught for it."

"That's tough," I said. "That's too bad."

"Max really likes you."

"I have a magnetic personality."

"You have a way with kids. You'd make a great father, Chico. I can tell."

"Well," I said, checking my Timex, "on that note, I better get going."

"Max is staying with me awhile."

"I know, you told me."

"As soon as my sister sorts through the funeral mess and she finds a job, she'll be back in Detroit. It's only for the summer."

"You told me."

"Max is really sad and confused about her father."

I nodded. "Tough break."

"My sister just wants me to look after her until things cool off and she's back on her feet."

"Good luck with that," I said, standing up and going for the front door.

But Max returned with a silver spoon and two flowery plates piled with two hunks of Mimi's flan. Max announced that there was only enough extra cinnamon for one serving. I looked down at my plate; my flan was the only one spattered with fresh brown cinnamon.

Charmer.

"You slept more than three hours," said Max, handing me my plate.

"And why not?" Willow said. "Sleep is good."

"You hardly moved or anything, sir."

"Sounds like me."

"We thought you was dead," Max said.

"*Were* dead," Willow corrected.

"We thought you *were* dead," Max repeated. "But Auntie said dead men don't snore like that. You snore like an animal!"

"Max!" Willow snapped.

"Sorry, sir."

"Stop calling me sir, Max. The name is Chico."

"Sorry, Uncle Chico."

"Turn on the TV, Max. So Uncle Chico can relax."

Before I could protest, Max grabbed the remote and flicked on the giant TV. Willow grabbed my arm in what felt like an attempt to break it. The girl was strong. Cherokee strong. She grabbed my plate of flan and dragged me down on the sofa beside her. As clumsy as a mother bear, Willow put her long right arm around Max's shoulder and her left arm around me.

Soon, Mimi ran in—snub nose, wide mouth, freckled face, thick black eyelashes, belly, breasts, gap-toothed smile, makeup, eyeliner, lipstick, rouge, powder, perfume, a plump jungle of red hair and cleavage in a bright green blouse and blue jeans that looked as difficult to get into as giving insulin shots to an alley cat—and yelled, "*Bueno!* Like a little *familia!*" before racing back into the kitchen.

Family. I had enough family trouble without Willow and Max. Back at the office was the Bronx River address that I had gotten for my own mother. I was finally going to see my mother again. I wouldn't know what to say first, where to start. She would not cry. She would be calm. I would ask if I had any sisters or brothers. I would tell her about the years that passed, St. Mary's, Nicky, John Jay, St. James and Company, my new business. I would listen and she would listen. We would understand. She would ask to see me again and we would meet regularly and continue our talks. I would sleep better. At least, that's what Nicky Brown kept telling me and nagging about whenever he called from Atlanta: "When are you gonna go see your mama?"

Mind your own business, Nicky.

I scooped up a spoonful of flan and shoved it in my mouth, wondered how to get out of my current mess. I swallowed a spoonful greedily, then a second, then a third. After a dozen spoonfuls, I felt sleepy again and sank back on the sofa.

"Watch this!" Max yelled. On Willow's giant television was an episode of *Smallville*.

Apparently, Max got the series on DVD from her dad last Christmas.

Small world.

"I love him!" Max said, watching the young, white, handsome, indestructible Clark Kent. First Pablo, now this. I couldn't seem to escape Superman no matter where I turned today. But what did it mean? What does it mean, Chico? Any of it?

"He's so brave," Max said. "It's so cool. I wish I was a boy."

"Don't say that," Willow said, "Being a girl can be an adventure, too."

"Sure," said Max, screwing up her face. "Like how?"

Willow looked at me and smiled all sweet. She took my hand gently and gave me that look and I jumped off the sofa like it was on fire and said, "I really gotta go."

"Won't you have some of Mimi's *pasteles* before you go?"

"No."

"Max, go get Uncle Chico some more flan."

Max beamed like the idea of getting me some more flan was equivalent to a trip to Six Flags, and ran out of the room again.

Willow stood up and shook her head.

"What're you doing with your life, Chico?"

"Let's see. It's August, hot, humid, and muggy—my favorite. The money from my last case is spent, and the economy is in the crapper and so I'm living in my office. I keep a sock with all

21

the pennies I have left in the world under my desk and I think about selling my bowling shoes or my father's baseball signed by Roberto Clemente. I live in my office. I shower at a friend's. During the day I create sculpture out of hot dog buns. At night, I get wasted on coffee and chocolate bars and play the harmonica in a hip-hop-salsa band. Same ol', same ol'."

"Sounds like fun."

"I am emotionally and financially unstable. Yeah, *fun* is the word I would use."

"Any lady in your life?"

"If there is," I said, "she's not talkin'."

"Look," Willow said, "I have to go to Spain."

"I've seen pictures. It looks like a nice town. I'm sure that Max will love Madrid."

"I can't take Max. I'm going to be spending most of my time in offices, in the middle of chaos."

"You want the name of a good babysitter?"

"No."

"Jesus Christ, I can't stay here, Willow. I can't do it. I don't like kids."

"Why not?"

"Because I don't like people, and kids are nothing but people waiting to happen."

"Shut up. C'mon, Chico. This apartment has three large bedrooms and a big remodeled bathroom with a walk-in tub. You could take bubble baths."

"If there's anything I dislike more than kids, it's walk-in tubs and bubble baths. I wish I could help you."

"Chico. C'mon. You're the only person I know in New York who can do this."

I hardly knew Willow. Yeah, she had risked her life on the Kirk Atlas case. Yeah, she had almost gotten killed while helping me but we're talking about babysitting—a child!

Willow stepped close.

"What?"

"Please."

"I can't."

Willow frowned and placed her soft hand on my chest. "Pretty please."

"Pretty no," I said.

"C'mon, you're not leaving town anytime soon. Mimi tells me you never leave New York. Stay here," she whispered. "You need that girl as much as she needs you right now."

"Says who?"

"Nicky."

"He's managing my life from Atlanta now?"

Willow pushed me away and made a fist. "I oughta bop you on the head!"

I thought about a book in my office that sat among the shaving cream, the razors and aftershave, beside the ten cans of tuna, two loaves of bread, one jar of jelly, two jars of peanut butter, two music tapes—one CD of Tchaikovsky's Four Seasons, another by jazz musician Ornette Coleman—and finally my *Don Quixote* (a gift from Ramona), turned to page 220.

What can ever cure my sadness?

Maybe I should get to Atlanta. Who knows what I could find? The ladies, the heat, lounging in a hammock in somebody's backyard as the sun goes down over Georgia. And New Orleans is coming back! That's what Nicky said. He's got people there. Mardi Gras! The colorful, ceremonial stuff! The crowds, the music! Jazz! Nicky went to a fortune-teller in New Orleans who told him to tell me, "Expect glorious things."

I didn't know what that meant. But I knew for sure, Max couldn't be it.

"Listen," Willow said forcefully. "This is the deal. I go to Spain for work. You stay here with Max. I'm going to be making a lot of money on this job. You will be paid."

My eyes popped. The magic word. Finally. "Paid?"

"Yes," Willow said. "Of course. You don't think I'd want you to do it for free. Lincoln died for a reason. I'll pay you whatever you charge for taking a case. The Maxine Johnson case."

"But I've never done any babysitting," I said. "What if I'm no good? No. I'm sorry. I can't. A kid. It's too much."

Willow looked at me, smiling and easy; she leaned in and kissed me. Willow Mankiller Johnson kissed me.

"I've been wanting to do that for a long time," she said.

"Oooh!" I heard someone yell. I turned and saw Max, holding my replenished plate of flan.

"You're getting your groove on!" Max yelled.

"Max!" Willow said, and laughed. "Nobody is getting any groove on. Where did you hear that?"

"School."

"Well," Willow said, "no more school for you."

"For real?" Max said, a bright light in her eyes.

"No," Willow said, "not *for real*. And nobody is getting their groove on. That's not a polite thing to say."

"Sorry." Max turned to me. "Sorry, Uncle Chico. Wanna see my room?"

"Chico isn't staying, Max."

"Why not?" Max said, looking at me all sad, like a Jewish kid on Christmas Day. "I got books and I'll let you play with Gizmo. You can hold him all you want."

"Sounds tempting," I said. "But I got work I gotta do, Max. I wish I could."

"Okay," Max said, handing Willow the flowery plate and putting out her chubby little hand.

I took it. It was small and brown and soft.

"Well," Max said, all eight years of her, "it's always pleasant to meet Willow's friends."

"Ditto."

I nodded at Willow and turned to go out the door again. But a sweet smell floated into the room and ruined everything.

Mimi holding a plate of *pasteles!*

24

"Why are you doing this to me, Mimi?"

"Nicky called me," said Mimi. "I am bored. It's hot. I got Yolanda watching the Cuchifrito and I can watch Max part-time babysitter whenever you can't. I'll spend more time with my Chico and talk and laugh and watch the movies and cook. It's good for me, Chico."

"Yeah. She cooks good," Max said, rubbing her belly.

"I will do all the cooking for you and Max," said Mimi, "while Willow is away. I can watch Max *and* Boo while you are out. So even with your case, you don't have to worry. You just have to get back here before sunrise, and I will take a cab ride home."

Willow added, "I would pay for that, too."

Now, as a rule, I don't like children. Even as a child, I didn't take to them. I found most kids mean and selfish and cruel. One of the rules of being a member of my childhood gang The Dirty Dozen was that you didn't act like a kid.

But there I was, trapped, with Mimi holding out her delicious *pasteles* and Max smiling expectantly. Her ridiculous black-framed glasses made her look like a miniature TV reporter from the sixties. We would have to do something about the glasses.

I looked into Max's big, anxious eyes and I thought about her dead old man and my dead old man and I couldn't help it—my heart broke. I took one more look around Willow's large co-op apartment. It wouldn't be so bad. I mean, I could have tried to run away, but Willow would have prevented me—by force. I was staying. But don't get me wrong. I wasn't doing it just for the kid. I wasn't doing it for Willow either. Or even for the money. No. I was doing it for the *pasteles*.

Mimi's *pasteles*.

Will work for food.

"Okay," I said, defeated, keeping one eye on Mimi's *pasteles*. "Here's the deal. I'm gonna stay here with Max. When Willow gets back, Max can stay with her. When Max's mother gets stable,

Max can go home to Detroit and by that time and Boo and I can go back to the luxurious comforts of my tiny office."

Max looked at me with worried eyes and said, "I don't wanna go home."

"Aw. Why not, Max?" said Willow.

"You like Chico that much already?" said Mimi.

Max shook her head and said, "They kill people there."

THREE

New York City was on fire, with temperatures in the nineties. I was sweating bullets like it was Christmas in the Congo. Thank God that global warming didn't really exist, or I'd have been worried. Esther Sanchez kept talking and poking me in the back with her steel cane as we drove all the way from Parkchester in the Bronx (where they picked me up) to her bingo joint in Washington Heights in Pablo's rusty white Ford Fiesta.

Pablo's driving and glancing at his mother in the backseat at the same time didn't make me nervous; a lot of the folks I grew up with did the same thing and somehow they never crashed. Well, hardly never.

On second thought.

"Keep your eyes on the road," I said. Pablo turned to look at me.

"Seat belt," I said.

Pablo fastened his seat belt. Mrs. Esther Sanchez tapped me approvingly on the back with her cane.

"When are you going to get married, Pablo?"

"Ma!"

"If you had a wife—"

"Ma, please."

"Children. Responsibility."

"Please, Ma!"

"Don't make the same mistakes I made."

"Shhh . . ."

I looked out the cracked car window, as the tiny white car bucked and bounced with every ding and dent in the street, and the probability of getting any real money out of Pablo Sanchez sped away faster than the George Washington Bridge.

So why did I go along with Pablo Sanchez and his mother? Well, sitting in Parkchester with Max, her one-legged cat Gizmo, and my cranky Chihuahua Boo, broke with no future money and no other case in sight, after a humid night of trying to sleep alone in a strange bed, and nothing but *Frankenstein* on TV until 5:00 A.M., was beginning to feel suspiciously like tragedy. So I had nothing to lose with Pablo but a morning with an eight-year-old in a red-towel cape doing magic tricks with sock puppets.

As we drove along Washington Heights, I remembered that I had left my Timex behind on Willow's round brown coffee table. Last night, I had taken off my watch, kissed Willow, and put on the radio, turned to the station where they played mostly Motown and oldies.

I know you wanna leave me, but I refuse to let you go . . .

Then Max came in and insisted that we watch *Chitty Chitty Bang Bang* and nothing happened with Willow and me and Willow was off to Spain by morning and she dropped Max off with Mimi on Brook Avenue and I was driving with a potential client who didn't get that I'm practically homeless and living in my dingy office and not at the location in Parkchester where he picked me up.

Just before Esther Sanchez closed the car door and went down into the Washington Heights Arcade Bingo Hall (a former bowling alley) on 181st Street and St. Nicholas Avenue, she said, "You watch out for Pablo, Chico. Pablo is very young at heart. He loves dogs and children. He's a hard worker. He deserves a real friend, *hijo*."

She called me *son* and she handed me two Tupperware bowls full of Dominican food (*sancocho* stew, mashed plantains, yucca, and *abichuelas con dulce* and rice) and I wish I could say that I didn't feel anything because I'm nobody's sucker. But I did.

Will work for food.

"I'll see what I can do," I said, holding that stupid Tupperware.

We dropped Mrs. Sanchez off, after sloppy kisses, a *"Dios te bendiga,"* and a "God bless you, *hijo*." We drove downtown, parked on a side street near Baruch College, and walked to a comic-book shop on 23rd Street above a nail salon in a redbrick building where Pablo said he was going to show me just how well Joey was going to take care of me.

Cosmo Comics.

I followed Pablo down a short blue hall and up a long flight of stairs, to the second floor.

"If everybody, including the police, says that Joey had something to do with his wife disappearing," I said, "what makes you think *you* can prove them wrong?"

"We," Pablo said, looking back at me. "We."

"We'll talk about that."

"No. You gotta help me, Chico. You seem like a good guy and an enthusiastic creative mind, and I think we could be comic-book partners, too, if you still like to draw. At the *momento* I realize this all has a very crazy feel to it—but I just want to say I do hope to become friends in addition to partners on this case."

29

"Partners? I got bills, Pablo. Can you pay?"

"We're gonna make a deal," said Pablo.

"Make a deal. Name that tune. Five hundred for things that don't pay."

Pablo took out a ring full of keys and unlocked the glass door.

"I thought you were a janitor?"

"I was," Pablo said. "TSP fired me. Don't tell my mother. She doesn't know. I worked here in high school. They gave me my old job back."

"Why did The Superman Project fire you?"

"It was over Joey. They said I was too close to Joey and a loose thread."

I admit it: I have a soft spot in my dusty heart for loose threads. But soft spots don't pay the bills. I needed to see some dead green presidents and soon, or it was back to the Bronx for Chico Santana, Joey Valentin or no Joey Valentin.

"You like comic books, right?" he said. "You can draw, right?"

"Long time ago," I said. I massaged my aching head. "You got any aspirin?"

Pablo opened up, hit the lights, which blazed white over a large green room. The walls popped with colorful posters of Batman and Spider-Man and T-shirts, shelves, racks, and glass counters filled with tons and tons of graphic novels and DVDs and action figures and mostly old or shiny brand-new comic books.

We walked past the stacks and went into a small back office, also green, with MANAGER on the door. The dusty room smelled of sweat and freshly printed paper. On a desk in the center of the room was an ancient IBM computer that only the Flint-stones could think of as technology without laughing. The room was filled with even more comic books tied and stacked along the walls. A red bucket beside the desk was filled with coins—pennies, nickels, dimes.

"My savings account." Pablo chuckled as he went into the

first aid box and handed me a couple of aspirin and a can of warm soda. Then he went into his Cosmo Comics bag and proudly handed me a thick stack of pages: THE ADVENTURES of CAPTAIN BRAVO and THE CUCHIFRITO KID.

There were two cartoon characters on the cover page: one short and fat superhero and one tall and skinny superhero. The tall thin character wore a Dominican flag mask and matching flag cape and the short fat character wore a Puerto Rican flag mask and matching cape.

"*Captain Bravo*," said Pablo, pointing a fat Dominican finger. "The thin Dominican superhero has to be beaten nearly to death before his super-strength kicks in. The fat Puerto Rican sidekick, *The Cuchifrito Kid*, can use anything oil-based as a weapon, from hot cooking grease to hair gel. They're Latino superheroes."

"Uh-huh," I said, glancing at Pablo.

"I invented them with my ex-best friend Elvis in high school. That didn't work out. But Joey was going to draw them. We were going to work together. I would write the stories and Joey would draw. I even got a nice letter back from DC."

"DC Comics?" I said. "That's big."

"I have great characters," Pablo said proudly, "and I'm determined my comic's going to be published."

"It's a little long, no?"

"What do you mean?"

"It could maybe use some cutting."

"No. Never. No editing." Pablo shook his head. "No selling out. No butcher called an editor taking the heart out of it. I've been working on that for ten years. It's not even finished yet. I don't sleep, I work. I'm here writing until six in the morning sometimes. Nobody bothers me here at night and when I work it has to be in a distraction-free environment and that's not always possible with my mother around. I'm creating something really special, Chico. Something that's basically not every other comic on the shelf. I wanna deliver something that'll knock your socks off and teach you a little something about life. I don't just need somebody to draw, there has to be character design. I have to go through sketches and sketches before I can really find what I'm looking for. I got everything in there—philosophy, psychology, sociology, Spanish history, African history, Dominican history, Haitian history, American history."

"Any superheroes?"

"Of course," Pablo said. "Joey was going to pencil, ink, and color it for me. It's gonna be big. The *Moby Dick* of comic books."

"So Joey was your partner?"

"He was my friend," Pablo said. "When I heard about him and Gabby, I swear, I felt like my heart was cut in two."

Funny. Once upon a time me and the Joey I knew also planned on breaking into the comic-book business. The other kids at St. Mary's would write the stories, and me and Joey would draw and ink and color them. We put together five issues of *St. Mary and The Dirty Dozen*, before Joey disappeared one Easter after a trip to Coney Island (which he treated everybody to with proceeds from the design money he got from Bomba's Auto-Body Shop) with a duffel bag, headed, he said, for Tahiti. But that was a long time ago. Now, I'm a private investigator and Joey is an accused something or other, and what's worse, he's too missing to argue otherwise.

Pablo sighed. He sat on the rickety chair behind the desk and pressed PLAY on an ancient answering machine.

Message #1: "Pablo. It's Elvis again. Call me."

Message #2: "Pablo, I'm calling you and calling you and you never call me back. It's Elvis."

Message #3: "What the fuck, Pablo?"

Pablo pressed ERASE on the answering machine three times.

"Who's that?" I said. "Let me guess. Elvis?"

"Yeah. My ex-best friend Elvis. He's an artist, too. His father was a wrestler. In Mexico. Remember *Lucha Libre*?"

Lucha Libre is the Latino version of the WWE.

"Elvis's father was *Blanco Diablo*," Pablo said. "The White Devil. Now he owns a bodega on a Hundred Sixty-third. I know wrestling's fake. But I still love watching them fight. It's that good against evil thing, you know? Elvis was drawing on my comic book all through high school before I met Joey. But we had a disagreement."

"What about?"

"It's personal."

"I'm a person."

"You wouldn't understand."

"Try me."

"Elvis said he liked *Superman Returns*."

"Everybody makes mistakes," I said.

"Exactly!" said Pablo. "Elvis said that not only did he *like* Bryan Singer's *Superman Returns* but that Singer had more genius in one pinky than Richard Donner, who made *Superman*, had in his whole body."

"Superman movies? You fought over that?"

"It's not just that," Pablo said, snapping the cap off a warm Coca-Cola bottle he picked up among a stack. "Elvis, he's a know-it-all. Ever since we were kids. He's got that hardheaded Puerto Rican machismo thing. He knows everything and I know nothing. He wouldn't apologize."

"Sounds like he wants to apologize."

"I don't care anymore," Pablo said. "I suffer from anxiety. I got it from my mother. Elvis doesn't understand that. He thinks I'm just complaining. That I got too much yin in my yang. That I think like a chick. Chick, that's the kind of word Elvis uses. He thinks it's okay to have sex with sixteen-year-old girls. That's not me. I'm classy. I haven't been to college yet but I read stuff. From the library. I know stuff. He's ghetto. He's not a sensitive person. I am. I'm not ashamed of that."

"Is Elvis a member of this Superman Project thing?"

"TSP?" said Pablo and laughed. "No. He's got a big mouth. He's nineteen and acts like a little kid. Arrested development."

"I like him already," I said.

"You wouldn't if you met him."

"Let's get back to business," I said. "What *exactly* is better than money?"

Pablo looked around the room and went over to a stack and from the bottom he pulled out a brown leather book bag and from the brown leather book bag he pulled out a photo, wrapped in plastic. He handed it to me. It was a photo of Joey holding up a comic book. A familiar red-caped hero lifted a green car above his head and smashed it into a boulder, wheel flying, one man nearly on all fours, two panicked witnesses running away in wild-eyed terror, one in the foreground, another in the back:

No. 1, June 1938, ACTION COMICS, *10 cents*

"Joey and a reprint of the first Superman comic book?" I said, holding up the photo. "So what? What's this got to do with my fee?"

A bell rang. Pablo went and huddled by the window with soiled green curtains to check. He turned to me and said, "It's not a reprint!"

FOUR

Pablo, his back to me, peeked out the window from behind the soiled green curtains and the doorbell started ringing and ringing but Pablo just ignored it. I could almost feel Pablo watching me watching him watch whoever was outside that window, ringing. When the bell rang six more times and died, Pablo Sanchez, his boyish face twisted with annoyance, turned to me and added: "I can get you Joey's comic book, Chico. The first Superman comic book. Mint condition. Joey'll give you triple your fee if you find Gabby."

I glanced at the photo.

Then I heard, "Joey could sell that comic book for about three hundred thousand dollars."

I looked at the photo again. "Three hundred thousand dollars for a comic book?"

Pablo nodded. "Maybe even four or five hundred thousand."

"Where did Joey get it?"

"An old TSP member passed away and left it to him."

I nodded. "And I thought comic books were just kid's stuff."

The bell kept ringing and Pablo kept ignoring it.

"I'd be an idiot to take your case based on the promise of payment from a comic book not already in your possession," I said. "I'll take it."

"Yeah?" Pablo said, excited.

I smiled. "It took you long enough, but by Great Caesar's Ghost, I think you've convinced me."

Helping an old childhood friend was starting to become a bad habit.

"Where is this Father Ravi of The Superman Project?"

"I don't know," Pablo said. "He hasn't been seen at TSP since Joey ran off. They just show recorded messages from Father Ravi now. TSP is very hush-hush at the top. They have a lot of secrets. Joey knew them all. My mother just thinks she knows. Joey knew."

"Uh-huh."

"Gabby just ran off," Pablo said. "I don't care what the police or anybody says or thinks. I've known Joey for over a year. We talked about everything, almost every day, five days a week. Somebody is trying to frame Joey. I'm nobody in the Project, not even a member, just the fat janitor."

Pablo patted his fat belly. "Joey was high up in the Project. Father Ravi loved him. Joey was next to become the president of TSP. He knew everything and everyone. Joey helped re-create The Superman Project. A lot of people said TSP would never have caught on if it wasn't for Joey. It would've died a long time ago. Everybody said so. Joey got new members, young members, artists, actors, writers, college kids, young businesspeople, female members, rich members, all kinds of donations. Father Ravi is the founder, the spiritual head of TSP. He started The Superman Project but Joey made it what it is today, everybody says that. Something happened. Joey can't be bribed. Joey isn't like that. He *believes* in TSP. They couldn't buy him, so they had to get rid of him somehow. When Gabby went missing, he was the last one to see her, because of all that domestic trouble, the scratches, the other women, he looked guilty, he got scared so he ran."

"Uh-huh," I said.

But if Joey *believed* in this TSP stuff what was up with the other women? Or was that part of the program? Hell, I know that program and I know the dues owed and there ain't nothin' *spiritual* about it.

"I don't have any money," Pablo said. "I'm managing this store. I have a sick mother. But as soon as I get that comic book from Joey, you're paid."

The bell screamed again and finally I said, "I think maybe you should get that."

Pablo nodded his head and said, "Hide that."

I shoved Joey and the comic-book photo nice and neat under the Tupperware bursting with Dominican food, placed them on my lap, and sat down.

Pablo went out and came back into the office with a kid as skinny as Pablo was fat. He was pale, good-looking, with dark blondish hair and sleepy blue-green eyes. He wore an X-Men T-shirt and colorful Hawaiian shorts, and a white baseball cap with a Puerto Rican flag that read *Puerto Ricans Do It Better.*

Elvis.

"What do you want from my life, Elvis?!"

"Why are you acting like this, sweetheart?" Elvis asked.

"I'm busy," Pablo said. "I need you to go away."

"I've been calling you for three days."

"The wait is over. You found me. I'm fine. Go home."

Pablo glanced at me. "I'm sorry about this, Chico."

I nodded and sized them up.

Pablo was fat, good-natured, simple, smart, melancholy but

friendly, short, and ambitious about nothing but friendship and comic books.

Elvis, on the other hand, was six feet tall and lanky, and you could tell by his swagger that he thought a lot of himself.

It was also obvious that Pablo had an allure for Elvis. Maybe because Pablo was not afraid to be himself and because he seemed as self-sacrificing as anyone I had ever met. You could tell that about the guy as soon as you met him and his mother, even before he opened his mouth. He was one of those guys. I wouldn't say he was a chump, but there was no dog eat dog in the dude, not an ounce that you could see.

Elvis turned to me and said, "Who are you?"

"He's a private investigator," said Pablo. "He's gonna find Gabby."

"Cool," he said and put out his hand. "I'm Elvis Hernandez."

Elvis had what our art teacher Sister Irene at St. Mary's called the face of classical beauty, everything in proportion to everything else, nose, eyes, lips. It was the textbook face of heroism, whether its owner was a hero or not, admirable or not, like it or not.

"Chico," I said, putting out my hand.

"Puerto Rican." He smiled.

"I've been called worse," I said.

"You know it!" Elvis laughed, hugged, backslapped, and fist-bumped me like I had just agreed to bang on a cowbell in the Puerto Rican Day Parade.

Chico don't do parades.

Elvis tapped a Newport cigarette out of a crumpled pack and offered me one.

"No, thanks."

"We're busy, Elvis. Will you please leave? You see? I'm not lying. We're having a meeting."

"You not my friend anymore?"

"No," said Pablo.

"So that's it? After ten years? Growing up together. Elementary school. Junior high. High school. It's over?"

"Yeah," Pablo said, holding the office door open. "If you see me on the street, don't stop to say hello, walk on, and remember the good times we once shared and remember that it was all your fault. You know it, homie!"

"That's fucked up," said Elvis.

"You're fucked up."

I stood up. "Maybe I should go."

"No, Chico, stay. You go, Elvis."

Elvis glanced at me and said, "Pablo thinks I stole his comic-book idea and his girl."

"Elvis!"

Pablo got red in the face. It wasn't anger; it was shame. The trouble between Pablo and Elvis was not simply the question of whether Bryan Singer or Richard Donner had made the better Superman movie. Apparently, it was a question of work and love, broken hearts, and loyalty. Same old song.

"I didn't *steal* your idea or your girl, Pablo. *Captain Bravo* was your idea. *The Cuchifrito Kid* was *my* idea, you just made him fat. My *Cuchifrito Kid* looks nothing like yours, he's skinny like me. Your comic book is science fiction, my comic book is a western. And, anyway, I'm not talking to DC, I'm talking to this brother at Marvel that Chase knows, and Chase was *never* your girl. It just beez that way, sometimes, *papá*."

"I told you, I don't wanna talk about Chase!"

"Who is Chase?" I asked.

Pablo said, "Chase Gupta is the sister of Gabby Gupta. Joey's wife. Father Ravi has four daughters. Gabby, the oldest, then Mara, then Chase and Zena—the youngest one. Chase was kinda my girl before—"

"C'mon!" Elvis said. "Let's be honest, Pablo. Your girlfriend? You're overweight. You got a funny hairline, you're one inch taller than a dwarf, the last girl you had was your left arm, and you have dimples, but in the wrong places. In any case, *papá*, the reason Chase rejected you and wants me is not because of any of that. She's looking for someone with potential to take care of her and protect her, and the probability of you doing that is, unlike you, slim. Don't you see that?"

Silence. Pablo's face fell. I couldn't believe the balls on that Elvis kid either. I saw Pablo's left hand balling into a fat fist he was too nice of a guy to use. In fact, I would find it hard to believe that Pablo Sanchez ever slugged or socked another human being in anger, no matter what the offense.

"I don't give a damn about Chase Gupta!" Pablo said. "Or you! You faker! You liar! You thief!"

"You should be happy for me, *hermano*."

"Happy? What do you have in common with Chase Gupta?"

"I'm a Cancer and she's a Pisces," Elvis said.

"You told me that Chase Gupta was too old and big and fat and hard on the eyes! That's what you said, Elvis! She's twenty-six and I'm eighteen. She's too old. That I shouldn't waste my time! That's what you told me!"

"That was just a first impression," Elvis said, looking at me as if for support. "It was late and dark. We were dancing. I was on a full stomach, dizzy on whiskey and that was my first time eating Indian food."

"When she said she had a thin beautiful woman inside of her," Pablo argued, "you told me she had at least three."

Elvis turned back to Pablo. "Chase is going on a diet. You know me. I got a big mouth."

"So what do you want from me, big mouth?"

"I want your blessing."

"I bless you for being a thief and Chase Gupta for taking up any stray that passes by. For choosing looks over sincerity."

"You don't understand."

"Oh, I understand," Pablo railed, as if he had forgotten I was in the room. "You take what's sacred: friendship, honesty, love, loyalty, integrity, and you throw it in the garbage. And then you come here looking for blessings! She was my girl!"

"She's in love with me, *papá*."

"She wasn't in love with you two weeks ago!" Pablo said. "Maybe she wasn't in love with me either. Maybe we weren't a couple yet. But we were going out on dates. We were talking. And you betrayed me! You betrayed ten years of friendship for a girl that you said was a dog!"

Elvis sighed and said, as if quoting from a book, "I have often laughed at the weaklings who thought themselves good because they had no claws."

Pablo's eyes shot wide open. "Oh, my God!"

"What is it, Pablo?" I asked.

Pablo stepped back and away from Elvis, and said, not without horror, "He's a member of The Superman Project!"

Elvis nodded and said, "Not only that. I'm running for president of TSP. It's Chase's idea."

"What?"

"As Father Ravi's former secretary," Elvis said, "your mother has a lot of old and influential friends in the program, Pablo. Chase and I would love to get Esther's support."

"Oh, my God!" Pablo pointed a thick finger at Elvis and said, "Come back here again, and I swear I will destroy you."

Pablo didn't have much force or believability in his voice when he said *destroy you*, as if he were a child repeating a line he had read in a comic book. There was no commitment, no fury or fire in it. He might as well have been saying, "Would you like fries with that?"

Elvis turned to me and said, "Pleasure."

"Likewise," I said, handing him my card. "Maybe I should meet with you and your girlfriend Chase and we can talk about your candidacy and her missing sister."

Elvis nodded and winked and pocketed my card and went out and before he could say one final word Pablo slammed the door in his face. He turned. "What's up with you, Chico? Why do you want to meet up with Elvis and Chase for? They're not on our side."

"Is that why you're trying to help Joey find his wife Gabby? To win her sister Chase back from Elvis?"

Pablo blushed again but said nothing—which said everything.

"Where can I find this Superman Project?"

Pablo went into a drawer, waddled over, and handed me four old *Black Falcon* comic books and a little blue and yellow card marked with red lettering:

> *THE SUPERMAN PROJECT*
> *EXPLORE YOUR POTENTIAL FOR ACHIEVING*
> *ENLIGHTENMENT*
> *CONNECT WITH OTHERS WHO THINK LIKE YOU*
> *FINALLY FIND THE RAINBOW AND THE BRIDGES*
> *OF DISCIPLINE*
> *YOU ARE LOOKING FOR*
> *1134 West 47th Street*
> *New York, NY*

"Tell me everything, Pablo."

"I've told you everything."

"No you haven't," I said. "But you will."

FIVE

Parkchester. 10:30 P.M. The air conditioner was chugging along nicely, pushing back the great big package of humidity that dropped on the Bronx.

Boo was asleep at my feet and I was skimming, eyes burning from lack of sleep, *Wrestling with The Superman* by Father Ravi to see if there were any clues in it that might help with finding or just understanding Joey and his missing wife Gabby. Father Ravi's #1 no-no was any kind of attack, physical or verbal, on any member of The Superman Project. This would result in immediate expulsion. Farther down the list but also prohibited was anti-TSP conversations or writings deemed subversive to "spiritual growth" and contradictory to TSP rules. TSP, the book said, was about "simple living and high thinking," and the removal of all sensual distractions, to focus the mind on The Superman. Also on the no-no list were drugs, promiscuous sex, smoking, drinking, sarcasm, and cynicism.

Father Ravi, The Wise and Magnificent Om.

There goes my membership.

I was on page 46, when Max, wearing blue pajamas and that red towel tied around her neck, came into the living room and insisted on doing her best dance moves in the Max Johnson Extravaganza, followed by impressions of Eddie Murphy in *Doctor Dolittle* and more magic tricks that mostly entailed my pretending not to see the coin she was hiding in her left hand as I drank my regular big cup of after-midnight coffee in front of the TV, saying, *"Wow, how'd you do that?"* as convincingly as I could muster.

As I watched Max I caught a movement through the glass sliding door behind her and saw an uninvited guest slumping through the short wooden gate leading into the backyard past an old barbecue grill. The way he was walking said that he had no intention of asking for an invitation, whoever he was. He meant business. What kind, I was not about to find out with an eight-year-old in the room. I stood up.

"Max."

"One more trick?"

"No more tricks," I said. "Boo!"

Boo woke up, yawned, and looked up at me with that sleepy, "Was'up, bro?" look.

"Gimme your hand, Max."

"Super Max," she corrected me.

"Super Max," I repeated.

Super Max gave me her hand, and I walked her and Boo toward the front door.

"Where are we going?"

"On a little adventure."

"I'm not dressed in my regular clothes!" Super Max said, pulling at her blue pajamas. "People will know my secret identity!"

"That's all right."

Max began sucking her thumb.

44

"Max, stop sucking your thumb."

"Why?"

"It's nasty," I said, unlocking the front door.

"Why?"

"Stop asking why."

"Why?" said Max and laughed.

"Stop it or I'm gonna cut your hair."

Max, taking my threat seriously, grabbed at her pigtails and stood by quietly as I pulled open the door. A girl, early twenties, dark, black, short, thin and athletic with a short Afro, stood blocking my way in jeans and a black blouse.

Boo started sniffing at her and wagging his tail.

Some guard dog.

Each time he went to the bathroom on the sidewalk and I picked up his deposit with a plastic bag, the ASPCA looked better and better. Now this.

Make sure you let her know where we keep the safe, Boo.

"Mr. Santana?" the girl said with a strong accent that I couldn't place. It wasn't Jamaican. I knew Jamaican. Some kind of African?

She smiled with big brilliantly white teeth.

"Yeah?" I said.

"We need to speak with you a moment, brother."

"Who is *we*?"

She signaled at the uninvited guest, a tall, thin, young white kid now standing outside the sliding door. He had long greasy hair and a pockmarked face and wore dark brown khakis and a blue shirt.

"That is my friend."

I let her "friend" in. He stank of cigarettes. Chain smoker. I knew the type. I was the type until recently. Very recently. He saluted me and then saluted Max, who saluted right back.

Boo growled and circled and barked at him.

It took you long enough.

The long-haired young man jumped around as if he were

45

being bit and his hand was shaking as if Boo were a pit bull and not a Chihuahua about three inches high.

A grown man afraid of a Chihuahua.

I took pity before the guy had a coronary or Boo got the wrong impression that he was actually a ferocious creature to be respected and feared and that he should be running things around here instead of me and pushed the little demon into one of the bathrooms.

"Your dog has got good taste," said the girl, glancing at her spastic friend with a little smile.

"No doubt," I said.

"Greetings, little lady," said the long-haired young man, a little embarrassed, catching his breath.

"Greetings," said Max. "Are you guys from the FBI?"

"No, we ain't." The young man smiled.

"You the ones who do the most-wanted posters in the post office on Brightmoor?"

"Not us, man."

"I'm interested in being FBI," Max said, then slit her eyes. "Are you two secret agents? What's your name?"

"We're not using names tonight, little sister," said the girl.

"Of course, you're not supposed to tell me your *real* name." Max laughed. "You're supposed to be a secret agent. How you gonna be a secret agent if everybody knows your name? But you can give me your secret agent name."

"Little sister has a good point," said the girl.

"You can call me the letter *L*," said the long-haired kid. "You can call my friend the letter *S*."

"What's this all about?" I said.

"Perhaps you would like to escort the child into another room, brother."

Max shook her head and went to suck her thumb, but stopped herself. I guided her to her bedroom, handed her a book, and shut the door.

"Did you hear from anyone with TSP yet?" said the girl calling herself the letter S tonight.

"I don't know TSP from ESP," I said. "I'm in with the out-crowd."

"Doubt that, brother man," said L with his speedy blue eyes.

"What's this about?" I asked. "Are you guys cops? Do you have a warrant?"

"We don't need no steenkin' warrants, man," said L and smiled like he knew me.

"Title 18," I said. "United States Code, Section 3107, empowers special agents and officials to make search and seizures *only* under warrant for violation of federal statutes."

"This is not a search or a seizure, man," said L as if he were familiar with the practice.

"What is it? Community outreach?"

"Chico," said the young girl. "May I call you Chico?"

"Sure," I said. "Call me anything you want. Just don't call me Shirley. I hate when people call me Shirley."

"Chico," S continued. "You are not being accused of anything."

"That's nice to know."

"This is a routine gathering of information, brother. There is nothing to worry about."

"You interrupt my quiet evening of eight-year-old entertainment. Why would I be worried? Oh, yeah. Let's see. Because I don't know what the hell you people are doing here."

"We understand that you are working for Joey Valentin."

"How do you understand that?"

L looked at S and then back at me. "Top secret, man."

"How did you find me?"

S looked at L and then back at me. "Also top secret."

"Do you guys come with batteries or are those sold separately?" I asked. "What do you want?"

S looked at L. L nodded.

"We're with Joey," said S. "It is our desire to help Joey."

"You do care about Joey, right, man?" asked L.

"Where is Joey?" I asked.

They both said, "We don't know."

"He contacted us, brother."

"On a disposable cell phone," I said. "Yeah. Yeah. Yeah. What does Joey want with me now?"

"Joey needs refuge," said S.

"Is he still in New York?" I asked.

They both nodded yes.

"A stick which is far away cannot kill a snake," said S.

"And washing down a bowl of beans with coffee is never a good idea," I said. "But what does that have to do with me?"

"Can Joey stay with you, man?"

"Stay with me?" I said. "Where?"

They both looked around the apartment.

"Whoa," I said.

"Not right away, man."

"Not tonight, brother," said S.

"Yeah," said L. "He has a place tonight."

"Where?"

"We don't know," they both said.

"Let me get this straight," I said. "Joey not only wants to hire me on an IOU basis, but he wants me to stick my neck out for somebody I haven't seen in twenty years?"

"If you do an illegal thing for a righteous reason," said S, "that is also justice."

"Right on, man!"

"I think that's about enough," I said, pulling the front door open and looking at L. "And you say the word *man* one more time, I'm gonna lose my mind and I ain't got much to spare, so *buenas noches* . . . Man."

"We are just talking about helping your friend," said S.

"Okay," I said. "I've *already* signed up to help Joey find his wife. But I'm not gonna stick my neck out for the NYPD chop-

48

ping block. I like my neck. It goes real nice with my shirts. So you tell Joey. You let him know when and if he calls you that I got his back in that department. But that's enough. Joey wants to hold hands, form a circle, sing 'Kumbaya,' and share old neighborhood stories, tell him to come see me at my office and personally tell me something I don't know about his missing wife's whereabouts. In the meantime, no sleepovers, and you two can just blow. You know how to blow, don't you? You just put one foot in front of the other and get to steppin'."

I stood there, waiting.

S finally glanced at L and said, "Let us go."

"Wait!" Max said, jumping into the room again, excited. "I'd like to join you! I know this kid who shoplifts. I could catch him first. I got a couple of criminal types in my family, too. Only not my uncle Dean. He works at the Joe Louis Arena. He's a criminal type, but he's real nice to me. I would give him amnesty. I would like to clean up Detroit. If you want me to clean up other cities, I could. I'm not a boy but I'm strong. But I would like to start with Detroit because . . ."

"We shall take your application into consideration, little sister," said S, who bent down and smiled with those brilliantly white teeth and hugged and kissed Max on both cheeks and rose again. "Let us go."

"Alright," said L, turning to me. "We'll go to your office next time, man."

"Whatever floats your boat," I said, opening the front door. "Next time don't be so shy and bring something that I can use. Maybe Ring Dings. I like Ring Dings."

As they went out, Max followed behind them spraying them with questions: "How much money you get paid for being a secret agent? I got Indian blood, is that okay? Could I tell people I'm with you? You want my fingerprints? Do you know the president?"

"Enough, Max!" I said, pushing her back and closing the door. Max looked up at me with startled eyes. And for the first time since I had been watching over her, she uttered those three words that mostly parents, if they are human, will hear at least once in their lifetime from a child they are merely trying to love, to protect, and to raise. Max looked up at me, tears in her eyes, pudgy little brown fists flexing, angry and insulted that her interview had been so abruptly cut short, and screamed, "I hate you!" And with that, she ran out of the room, weeping. And now I'm hated by the eight-year-old entrusted to my care. Things could be worse, Santana, I thought. Worse? Man, I had no idea . . .

I waited ten seconds and went out after S and L to see if I could catch some license plate action and get back to Max before somebody called CPS when my cell phone rang. Someone on the other end was screaming.

"Somebody killed her! Somebody killed her, Chico!"

I recognized Elvis's voice.

"Killed who?" I asked, stopping in my tracks. "Who's killed?"

SIX

In forty-five minutes I was at the scene. The big postwar tenement was on Broadway and 162nd Street in Washington Heights (which Officer Samantha Rodriguez called Santo Domingo West) across from Flaco's Pizza.

Elvis was scared. Elvis needed help. He was sitting in a room with a dead body. He was covered with blood, and she was dead. He needed somebody on his side, somebody who wasn't connected to The Superman Project. He was afraid of the police. He had had bad experiences with the police. He couldn't reach Pablo. He needed my help. I told him that I would get there as fast as I could.

I hung up and called Mimi to watch Max and then I put out an S.O.S. to Officer Samantha Rodriguez, and using terms like *help* and *emergency* and *I'll owe you and make it up to you, I swear* and *please, baby, baby, baby, please,* I convinced her to meet me in Washington Heights.

Before the crime-scene tape went up; before the police kept the crowds back; before forensics took what evidence it could; before the medics pulled up and were told this wasn't their day; before the police photographer took pictures of the victim, there was just me, Elvis, Samantha, and the body.

I jumped out of the gypsy cab into the humid night. Some dropped-out and unemployed teenagers in sandals without socks were interrupted from selling nonprescription drugs to night-crawlers and sleepwalkers and exhausted workers who mostly looked at them like pariahs.

Knowing that poverty and need, like pain, breed all forms of doubtful escape routes, I went past a dark young man about five-foot eleven, around 117 pounds, in dirty rags and sobbing, crap in his wooly hair, pulling a small shopping cart filled with pieces of metal, wood, wire, and a plastic bag packed with empty bottles and cans. A skinny pit bull was hitched to the young man's shopping cart by an electric cord, which was tied to its rope collar.

I walked past them all toward Officer Samantha Rodriguez, petite, long black hair, lovely brown skin, off duty, in civilian clothes—a charcoal gray ruffled blouse and blue jeans and open-toed shoes. She had pretty feet, small, pretty brown Mexican feet.

Focus, Santana.

"A dead body," she said as I approached. "Is that what it takes to get you to call me?"

"No," I said. "But it helps."

She threw a fake punch at my chin. "Good to see you, too. But I don't like this. Why am I here?"

"This Elvis kid doesn't trust cops. No offense. He's hysterical and afraid to make the call. Afraid he's going to be blamed or something. And you're here to help me have a look around. Make sure your brothers in blue understand I'm one of the good guys."

"I wouldn't call you one of the good guys but I would call this a misuse of my badge."

"Happens every day for the wrong reasons," I said. "You're helping to even the score."

I grabbed her hand and kissed it.

"*Cholo*," she said, snatching her hand away.

"No," I said. "Chico. Shall we?"

The elevator was busted, so we walked up to the fifth floor.

I heard barking from the Sanchez apartment. Samantha knocked, and Elvis answered, crying. Three pug dogs sniffed and barked, trying to get past him.

"Oh, Chico!" he said, weeping like a child. He smelled like beer. I saw two popped caps and bottles of Presidente sitting on a coffee table. Could you blame him?

"What happened?"

"She was in Pablo's room as usual," he said, between hysterical sobs. "Playing country music on the computer."

"Country music?" I repeated.

Elvis nodded his head frantically. "I know. The door was open. I came in, with my flowers and candy. I went into Pablo's room and found her there on her stomach."

There was blood smeared on Elvis's white baseball cap, X-Men T-shirt, his Hawaiian shorts, and caked on his hands and under his fingernails.

He noticed me and Samantha staring.

"I touched her, Chico," said Elvis. "I panicked. I tried to see if I could help. She's dead. There's blood everywhere."

"What happened, son?" asked Samantha. "Was she shot? Stabbed? What?"

"I don't know," said Elvis. "I didn't see a gun or a knife or anything. They're gonna think I did something, huh? They won't believe me. I was the only one here. They're gonna think I did it, huh?"

"I'll see what I can do, Elvis. You stay here."

I patted Elvis's shoulder and slipped on the blue plastic gloves that Samantha handed me and we went down the Sanchez's living room, which was filled with multicolored furniture

53

and dominated by a Dominican flag and a giant watercolor print in a gold frame—Jesus Christ, white clouds, blue sky, brown mountains, with children and animals gathered around him, and white doves hovering above his head. He looked as though he was laughing at something a child had said. It occurred to me that I had never seen a picture of Jesus laughing in all my time at St. Mary's.

I moved along a hall behind a trail of bloody footprints. A foul stench emanated from a room with a white door and a sign that said:

Fortress of Solitude

Do not Enter without Knocking

Please

I heard the trembling falsetto of Freddy Fender singing "Before the Next Teardrop Falls." Fender, a Mexican-American, was one of the few country musicians my folks ever listened to (ex–Negro League baseball player Charley Pride was another), so I recognized it. He always sounded like he was crying, whether he sang in English or Spanish. I didn't mind Freddy so much, I thought, as I turned to Samantha and said, "I bet that brings back some memories, huh?"

"What do you mean?" asked Samantha.

"Freddy Fender," I said.

"Who's Freddy Fender?" said Samantha, adjusting her gloves.

"Bad Mexican," I called her as we followed the bloody footprints and pushed open the door to Pablo's room and stood in the doorway. The light was on, and the TV was, too. *Superman II* on DVD, frozen to the scene at the start where three villains in black leather, two males and one female, stood under a blinding white light. I vividly remembered watching that movie years ago, Joey and Nicky sitting to the left and right of me. Next, the three villains would disappear, punished. A voice, like the voice of God, would intone: "Guilty. Guilty. Guilty."

Pablo's bedroom was a mess. A mattress lay on the floor, and the room was filled floor to ceiling with comic books.

The victim, or what was left of her, was on her back, on the floor, beside a plastic bowl of potato chips, a forty-ounce Coca-Cola, and a half-eaten package of Twinkies. Elvis's flowers and chocolates were sitting in a pool of blood at her side. Even before I looked at her face, I knew.

Samantha began to examine the crime scene from a safe distance in the doorway.

"Whoever did this doesn't seem to care about being caught," said Samantha, pointing at the bloody footprints leading into and out of the room. "How do you know this man?"

"Elvis? He's the friend of a client. Kid who lives here."

"Looks like somebody was searching for something."

Everything in the room had been smashed, ripped, stepped on. The poster of Lynda Carter (the half-Mexican beauty who played Wonder Woman in the 1970s, all hips and breasts, wrapped in patriotic red, white, and blue—the first American female superhero, with a golden lasso and permanent wedgie, spinning like a dreidel at a Hanukah dinner, Wonder Woman teaching Catholic Bronx boys that superheroes and lust could go together) was torn to shreds. Pablo's CDs—Johnny Cash, Willie Nelson, Dolly Parton, Tammy Wynette—were all cracked in half. His superhero dolls were busted up and scattered everywhere. There was one book among the mess, *Moby Dick* by Herman Melville. The smell of blood flooded my nostrils.

"You think he did it?" Samantha said, signaling over her shoulder in Elvis's direction.

"He's the only one here, still alive, and covered in blood," I said. "No."

"Who is she?" asked Samantha.

I looked at Samantha and then at the corpse and whispered, "It's Pablo's mother. Esther Sanchez."

Esther Sanchez had been killed. There was no knife or gun to be seen but I noted the TWO SETS of bloody footprints leading away from the body and out of the bedroom. There was only Elvis with his shirt and hands caked in blood. But if you found your friend's mother like that, wouldn't you try in your panic to help her, with no thoughts of prints or evidence tampering, before you finally realized that there was nothing to be done?

Samantha crossed herself and kissed her *Lady of Guadalupe* pendant. "Honey," said Samantha. "We should call."

Pablo's home phone rang. It was a big red and translucent plastic job. I froze. Samantha shook her head for me NOT to enter and pick it up.

I entered, stepped around the bloody footprints, and carefully picked it up and heard a calm male voice say, "Pablo?"

"Yeah?"

I looked for the caller ID. There was no caller ID.

"Hello?" I said.

Nothing.

"Hola?" I said.

More nothing.

I heard a voice. "Chico?"

"Joey?"

"Are you alone, Chico?"

"Uh." I glanced over at Officer Samantha Rodriguez in civilian clothes.

Dial tone. I put the phone back down.

"Who was it?" asked Samantha from the doorway.

"Joey Valentin," I said. "He sounded shaken up. He asked for Pablo and changed his mind. Joey Valentin."

"Who is Joey Valentin?" asked Samantha.

Elvis came over and stood in the doorway.

"Is there something you're not telling us, Elvis?" I asked, carefully slipping out to the doorway again.

"No," he said and began to weep hysterically.

Samantha found something on the floor, left of the doorway. She handed me a business card covered in blood. I read the card, holding it between two fingers and the latex.

The Superman Project
Joseph Valentin
1134 W. 47th Street

I thought about what Esther Sanchez had said about her old employer: *"The secrets I know about TSP. I could take that place apart brick by brick."*

Then I heard Officer Samantha Rodriguez say into her cell, "I'd like to report a homicide."

I took out my Zippo lighter and flipped it open and closed. I wanted a Newport cigarette. I wanted a White Russian. I wanted. I wanted to be a farmer, to walk in the green fields, graze with brown cows, build red barns, raise cabbage. Chico Santana had had enough murder. What the hell do you know about raising cabbage, Santana?

I'll read a book. I'll learn.

Right.

Terrorists strike. War sucks. Life is hard. Death, like bad milk, happens. People die. It was simple. It didn't matter who you were, or how you went, rich, poor. You would eventually take that trip to the graveyard. It was a party we all had to attend. And one day you'd be the guest of honor, Chico. Today was Esther Sanchez's day. And the not-so-funny thing was, I never did get a chance to tell her that I had, after all, taken the Joey Valentin case.

Hijo. Son. She had called me son. I thought about my own mother and Esther Sanchez's stupid Tupperware full of Dominican food.

No time for tears, Santana.

It was 4:25 A.M. by the time they arrived for the body.

SEVEN

Elvis was in jail and I was chowing down on a cold *pastele* for breakfast, after polishing off my fifty punishments—I mean, push-ups and sit-ups—of the day, waiting for Mimi, already wearing a black suit, when I got a phone call from Officer Samantha Rodriguez. The NYPD had another possible suspect besides Elvis Hernandez. Thirty-nine neighbors were questioned and nobody heard anything except for one who reported seeing a man, not Elvis, running out of the apartment some time after the killing.

Joey?

Esther Sanchez's brand-new two-hundred-dollar cell phone was missing and Pablo Sanchez, before suffering a chronic asthma attack during questioning and being taken to Roosevelt Hospital, reported that he had not returned directly home from Cosmo Comics the night of his mother's murder because he was working on his comic book, *Captain Bravo and The Cuchifrito Kid*.

Esther Sanchez was dead. She had been stabbed in the back. Esther Sanchez was a good woman, active and beloved in her neighborhood. One year short of her sixtieth birthday. The police weren't interested in any private investigator or his mysterious visitors in the Bronx called S and L but they were interested in Joseph Valentin and his business card found at the scene. Pablo confessed to the police during interrogation that Joey had called him that night from a disposable phone looking for a place to hide out. Pablo said that he had refused the request and had walked home from 23rd Street to Washington Heights, for his new self-imposed weight loss regimen, starting out at 1:00 A.M.

I looked over the detecting truths that hung on the wall of my mind. One: There is no such thing as coincidence when it comes to murder. Two: There is such a thing as coincidence when it comes to murder. Two: Never try to predict the weather or the future. Five: Maybe look into taking an adult-learning math class.

I guzzled my cold, sugary Malta.

My cell phone rang.

I answered.

It was her.

She had called the morning after the murder.

I confirmed our meeting and hung up.

I made the next call. "Hello, *Caliente*."

"Would it kill you to press your pants and change your shirt once in a while, maybe shave regular, cut your hair, Santiny?" Joy said.

"How do you know I haven't?"

"How do I know that crawfish soup is spicy?"

"How does the New York police force get on without you, Joy St. James? You and Hank should go back to active duty."

"What?" said Joy. "And give up helping my former John Jay pupil Chico Santana for free with stuff I taught him to do for himself? Never."

I had called Joy St. James, Ebony, ex-cop, my old boss and professor when I studied criminal law at John Jay, and her husband Hank Murphy, Ivory, also an ex-cop, also my old boss at St. James and Company private investigations where I was one of nine independent contractors before I started my own detective agency, last night. Ebony asked me to join her for a Stephanie Mills concert at the Paradise Theater on the Grand Concourse because Ivory was in Ireland tracing his family tree or something. I politely declined and asked Joy if she could have Office Manager Kelly Diaz go home a few minutes later to her husband and children in Sugar Hill and check out Pablo Sanchez, Esther Sanchez, Joseph Valentin, Elvis Hernandez, Father Ravi, and The Superman Project.

"I need the dirty," I said.

"I need the rent," she said, after cursing me for not having a computer yet and threatening to send me a St. James and Company bill.

"Kelly's got nothing on most of your people so far," she said. "But she did some criminal background checks on Valentin and Gupta. There were some domestic violence reports."

"Against Joey?"

"No," she said. "Against his wife Gabby Gupta. Let me get this straight. You knew the murder victim?"

"Esther Sanchez," I said. "Not really. Her son Pablo Sanchez hired me."

"Who do you think did it?"

"Pablo Sanchez thinks somebody's trying to make Joey Valentin look like a kidnapper and a killer," I said. "The coppers have another suspect besides Elvis Hernandez but won't share."

"And now you're caught up in the mix," said Joy. "Stepped right in the poop with your Rockports and your eyes wide open. Again."

"Joey Valentin called Pablo the night Esther Sanchez got permanently retired and I found his business card at the scene."

"How do you know this Joey Valentin again?"

"Childhood friend."

"Not one of those Dirty Dozen boys you always go on about?"

"Yeah," I said. "Maybe Joey did do this. Or maybe somebody wants the police to believe he did."

"Anyways," Joy continued, "Kelly got hold of a former TSP member. It's some kind of school. It's run by that Father Ravi and meets every Tuesday and Thursday night or Monday and Wednesday night. New people are recruited by current members who strike up conversations in coffee shops and bookstores and colleges and invite them to lectures. If the potential recruit expresses interest in the topic, they're contacted and interviewed. The recruitee thinks they're joining a group devoted to increasing consciousness."

"They're not?"

"Kelly's source said that they're being recruited into a cult, with all the markers for manipulation and mind control. But this is not evident to new people or to long-term people who are still members."

"So it's a cult?"

"Well," said Joy, "members are not what you typically think of as cult members. They're not only college students but professionals, doctors, nurses, architects, engineers, teachers, artists, businessmen."

"With a hankering for some Kool-Aid?"

"Apparently," she said. "My favorite is lime. Yours?"

"Anything blue," I said. "If it's blue, I'll drink it."

"Toilet water is sometimes blue."

"No comment."

"Some members of this TSP, many of whom belonged for decades, have given hundreds of thousands of dollars, married, divorced, and gave up family, friends, and children at the whim of this Father Ravi."

"Nice," I said, pacing.

"Apparently, some of his followers treat him as a god or something. They believe this Ravi had spent a year meditating without food and water."

"That's some diet," I said.

"I'll put Kelly on," said Joy. "She'll fill you in on the rest, I gotta go get my hair did. Later, Choco."

"Later, chocolate."

"*Hola*, gorgeous," said Kelly Diaz, coming on the phone.

"Still married?" I asked.

"Until you say when, *papi*." She laughed.

"I'll check my calendar," I said.

Kelly Diaz was filling me in on Father Ravi and his four daughters and the main players at The Superman Project when I heard banging coming from Max's room. I thanked Kelly and rushed down the long hall and into the bedroom and saw Max at an open window, red towel tied around her neck, jumping up and down on the wood floor with all of her weight, arms outstretched.

"What're you doing, Max?"

"Tryin' to fly," she said, turning from the open window, screwing up her face like what a stupid question. "I prayed and prayed to God every night now, hard, real hard, I cried and everything, and I asked God, I begged God, to make me Superman and every morning I wake up and I know he'll do it soon so I open the window and try to fly and then I thought maybe he'll do it at night and now I feel real stupid because he didn't. I prayed to God that when I woke up he'd really make me Superman and I'll help everybody, the whole world, and I'll get rid of all the bad people with guns and I'll catch the guy who killed my father and I'll save all the good people and there won't be no more war or people dying and everybody'll be happy and safe."

She had tears in her eyes. "I prayed real hard that in the morning tomorrow I'll really be Super Max. That everything's gonna be alright, Uncle Chico."

"Everything's gonna be alright," I said and picked her up and put her back into bed.

"I forgot to feed Gizmo his breakfast!" she said, trying to rise up.

"I'll do it," I said, pushing her back down.

"Okay," she said, and leaned back.

I pulled open the top of the box sitting on the floor in a corner of her room. As soon as I looked inside, the three-legged black kitten started meowing, blinked its big eyes, happy to see me, maybe complaining a bit about the service in this joint.

"Okay," I said. "It's comin'. Keep your fur on."

I changed the cat's water, gave it some food, and went out to feed Boo who kept me busy trying to keep him out of Max's room where Gizmo had three good cat legs left for a crazy high-strung Chihuahua to nibble on.

Then Mimi finally arrived all red mane and cleavage.

I told her what had happened, handed her my father's old baseball, and asked her to check with that friend of hers Dolores who worked for the Yankees if she knew or could check with somebody about its worth and hit the door.

"Where are you going, Chico?" Mimi asked, glancing curiously at the signature on the baseball.

"Funeral," I said.

Mimi crossed herself. "Are you coming back after that?"

"No," I said. "After that, I got another appointment."

"Where?"

"India."

The crowd of mourners walked into the crematorium behind the small church on Fire Island, where candles were lit and a Buddhist monk in saffron robes said a prayer. The incinerator was built into the wall, and Esther's closed coffin, a box of light wood or cardboard, was on a platform with small wheels, like the ones you see in those bakeries in Little Italy, leading into the hot furnace.

Esther Sanchez was loved. People lined the walls to bury her. So many turned up that mourners had to take turns going in and out.

Among the people were neighborhood friends, local Dominican politicians and wannabe politicians, social workers, community activists, some organizers of the Dominican parade, and employees from Cosmo Comics.

Pablo—slicked black hair, decked out in a cheap blue suit, yellow polyester shirt, red polyester tie, and red polyester handkerchief, looking like a plump Mafioso on welfare—signaled for me to go closer to the casket. I don't know how it is for some, but something awful happens to me every time I come face-to-face with death.

"Thanks for coming," said Pablo.

I nodded.

"It's my own fault," Pablo whispered. "I should've sent her back to Santo Domingo when she first got sick."

I nodded. I stood there looking down at the box, holding the eternally closed eyes, ears, and lips of what was once Esther Sanchez. My own mouth ran dry. My palms sweated. My knees went soft. I had that pain in my chest and my voice trembled every time I tried to speak to Pablo, so I stopped trying.

What are you afraid of, Santana? Death is not a failure on the part of the dead. Death is just as natural and even more common than life. Get used to it. So why couldn't I get used to it? Hell, in terms of death, I started young with my own father's murder, then the others, and now Esther Sanchez. So many gone, and with so much war in the world, even more going, every day going, so much going, and I still was not used to it.

Maybe I never would be.

As the coffin started rolling into the fire, Pablo held on and squeezed his pudgy fingers into my forearm. And when the door of the incinerator closed, you could watch the flames through a small glass porthole as they engulfed Esther's coffin like a giant tongue of red fire, until everything turned to black ashes.

Pablo wept and turned away and was consoled. I did not turn away. I was not consoled. I watched the fire. The heat coming from the incinerator was warm and inviting, not like nasty New York heat and humidity. It was a gentle and inviting warmth. Cremation. Pablo's idea. Something he got from Joey and The Superman Project. That's why I was there. Because Joey couldn't be. Because Elvis certainly couldn't be, even if Pablo wanted him to come. Because Chase Gupta refused to come. Cremation. It didn't seem like such a bad way to go. With the stipulation, of course, that you were dead before they put you in.

Afterward, outside, Pablo and I walked toward his little Ford Fiesta.

"Good turnout," I said.

Pablo nodded and wiped some tears.

"She was good people, huh?"

"She was a fool like me," Pablo Sanchez said, wiping more tears. "She couldn't just save herself. It's a family thing."

"What do you mean?"

"My grandmother didn't come here from D.R. because we were poor," said Pablo. "She came to escape that bastard Trujillo. My grandfather was political. When Trujillo ordered his army to kill twenty or thirty thousand Haitian workers in 1937, my grandfather and some of his friends disagreed with that."

"What happened to your grandfather?"

"Trujillo disagreed that my grandfather should keep breathing. He was marked as undesirable and died in a prison. So my grandmother escaped D.R. with her three children and the clothes on her back, and landed in Washington Heights. Those were hard times, but simpler. I'm like my mother. I'm Sanchez. We didn't belong in Santo Domingo. We don't belong in New York. None of us belong. We never have. We never will. Why didn't I see it coming, Chico?"

"See what?"

"You think Elvis killed my mother?" said Pablo Sanchez for the first time. "You think Joey did it?"

"Too easy," I said. "Elvis killed your mother because she refused to help him in his run for TSP president. Joey killed your mother because she refused him shelter and he even drops his old business card at the scene of the crime. Too easy. I don't like easy. Why would Joey hurt your mom? Your mother was on his side."

Pablo shook his head. "It doesn't make sense."

"No," I said. "It doesn't. Elvis doesn't strike me as the type and Joey's been real good at avoiding the police and TSP and then he does something as dumb as dropping his business card at the scene of a crime?"

"I used to just mop floors at TSP," said Pablo, shaking his head. "I think I wish I had just kept mopping floors."

"Do you know where Joey is now?" I said.

"No," Pablo said, getting out his asthma pump. "He hasn't called back since that night."

"Why didn't you tell me about Joey calling you to hide out?"

"I didn't want to get Joey in more trouble," he said. "I knew what they would think. The cops made me tell."

"Let me ask you something," I said. "You didn't really turn Joey down the night he called and asked to stay at your place, did you?"

"No," said Pablo and inhaled. "How did you know?"

"Some things I know."

We got in the car and didn't say one more word all the way back.

After the funeral, I didn't go to India. Well, not exactly. I went to Indian row on East 6th and 1st Avenue to be more precise. I went to meet *her.*

I went past a black Porsche with plates that read DESI into the

66

Madame Curry restaurant and walked over to where Chase Gupta—an Indian girl (not Native American but Indian-Indian), a little diamond stud in her nose, short of stature, short of limbs, thick, jet-black hair, rings that looked like giant chunks of golden popcorn, diamond-encrusted watch—was seated before a giant bowl of lentils and a large plate heaped with fluffy bread and shrimp.

Kelly Diaz had told me all about the third of the four daughters born to Father Ravi. As far as Kelly could tell from investigating various Internet social networking sites, Chase Gupta was twenty-six years old, college educated, and her hobbies included henna tattoos, younger men, wearing fifty shades of eye shadow, and blowing daddy's money on shoes and clothes. All the Gupta girls were thin, like their father. But unlike the other three Gupta sisters, Chase Gupta was fat.

Lovely and fat.

Chase Gupta waved and I saw that she wore a short skirt wrapped around her enormous legs, red sandals, and bright red lipstick for our meeting.

Chase popped up and kissed me hello on the mouth and held the kiss a little too long before she dropped back down.

I would regret anything I did with Chase Gupta, I thought as she kissed me. But that never stopped Chico Santana. No, as much as he tried, it never did. I sat.

She said, "You must be Chico. Elvis told me all about you. You're like a little too dark for my taste but cute. How old are you?"

"Over nineteen."

"You don't look too much over nineteen."

"That's because I'm very immature."

"Well, you and me got like a lot in common," Chase said and laughed and jiggled like brown pudding.

I like brown pudding.

But this is not your night, kid.

Concentrate, Santana!

"Yeah," she said, adjusting her big, round, brown, and I must say, quite solid breasts.

She asked the waiter to bring out two wineglasses and pulled a bottle of Masseto from her Coach bag, a two-hundred-dollar wine, she said.

Then she held up a brown box of cigarettes marked *Djarum* and said, "Do you like cloves?"

"Only on salad," I said. "And I hate salad."

"Please take them," she almost pleaded, holding out the brown and white box of cigarettes. "I can't bring myself to throw them away. I'm trying to throw away a pack a day. I have like twenty cartons stashed in my apartment."

"Why don't you throw away all twenty cartons?"

"I'm trying to quit," she said. "Not commit suicide."

I took them and shoved them in my pocket like a ticking time bomb. I know. I know. I know.

"So." I scooped up a shrimp.

"So." She smiled. "How was the funeral?"

"Dead."

"Did you tell Pablo about my calling?"

"No."

"Thanks."

"What do you love so much about Elvis?" I asked, hoping to soften her up by talking about her favorite subject.

"I don't know," said Chase Gupta, spilling. "He's like too young for me and not very educated, and then there's that awful black SUV he drives with the green cooler in the back full of Budweiser beer and those stupid cartoons he draws and that horrible comic-book collection that takes up every wall in his room. Comic books and cartoons are for children, don't you think?"

"I just got back from a funeral," I said. "I'm thinking about other things."

"I like totally understand," she said, and continued. "Well, I guess Elvis, he's exciting to be around, and a big talker. He only listens to rap and top forty. But I'm no snob about music. He's a city boy; he loves to explore, and to sit and people-watch all day. He's artistic. Not the most smartest. Arrogant, proud and passionate, not about what he does at his father's bodega, but about who he is. Elvis is not a grocer. Elvis knows who he is. He's good-looking and he can be suave when he wants to be. Maybe that's what I love about him."

"What's up with you and Pablo?"

"Pablo?"

"I think he's in love with you."

"Pablo and me were like *just* friends."

"Not what it sounds like to me."

"Well," she confessed. "He thought like because he took me out to the movies at Imaginasian and dinner here and ice cream at Serendipity sometimes that we had something."

"That's usually called dating."

"I never like led him on, if that's what you mean."

"Why let him *like* pay for movies and dinners and ice cream?"

"He wanted to."

"Because he cared for you."

"I never asked for it."

"You must have known."

"I couldn't tell him how to spend his money. If he wanted to spend it on me, that's his business. What?"

"It's not nice to use people."

"I didn't use him. Pablo is like so not in my league."

"You play baseball?"

"No."

"Then what league are you talking about?"

"You know," she said. "Pablo is fat."

I opened my eyes wide and leaned back to get a better look at her wide hips, which hung off her sides like saddlebags—not that I minded that sort of thing.

"What? Oh. Yes. I'm a big, beautiful woman. But I have a

pretty face. Pablo is just fat. I like thin, athletic guys, tall guys. Like Elvis."

"He's too short?"

"Short and like fat. That's not my type."

"What about tall and fat?"

"I don't do fat," she said and stuffed shrimp, dripping with some kind of green sauce, in her mouth. "Have you seen Elvis? He's prettier than I am. He's beautiful."

So Chase Gupta loved Elvis Hernandez because he was, for her, a symbol of ideal beauty; because in her mind Elvis carried a gun, a sword, and an impenetrable shield, a license to kill, to punish and to save.

People never ceased to amaze me. Here was a woman who weighed at least 220 pounds, flesh spilling everywhere, and she didn't "do fat." Pablo, seemingly one of the sweetest, most decent people who has ever lived, was not in her league. She wasn't against letting him spend his money on her, the little he had. But a kiss, a hug, a touch, some lovin', that was out of the question.

"When Elvis and I walk down the street, people turn their heads to look at us, and I know they're thinking, there goes a beautiful couple. When Pablo and I walked down the street, people never turned their heads—or when they did, I know they were thinking, what's she doing with him?"

"You really care about what people think, don't you?"

She snorted. "Don't you?"

"Depends on how much they're paying."

"Well," she said, "sometimes things like don't work out with couples. But Elvis and I will. We are getting married as soon as this horrible nightmare is over. I'm going to lose weight. We're going to take our share of TSP, and we're going to be very comfortable. I know I'm fat. I'm a fat Indian chick. I'm chubby or chunky or whatever you wanna call it. But I don't mind being fat so much. In fact, I sometimes feel so sexy I could burst."

"What do you think happened to Pablo's mother?" I asked. "If Elvis had nothing to do with it?"

"I almost can't even tell you what Elvis and I suspect," Chase Gupta said. "First Joey, now Elvis. I can't like almost say it."

"Say it," I said. "You can trust me. I'm from the Bronx."

"I like can't," she said. "It's like too evil."

"Okay," I said, rising. "Don't tell me."

"I want whoever took Gabby caught as much as you do," she said. "I'm her little sister. More, even."

I sat back down. "Talk to me."

"You're looking for the truth," Chase Gupta said. "I need the truth, but we have to tread carefully. There's too much at stake. We can't like run around accusing people without proof, and we don't need any outside attention destroying what my father has worked so hard to build."

"Your sister is missing!" I snapped.

"Hari," she said. "Hari Lachan."

"Hari?"

"Hari Lachan's family was Untouchable."

"Untouchable?"

"Hari was born into the Mahar caste of Maharashtra. Untouchable. Do you know about the Untouchables?"

"TV show. 1960s. Produced by the Cuban bandleader Desi Arnaz, who was married to comedian Lucille Ball. They did a movie with Kevin Costner, Sean Connery, Andy Garcia, and Robert De Niro in the eighties."

"The Untouchables of India."

"Oh, those Untouchables," I said. "Sorry. No."

"As many as three thousand castes exist in India today," said Chase Gupta, switching from out-there girl and airhead to historian with surprising ease. "They are Hindu. Hindus didn't like become Untouchables by chance. Their activities and occupations made them considered being so filthy that they were unable to be touched. There are certain jobs and behaviors that make a person an Untouchable. If a Hindu has like the occupation of taking life for a living, like fishing, killing, or disposing

71

of carcasses, then he or she is considered an Untouchable. If a person's job involves any contact with things like sweat, urine, feces, or saliva, then they're considered to be Untouchables. Also, the activities of people that include eating meats like cattle, pigs, and chickens make them Untouchables."

"I guess that would make most of the people I know way Untouchable," I said.

"The total number of Untouchables in India," continued Chase Gupta, "is like one hundred million. Being considered an Untouchable makes you part of this large group that has almost no rights."

"Sounds familiar," I said. "Was your father an Untouchable in India?"

"God no!" said Chase and laughed. "The Gupta family was higher caste. We were a family of lawyers and doctors and writers and teachers and engineers."

"Of course."

"Hari Lachan's a nothing," Chase said, "whose main interest in life is making and collecting cuckoo clocks. He's milquetoast. What I liked about him in the beginning, when my father first introduced him to us, was that he knew it. But now, though, he thinks, since Joey is gone, that he really is the next Father Ravi."

"Where is your Father Ravi?"

"Can I trust you?"

"You want me to help Elvis or not?"

"My father has Alzheimer's. He hardly knows where he is most of the time."

"Where is he when he doesn't know where he is?"

"My older sister Mara has him staying somewhere safe. His current condition doesn't quite fit The Superman image."

I thought about Chase Gupta and how *she* could possibly fit The Superman image.

"My older sister Mara is coordinating like the forthcoming worldwide publication of my father's book *Wrestling with The Superman*. There's like a lot at stake."

"Money?" I said.

"Yeah," said Chase.

"So this whole Gabby and Joey thing has everybody by the neck, huh?"

"Stressed," said Chase, nodding. "That we could lose everything. Especially Mara."

"What about Hari Lachan?"

"I despise Hari Lachan," said Chase. "He plays Mr. Calm-Soft-Voice-Spiritual-Vegetarian-Pacifist, but I know the truth about him."

"What's the truth?"

"He pretends to be Joey's best friend but I think Hari feels he got screwed because of Joey. He was once my father's favorite member, he was with TSP from the start, and then my father started talking about making Joey president of TSP after he retired."

"Uh-huh."

"The truth," Chase said, stretching a thick arm and pointing at the map of India over her head. "All the stuff happening at TSP is like India in 1947 with the nonviolent resistance to British colonialism led by Gandhi and Nehru that brought independence to India. Do you know the history of India?"

"I'm more of a geology buff," I said. "I know tons of stuff about slate; Indian history, not so much. You seem to know more than you pretend."

"No man likes a know-it-all." Chase Gupta smiled coquettishly and leaned her enormous bosom on the table. "I actually have a degree in history and I'm head of the archive unit at TSP but more flies with sugar and all that."

"Back to the vinegar," I said.

Chase dropped the act and shook her head. "India was like divided into the secular state of India and the smaller Muslim state of Pakistan. There was like so much killing. One million Indian people were killed by other Indian people. Then there was like even more killing between the two divided countries of Pakistan and India in 1971. This like resulted in East Pakistan becoming the separate nation of Bangladesh."

"So three separate countries came out of India?"

"Three countries," said Chase. "That's what we're dealing with at TSP now, three countries. Hari is one. My older sister Mara is another. And Joey was the third. With Joey and now Elvis gone, Hari has a fifty percent shot against my sister Mara at becoming president."

"What has this got to do with Esther Sanchez?"

"We think Hari may have been involved with why Esther was killed," said Chase. "Elvis says that Esther was always going on about the secrets she knew. We think she knew something about Hari, something that would destroy his chances of winning the presidency."

Chase Gupta nodded as if the case was all wrapped up, and all there was left to do was trap Hari Lachan.

"Hari did it," said Chase, "because of what Esther like knew or to scare Pablo off because he found out that Pablo was working on Joey's behalf to find Gabby and bring Joey back. I'm not saying Hari killed Esther personally or took Gabby, but he had something to do with it."

Chase nodded and sneered. "It was Hari or somebody working for him. My sister Mara's probably next. Or any one of us. Hari Lachan did this. To take it all. Gabby. Joey. Esther. Now Elvis. Hari Lachan, Chico. It's Hari Lachan you want."

EIGHT

The TSP building on West 47th Street was five stories high with three short steps and a handicapped ramp, opposite what looked like an abandoned building. It was a stunning white neoclassical mansion with a row of small white columns and tall, beckoning, polished, green doors. There was a storefront marked *TSP Artist's League Gallery* (products for a new age) where The Superman Project sold and displayed original art, clothing, crystals, candles, tapes, videos, tanning booth, skin lightening cream, yoga mats, and new age self-help books. There was signage in the window marked PREMISES UNDER SURVEILLANCE.

Where's the trust, baby?

That's some new age.

A gold plaque under the green doorway read:

The Superman Project was established by
the honorable and beloved
Father Ravi

I went through the tall green doors and was greeted by three massive security guards who looked like bodybuilders, two white and one black, standing before a red-carpeted spiral staircase was flanked by a cuckoo clock—probably courtesy of Hari Lachan. One short and bald white guard sat on a wooden high chair, and the other two guards stood beside him, hands crossed in front of them. They all wore slick red blazers, blue slacks, and yellow silk ties; they were handsome and smiling and perfumed, and looked more like bouncers for the Copacabana.

The sitting guard had a gold badge that read DOYLE. He smiled at me.

"Just sign right in, pardner," Doyle said with a strong Texas drawl and an officious-prick smirk on his face like a math teacher I had once at St. Mary's but worse. He pointed to a reception desk about twenty feet from the front door.

I approached the young woman who sat at the long oak reception desk, behind a basket of red apples, reading a *Rolling Stone* magazine hidden beneath a yoga magazine.

A ten-foot photograph labeled *The Honorable Father Ravi* hung over the reception desk. Father Ravi was an Asian Indian man with a gray beard and long gray hair. He looked to be a healthy and strong old man. He sat in a straw chair and wore red, blue, and yellow flowing robes, hands folded in his lap, surrounded by three beautiful, thin, young Asian Indian women, standing, also in flowing robes. I recognized Gabby Gupta. The other two were probably her younger sisters, Mara and Zena Gupta. The "fat" daughter Chase Gupta was not in the photo. Father Ravi sported a beatific smile and a red dot on his forehead. Below, his message was printed loud and clear:

"You are The Superman!"

The young woman greeted me with a cheerful, "Howdy!" She was a thin, tall, pretty blonde, wearing a red blazer and a gold badge that read TSP GUIDE: NARADA.

"Do you need any help, sir?"

"Where should I start?"

"Anywhere you'd like."

I looked around. The air-conditioned foyer was full of blinding sunshine that streamed in through the windows. The inner walls of the TSP building were gleaming and spotless, all dark wood and marble. I recognized Wagner playing over the loudspeakers, as seemingly happy and healthy people (mostly white) buzzed in and out of doors carrying flowers and files and fruit. I noticed that no one was overweight. All of the women were at least five-ten, and no man stood under six feet. And not one looked over the age of forty.

"It's funny that all your members look so . . ."

"Perfect?"

"That's a word."

"Darn tootin'," she agreed with a bright smile and a slight Southern accent. "We have a gymnasium on the fifth floor, and trainers. But no worries, everyone who is worthy of membership is given a probationary period to lose extra weight."

I sucked in my gut and planned on adding to my usual routine of fifty push-ups and sit-ups a day.

She picked up a big red plastic container. "This Superman powder makes losing weight easy. You put it in a blender with milk, soy or rice, or fruit juice. It's got antioxidants, vitamins, and other good stuff."

"Does it work?"

"I've lost fifteen pounds on the Superman Smoothie," said the tall blonde. "Since I was laid off, I've gotten my résumé out to one hundred companies. I've had high returns on my investment in the TSP loan program which not only benefits poor people in India and around the world but guarantees us, as members, the highest returns possible. I feel absolutely fabulous. Wealth, health, success, that's what TSP is all about. My dreams are coming true. Yours can, too."

She handed me what looked like a menu. It read:

A personal visit with Father Ravi
10 Minutes for $5
60 Minutes for $15
240 Minutes for $45
480 Minutes for $75
1,440 Minutes for $145

"Unfortunately," she said. "Those are the old rates and Father Ravi is away on business. But he'll be back."

She clapped her hands together. "All righty, then, I know what TSP can offer you. What can you offer TSP?"

"Besides creative spelling?" I said. "Not much but I'm a hard worker and willing to learn."

"My Super name is Narada," she said. "You can call me Narada." She giggled at her own little joke. "My street name is Kirsten."

As Kirsten began opening drawers, I glanced around.

"Now," said Kirsten, handing me a blank application. "There is a small cost for meals and gym membership and workshops at the Project. But all the workshops are reasonably priced."

"Workshops?"

"Anything from dating to real estate."

She handed me a golden flyer marked WORKSHOPS:

THE SUPERMAN WAY

Biting the Bullet of Love and Commitment, The Locomotive of Financial Security, Basic Emotional Flight Training for Men, Seeing Through His Walls, How to Eject the Kryptonite from your New Real Estate Investments, Confessing into the Sun, Accessing the

Stock Market's Phantom Zone, The Birthing Matrix, Color Therapy, Yoga, Whirlpool, Sauna, and Massage.

"All of the workshop engineers are super-successful experts in their subject. All are guaranteed Supermen, male and female at level F in their spiritual practice. At level F everybody is vegetarian and chaste and all that stuff. There are six levels, A, B, C, D, E, and level F is the highest, A is the lowest. A is *achuta.*"

"Bless you," I said. "You need a napkin?"

"You're a joker," she smiled. "*Achuta*. It means polluted and unclean."

"What level am I?"

"*Achuta*. Everyone outside the program and when they begin is *achuta.*"

"How long does it take to reach level F?"

"Oh," she said, waving her hand at me. "It depends. Honey, we have members who've been here twenty years and are still not at level F. We have members who joined within the last year and they're already at level F and running workshops. It all depends on how quickly you absorb the material and put The Superman tools and techniques into practice. Would you say that you're a go-getter?"

"Well," I said, "I guess if the go is there to get, I'll try and get it."

"Do you speak any foreign language?"

"A little Spanish," I said. "Mostly in my sleep. But I'm illiterate in five other languages. Why?"

"Oh," she said, making a note. "We're expanding all over the world. Latin America, India, Pakistan, Bangladesh, Russia, China, Africa, Israel, the Middle East, Europe, Canada. We need members with language skills. I made a note."

She handed me a form, labeled TSP DIAGNOSTIC, and an apple and said, "Fill that out and follow me."

"Actually," I said, "I'm not here to join. I'm looking for Hari Lachan or whoever's in charge of this Taj Mahal. My name is Chico Santana. I'm a private investigator."

"Oh," she said. "Is this about Gabby?"

"Yeah," I said. "And Esther Sanchez."

"Follow me," she said sympathetically.

I followed Kirsten to the back, past some elevators, an empty coat check section, and a mail room, to a bustling administrative area.

I smelled something.

I turned. A dark Indian girl in a yellow sundress dotted with blue and red flowers, a little diamond stud in her nose, moved past like she owned the joint. She stopped and looked at me directly, and smiled like she had known me in another life. She looked familiar as if we'd already met. And I felt it: an electrical charge that shot from my eyebrows to the balls of my feet. The same buzz I felt the first time I saw Ramona's cynical gaze turn from the Benin masks at the Metropolitan Museum and land directly on my cornea. But this girl was not Ramona; she was taller, younger, limbs a bit long, a bit too thin for my taste. Ramona always accused me of having a weakness for women who resembled my favorite beer—aged just right (somewhere over thirty or so), a bit cold, and robust. Anyway, the Indian girl went past me, with a smile and moving like a proud and confident brown cat, sashaying like a Bollywood starlet; intelligent, almost black eyes, jet-black hair, thick sensual heart-shaped lips, and very gifted in the face department. She marched into an office marked MARA GUPTA.

Thank God I was a professional private investigator and it wasn't love at first sight.

Kirsten, my TSP guide, caught me staring. "Ahem," she snapped, fake clearing her throat and grabbing my arm. "Are you okay there?"

"Yeah," I said, awakening from my daze. I pointed at the girl who had just passed. "Who's that?"

"Oh, her," Kirsten said, as if experiencing great fatigue. "That's Zena."

"Zena?" Zena Gupta. Of course. I recognized her from that photo in the hall with her Father Ravi.

"She's the head of the Library and Literature Unit. Kryptonic, if you ask me."

"Kryptonic?"

"Oh, I'm sorry, honey," Kirsten said. "You're not familiar with our terms yet. Kryptonic meaning toxic. Any behavior or people who are off the path to becoming The Superman."

"Is Zena off the path?"

"Way off. Don't let the pretty face fool you. That girl has not worked an honest day in her life. She's a devil wrapped in a woman's body."

"Really?"

"Darn tootin'," Kirsten said, scowling, her gossip meter on go. "I'm from the South. We don't play that. She's one of those rich, lazy, selfish girls—"

Kirsten stopped herself. She put on her best smile again. "You're not an artist, are you?"

"Well," I said, "if you consider cartoons an art form, I used to be."

She took a deep, defeated breath. "Too bad for me, artists never seem to end well."

"Is Zena an artist?"

"No way," she said. "She has some kinda useless degree in English or something. Makes fifty grand as a project manager here, doing a lot of nothing. That girl is bad luck and of dubious reputation."

"What do you mean bad luck?"

"I am so sorry," she said and reached out and touched my Northern cheek with her Southern fingers and pinched lightly. "I'm gossiping. That's old Kryptonic behavior. That's no way . . . I apologize."

"Oh," I said, "you're just talking."

"Right," she said and winked. "Just talking. Just between me and the private investigator, right?"

"Right."

Kirsten made for a door in a corner of the room.

I turned and saw bad-luck Zena of the dubious reputation and the useless English degree storm angrily out of the office marked MARA GUPTA carrying a Jim Croce CD and a paperback novel called *The Good Soldier* by Ford Madox Ford. I remember Ramona had read it in college for some paper she was writing. It was about apples or something. Anyway, Zena stormed through an outdoor garden with fountains and potted plants where young people seemed to be studying, relaxing, and making with the jibber-jabber. There were firecrackers in her eyes now. She was pissed.

After I got through with Hari Lachan, Mara Gupta was next. Maybe Zena Gupta, too. There was plenty of Chico to go around.

Kirsten led me into a room marked CONFERENCE. It had a long wooden table, leather chairs, a bookshelf full of videotapes, books, a television, and another cuckoo clock. That Hari Lachan sure do like him some cuckoo clocks.

Kirsten pointed at a bookshelf full of tapes in black cases. Four years' worth of messages from Father Ravi, she said, and pointed at another ten-foot blowup of Father Ravi. In this one, Father Ravi wore a tight-fitting blue body suit, under a red flowing robe, with a yellow sash at the waist, hands at his hips, legs apart. He smiled a brilliant happy smile, promising you his secret of youth, a sort of Asian Indian Superman look. He also reminded me of my old karate teacher Mr. Chang. I thought about going back to Fordham Road and finding Mr. Chang of Tiger Chang's Martial Arts and Chang's Sporting Goods—peddling sneakers below the training studio above it.

"Can you believe he's eighty years old?" said Kirsten.

I glanced at a sculpture in a corner of the room. The sculpture, spotlighted by the sun shining through a tall window, was a dream, six feet high: two figures, one with wings, wrestling.

"Beautiful," Kirsten said. "Isn't it?"

"Yeah," I said, and casually got closer. "Who did it?"

"A feller by the name of Giovanni Vaninni. He's no longer a member of TSP."

"What'd he do?" I said. "Tug on Superman's cape?"

"Worse. He stopped believing in the principles of TSP."

"You don't say?"

"Yup," said Kirsten. "You stop believing in TSP; well, that's like you just plum stopped believing in yourself. It was as if he was already dead."

"Is he dead?"

"Yup," said Kirsten. "Spiritually."

"Truth?" I said. "It's the physical part that bothers me."

"Follow me, joker," she said.

I followed Kirsten through another door at the other end of the CONFERENCE ROOM, down a long hall, to another green door marked *Men's Orientation Meeting*.

"Don't take this first step lightly," said Kirsten, holding the knob to the green door. "Not everyone has TSP potential, but everyone is afforded the opportunity to try. I know you're not here for membership, but this may be your opportunity. You never know."

"Uno nunca sabe," I said.

"Are you ready?"

"I think so."

She smiled coquettishly and she batted her lashes and I said, "We going in?"

"Oh, no," said Kirsten. "I can't guide you any farther than this. You gotta go on alone."

She pulled open the green door and said, "Go on now. You wanted Hari Lachan. You got him, honey. Toodles. Go on."

So I did.

NINE

I entered the dark, air-conditioned, blue and yellow auditorium with red carpet and was guided to my chair by another TSP GUIDE in a red blazer and gold badge. I sat. Music played. I recognized it. Strauss. Ramona played Wagner and Strauss and Count Basie and Duke Ellington when she worked on her books. Strauss played, and the hall smelled of burning incense. Men, mostly in business suits and, again, mostly white, sat in rows of folding chairs facing a stage where a simple table, a chair, and a microphone sat before a giant painting of a yellow sun so realistic-looking that if the real sun knew it existed, it might just get jealous and refuse to shine until the fake sun was destroyed.

I wanted to see firsthand what TSP was all about and I was getting my shot. The lights cut off.

I heard in the dark a giant "Ommmm . . ."

Soon, the TSP GUIDES in red blazers moved out of the room,

the music stopped. From the darkness came a booming male voice: "What is The Superman Project?"

No one in the dark seemed to know the answer.

"YOU are The Superman Project."

The lights snapped suddenly on and like magic a muscular Asian Indian man appeared. He was dark brown, very dark brown. So dark that if he were American born, you'd say he was black, in his thirties, onstage, behind the microphone, seated at the simple wooden table in a gleaming wheelchair, grinning in a dark blue suit, yellow handkerchief, and a red tie.

"My name is Hari Lachan," he boomed into the microphone. "If you've come looking for a religion, you've come to the wrong place. TSP is not a religion. We are a vision of the future for people with superior knowledge of what that future will be. You are here because it is not enough for you to live and die in the cycle of suffering. Mere living is not enough. You want glory, greatness, and POWER. You want to overcome your fear. To go from self-indulgent to self-disciplined, from unhappily alone to happily in community, from unemployed to working in abundance. You want THE SECRET."

A giant GONG went off and everybody jumped a bit in their seats. Or was that just me?

None of the wannabe members said a thing, but everyone seemed to be impressed by the dramatic beginning. I know I was.

"SUPERMAN," Hari Lachan continued, "is a translation of the German word *Übermensch*. A German philosopher once explained that man's destiny is power. Father Ravi has identified the Twelve Steps to Power through which anyone can become The Superman. Are you ready?"

Everyone nodded.

Hari Lachan said, "I was born in Bihar. Go to Bihar. See the poverty there. See how people sink into the mud. Then look at me. Who is worse off? I know what you're thinking. This man is in a wheelchair. But the path is a difficult path for everyone. Many may attempt to pass this way, few will succeed. Tear to pieces the idea of what you think you are. The things you are have made you sick. Your desire has made you sick. If you wish to be well you must give up your love of sickness. You must become The Superman. TSP is a revolution. We must get back to the male-female models. We must defeat the modern-day childless and miserable women. We must become as creative as soldiers at war in our will to power. We must do away with the deadly sexual practices which threaten mankind's survival. We must identify people deemed hostile to our way. We must spread our pro-Superman ideology. Kryptonic practices must be wiped out. Smoking, drinking, drugs, promiscuous sex, the eating of dead flesh. They are incompatible with the beliefs and practices of The Superman Project. The question is, Are you ready?"

"Yes," said one man.

"Yes?" Hari repeated and shook his head judgmentally.

"YES!" said more would-be members.

"Gentlemen," Hari yelled. "I need more. ARE YOU READY?"

The room exploded with male voices. "YES!"

"Better," said Hari and signaled with a loud rapping on the desk. Another loud GONG went off and the troop of TSP GUIDES in red blazers stormed back into the room and passed around handouts that read: 12 PERSONALITY DEFECTS.

"You think you know yourself," said Hari Gupta. "You don't know yourself. You don't know your power."

Two men started nodding.

"Some of you have been hurt, beaten, and rejected, by your mothers, your fathers, your brothers, your sisters, your wives, your country, your culture."

Some more men nodded.

"You've overcome the odds because you always suspected the truth," said Hari. "They told you all your life that you must be weak to inherit the earth."

More nods.

"But you are NOT weak."

Yes, a young man in a gray suit nodded.

"All along you suspected you had The Superman in you. You achieved, you worked, you succeeded against the odds and you didn't even know why. They didn't want you to know. They still don't. Because if you know, that's knowledge, and knowledge is power, and they are all afraid of YOUR POWER."

Almost every potential member in the room was now nodding along to the sermon, and all I kept wondering was who "they" were that didn't want a room full of mostly young white men in suits to know they were powerful Supermen.

"The Superman is wholeness," Hari Lachan rattled on. "If you want to get to The Superman in you, you must first accept that you are being trained by society, your parents, your teachers, your religions, to be The Little Man. But the day you decide to leave The Little Man, with our help, you will be on your way to more, more love, more friendships, and more financial abundance than you have ever known before."

The lights cut off again and the loudest GONG yet sounded. Everyone gasped, even me, and I'm no gasper. Suddenly a tiny spotlight shone on the center of the yellow sun painting, and out of this spot grew a twenty-foot projection of Father Ravi: a wise-looking, bearded gent, owlish and studious now in glasses, a touch of the Asian Indian saint about him. He stood in a courtyard full of sumptuous fabrics, plants, caged birds, reading, surrounded by books, and what looked like thin young models, wearing colorful robes. A question ran across the image: "WHO IS FATHER RAVI?"

The questions running through my head were, Where is Father Ravi? Where is Gabby Gupta? Where is Joey Valentin?

A recorded message, a feminine, soothing, and melodic voice began to play.

"Father Ravi is a dreamer," said the seductive voice, as slides were projected on the yellow painting. "The dreamer was found in a field in New Delhi by a kindly tea merchant from Uganda."

A slide of India and Uganda and a kindly tea merchant flashed onto the painting. The voice continued.

"Father Ravi was flown to the tea merchant's wife in Uganda, who named him William. The merchant's wife raised William, and soon found that he was brighter, stronger, and wiser than all of the other children. He had read the Vedas, the Sutras, the Tanakh, the Bible, and the Koran by the age of five. He played on the piano that same year. He was plowing fields at six, and correcting the logical mistakes of wise men at seven. A brilliant young man, William Gupta, as he was known then, won a scholarship at Cambridge. In England, he excelled in English literature and physics and wrote novels. Perfect man, perfect son, perfect student, always right, never wrong. It was not simple but he finally found unconditional love, married, sailed off to America, had four children, and discovered success in the transportation industry."

I made a guess that *transportation industry* really meant *cabdriver.*

"William Gupta had all the trappings of happiness. And yet, he still felt empty inside. Until a voice came to him. The voice told him that his destiny was to create and to lead something called The Superman Project. The Superman Project would empower people from the inside out. Father Ravi went to work, and the fruits of his labor, after many struggle-filled decades, are all you see before you today—from the beautiful urban luxury of the TSP mansion to the idyllic green of Utopia Farms. If you should be accepted as a member of this project, you will be one of the privileged few, the chosen, to take a step on a glorious ladder called The Superman."

Some final images of the ancient Egyptians, Greeks, and Romans were superimposed over Father Ravi's twenty-foot image and as they faded the lights snapped back on.

"Welcome to The Superman!" said Hari Lachan, still on stage. "Applaud yourselves, gentlemen, for making the best, most profitable, and powerful move of your lives!"

The recruits in the room applauded weakly.

"You are not pygmies," said Hari. "You are giants. You are not ants. You are The Superman. And now, you are not alone. Applaud!"

More weak applause.

"Is that all you got, gentlemen?"

More applause.

"Is that it, ladies?" Hari Lachan said, veins in his neck popping.

Harder applause, almost angry, almost frightening.

"C'mon!"

The mob, furious with applause, whistled and stomped their feet.

"That's better," Hari Lachan yelled. "Repeat after me. I can. You can. We can!"

"I can. You can. We can," they chanted.

Chico don't chant.

"People say you can't," said Hari. "You can. Doctors say I can't walk. I say that one day I WILL. Why? Because I want to, and if I want to badly enough, Father Ravi teaches, I can do anything. Anything I want to do. I CAN! That is the secret to The Superman!"

Music came back on again; but this time it was a pumping hip-hop beat, and a short, muscular white man with a long blond ponytail came onstage wearing a skintight bright blue leotard with red and yellow trim, clapping his hands, yelling, "Everybody move your chairs! Move those chairs to the edge of the room! DO IT!"

We moved our chairs.

"Now follow me!" said the tiny blond Hercules, leading us to remove our jackets/ties/shoes and then into the quick performance of jumping jacks, then push-ups, then sit-ups on the red carpet, like some speed-freak version of a high school gym teacher.

Soon, the crowd, minus a few skeptics, myself included, was chanting, jumping, sweating, for almost half an hour. I couldn't tell what the new believers were feeling. Maybe hungry? Maybe heads spinning? When they were out of breath and dripping with sweat, the tiny torturer said, "Now, give yourselves a round of applause!"

They applauded themselves.

"Now hug! Hug!"

Breathing like Boo after a good brisk walk in Parkchester, each person turned to the person on their right and hugged, then turned to the left and hugged.

"I'm good," I said, politely declining.

The tiny blond Hercules stamped his foot three times, and the green doors of the auditorium swung open. A sea of Amazons wearing robes in many shades of blue and red and yellow entered with trays of iced yogurt drinks, baskets of mangoes, and platters of bread and cheese and lentils and some brown paste called hummus.

"Drink this," the women said. "Eat this."

And the men did.

I thought about what Chase Gupta had said about her father Ravi. Mara has him staying somewhere safe. His current condition doesn't quite fit The Superman image.

I thought about Hari Lachan now in his wheelchair and how *he* could possibly fit The Superman image.

Five minutes later, the three massive guards from earlier entered, still smiling, and the bald one called Doyle launched straight at me and whispered, "Can we have a word with you, pardner?"

"What about?" I said as they backed me away from the others to a corner of the room by an emergency exit.

"Dr. Mara would like to speak with you in private," whispered Doyle the bald guard. "Can we see some identification to make sure you are who you say you are?"

"Sure," I said, but as soon as I reached into my pocket, Doyle the guard produced what looked like a large cell phone and pressed it like lightning against my ribs. Four electric currents hit my spine like a hot bull on a rodeo clown so hard that for a minute I forgot my name and I dropped and tasted the red carpet . . .

TEN

I was dragged like a rag doll up some back stairs to an office on the second floor, my legs like boiled vermicelli and my head on fire.

"Sleeping beauty," said Doyle, snapping his fingers in front of my face and snapping me back to the TSP office.

I was reassessing my career choice of private investigator as Doyle's fellow goons in red blazers tossed me onto a plush red chair.

"I'm Doyle," said Doyle, the third guy, the little guy with the strong Texas drawl. A toothpick dangled from his lips now, and he had cowboy energy like he was hunting for buffalo. And I was the buffalo.

"This is Lieblich and Big Man."

"I heard trouble came in threes," I said.

Big Man was big, black, stiff with muscle. And Lieblich was smooth, white, drunk with testosterone. They worked for a "spiritual program," but I didn't let that fool me, Lieblich and Big Man were well-made, break-your-back, snap-your-neck-if-you-even-think-about-it machines.

"Hi, fellas," I said.

Lieblich and Big Man stood there like two concrete pillars, no smiles, no nods, nothing—just a mixture of water, sand, cement, and crushed stone with eyes.

"I'm head of TSP Security," said Doyle.

"How's it hangin'?" I looked at Big Man. "You wouldn't happen to have a spare spinal cord in your pocket, would you, brother?"

"You have any questions," said Doyle, "you direct them at me."

I turned my head and looked into the cold brown eyes of Doyle. "First question. How did you get so pretty?"

"How'd you like a knuckle sandwich?"

"No thanks," I said. "I'm watching my figure. Maybe some peanuts or Cracker Jacks."

"You want a snack?" Doyle said, and lifted both meaty hands. "Which one would you like first? The left or the right?"

"Ooh," I said. "You must be the alpha male."

Doyle smirked. "You got something to tell me?"

I looked at him, bulging out of his clothes. "Get yourself a shirt that fits?"

He turned to his partners and smirked some more.

They looked at each other and shook their heads.

Then Doyle looked at me and smiled, face going all soft. He passed a weary hand across his bald skull, leaned in, sitting at the edge of the office desk, and looked at me all unsympathetic.

"You know what, guys? This trespasser looks kinda familiar," said Doyle.

"I have one of those common trespasser faces," I said.

"Well," said Doyle. "Dr. Mara needs to have a word with you, common face. What were you meeting with Chase Gupta about?"

"We were trading tandoori shrimp recipes," I said. "Why?"

"Where is Joey Valentin, wise guy?"

"Don't know, big shot."

Doyle clenched up, from his BVDs to his toothpick. "What the hell, Santana? Are you with the law or against it?"

"I'm on a missing persons case."

Doyle took the toothpick that was hanging from his lips and poked my chest with it.

"Have you heard of the Patriot Act, son?"

"I believe so," I said, pushing his hand and toothpick away. "It's got a nice beat, but it's kinda hard to dance to."

"You always this glib, Santana?" said Doyle.

"Yeah," I said. "And don't think it's easy. This kinda glib is exhausting."

Lieblich and Big Man shook their heads some more.

"Egyptian!" Doyle said suddenly, placing the toothpick back in his mouth and clapping his hands. He looked at Lieblich and Big Man. "Doesn't Chico here look like that Egyptian trouble-maker wanted in Brooklyn? The Muslim?"

Lieblich and Big Man nodded in agreement and Doyle twisted his head as if to get a better look at me. "You know what? Under the right hot light, Mr. Santana does look exactly like that Egyptian Muslim."

"Aw, man." I laughed, pretending I wasn't spooked, but I was. "Do I look like I just got off a boat? You think I swam to the Bronx or jumped a fence or something? You wanna see my birth certificate? I'm an American."

"American," said Doyle. "You think just because you were born here, that makes you an American?"

"Yeah," I said. "And if I was born in an oven, I'd be a muffin. I got other songs like 'Yankee Doodle' and the Bill of Rights. I can hum a few bars."

"Bill of Rights?" Doyle laughed. "It's been suspended, son. We're talking about national security here. We know people.

They've got some nice prison cells where they could stuff you to think over what you do or do not know."

"Are you threatening me?"

"We're TSP, son," said Doyle. "And you're a trespasser. We don't have to threaten you."

Doyle smiled. Lieblich and Big Man stepped closer, boxing me in. Doyle talked at me like a rapid-fire machine gun.

"We know you met with Chase Gupta. We want cooperation. Information. Everything you know about Joey Valentin and Gabby Gupta. About Pablo Sanchez and Esther Sanchez. About Elvis Hernandez and Chase Gupta. Everything. Everything you know."

"Met Chase Gupta once," I said. "And the truth is I love Gladys Knight but I'm still trying to figure out what the hell a Pip is, so I'm not the best at answering the tough questions."

"And I'll tell you the truth," said Doyle. "I'm tired of your kind."

"What kind is that?"

"The kind that obstruct justice and the law."

"Why don't you go find your bad guys on your own and leave me alone, Doyle? I'm just some chump with his own little private investigation firm."

"Look, Santana," Doyle said, easing up. "We don't want to interfere with your investigation any more than you want to interfere with ours. You've heard nothing from Joey Valentin?"

"No."

"Why are you trying to infiltrate TSP?"

I tried to get to my feet. Lieblich and Big Man pushed me back down. "Look, I don't care if you guys are TSP, CIA, or ABC. I don't know where Joey Valentin is and I've only *infiltrated* two groups in my life. One was so secretive, I didn't know where the meetings were even *after* I infiltrated. The second was a hate group composed of anybody who saw Billy Baldwin and Big Daddy Kane in the movie *Posse*. But I couldn't keep up my anger.

I'm just not a good infiltrator. And until I figure out what's up with your group, you get nothin' from me unless you give."

The three guards closed in on me.

"That's enough!"

Doyle and his goons turned.

A woman, holding a clipboard, Asian Indian, late thirties, entered. She wore a severe expression, unsmiling, cold, in a tight dark blue suit with a yellow blouse and a red handkerchief. This case had more suspicious personalities than Nabisco had crackers.

"Dr. Mara, I presume?" I said and stood up on my shaky legs.

Mara Gupta walked in and the guards pushed me down into the plush red chair again.

She closed the door after Doyle and his goons filed out.

I stood up.

"Sit," she said. "The guards are still just outside the door."

I gladly dropped back down. "Is there something wrong with my credit rating? Besides the fact that it's nonexistent?"

Dr. Mara didn't waste any time. "What brings you to TSP, Private Investigator Chico Santana?"

"Actually," I said, "I was in the neighborhood. My first choice was *Lion King* but somebody told me about your show and I thought why not?"

"That's a lie."

"I don't appreciate being called a liar until you *really* get to know me."

"Chico," she said. "That's a child's name."

"I'm big for my age."

"I know why you're here," she continued forcefully. "We know everything."

"So what do 'we' want?"

"You seem relatively bright."

"Thank you?"

She stretched and handed me a sheet of paper from her

clipboard. It was the form, labeled TSP DIAGNOSTIC, which asked, among other things, how many hours a day you watched TV, how close you were to your mother, and the number of friends you had.

"Don't tell me you want me to fill this out?"

"We already filled one out for you," said Dr. Mara, calmly glancing at her Cartier watch.

And to prove it, she looked down at her clipboard and quickly diagnosed me. "Your name is Chico Santana, son of Adam and Gloria Santana. You're a private investigator, formerly of St. James and Company. You're temporarily staying in the Parkchester section of the Bronx with a dog and a cat and a little girl named Maxine Johnson. You're estranged from your wife Ramona Guzman Balaguer. You have a problem with alcohol, cigarettes, anger, attachment, and dwelling on the past. You are overly sensitive and you lack a stable home life and security. You are a man adrift in the world, floating from one thing to the next with no real focus, goal, or direction."

"Sounds like me," I said, handing back the blank form, angry but impressed by the detective work. "Is that bad?"

"Oh, no," she said. "That's the good news."

She tapped her clipboard with a long strong finger. "We'll save the bad news for later if we need it."

"Uh-huh."

Then she added, "Your father went to Vietnam. He was a patriot."

"What?" I said, straightening up. "What the hell's my father got to do with anything?"

"Your father helped his country when his country needed help. He was a hero."

Hero. I don't know from heroes. But it was true. One day, parked outside our building on Brook Avenue, hot summer, garbage steaming, fire hydrants blasting water, kids racing, radios beating with the salsa of Hector Lavoe and the soft, sugary love songs of Sam Cooke, on an overheated morning, motor running, heading for Orchard Beach, my father in shorts with his short-sleeved summer shirt rolled up, sitting in the driver's seat of his sea-blue Charger with white racing stripes. I saw the letters USMC on his dark brown upper arm and asked what they stood for, and he said, *"El pasado.* The past." And I was still outlining the anchor of the tattoo with my finger when my mother came out of our building, smeared shiny with suntan lotion, her short dyed blond hair braided like a crown of thorns on her head.

At Orchard Beach, my father and his friends—mostly black and Puerto Rican or both, the only exception being Mr. Herman, who was Jewish, a ghetto doctor like my father who played the conga like nobody's business—slapped down ivory dominoes and drank rum and beer, as the smell of pork roasting on a nearby grill spilled up past the summer trees into the blue sky. At some point, my mother separated me from the other children tossing a Frisbee and scolded me and told me that I was never to talk to my father about the tattoo or Vietnam because it made him sad. She told me that he had gone into Vietnam, volunteered, happy to serve, believing in America and Puerto Rico and progress and democracy, waving two flags, hating communism and what Castro had done to Cuba. She tried to explain, for the first and last time, she said, that when he came out of Vietnam, he was not cursing Castro and he was not waving any flag, American or Cuban or Puerto Rican. And the world made little sense.

My mother never told me what it was that my father had done in Vietnam or what had been done to him. I do know that his brother was killed in Vietnam by a grenade he jumped on to save the lives of his fellow soldiers and friends. Another brother was stabbed the day he came back from war, fighting some muggers for his wallet fat with thirteen dollars on the 6 train. A third brother, the funny one, was shot in an Irish-Italian bar in Queens for laughing too loud with some white girl he was dating. All of the Santana boys were dead. And my father had his painkiller until he was murdered, too.

Dr. Herman did confess to me once that my father earned a medal for heroism when he served fourteen months as a medic in Vietnam. I never saw any shiny medals anywhere in our apartment. In fact, the only thing I ever heard my father say in relation to Vietnam was, "Don't let anybody tell you you're not anything you want to be, tell them you are anything you decide to be as long as it helps and doesn't hurt life. Tell them your father learned that in Vietnam. Tell them your father said so."

I didn't like that Mara Gupta could pull information about me off her little clipboard like it was the most natural thing in the world.

"This is bullshit," I said, glaring at her. "You leave my father outta this. Why exactly am I here? What have I done? Have I offended you in some way? I can run out and buy some mints."

She grinned and said, as if reading from a brochure, "TSP is a professional self-help program, operated by men and women seeking a stronger way of life. Members engage with each other to strengthen their productivity and self-confidence, empower their lives, and change the world. We have a total of more than ten thousand members in New York City and we are planning more than sixty similar Superman Project satellites in host countries around the world starting with India, which will assist some six hundred thousand men and women. My job is to find Joseph Valentin and my older sister Gabby while protecting that mission."

"Mission?"

"Human happiness can be improved. The Kryptonic treadmill of divorce, smoking, TV, drinking, drugs, overeating, sexual deviance, and promiscuity is breaking the world down. It's literally killing us. We just want the killing to stop. If you have something better to offer, Private Investigator Chico Santana, speak now. Life is short."

I paused. "Bowling?"

"I didn't think so," she said. "Are you familiar with the whereabouts of Joey Valentin?"

"No," I said. "Are you going to ask me about your sister Gabby?"

Long pause. "Why?" she asked. "Do you know where she is?"

"No," I said. "But you seem relatively unconcerned about her being missing."

"Why did you meet with my sister Chase?" said Mara Gupta, ignoring my question. "What did she tell you?"

"I met Chase's boyfriend, Elvis," I said. "At a comic-book store on Twenty-third Street. Pablo Sanchez manages the place. I also met Pablo's mother, Esther Sanchez. They wanted me to find out what happened to your sister Gabby. Now Esther Sanchez is dead and Elvis is being accused of doing the dirty deed and Joey is being sought for questioning because his TSP business card was dropped at the scene but you probably already know all that, since the police have probably already been by here to say hello and *como estas*."

"And why did you want to see Hari Lachan, Mr. Santana?" she asked.

"I heard he had a way with cuckoo clocks and I'm cuckoo for cuckoo clocks."

"Are you investigating TSP or looking for Gabby?"

"Maybe they're not mutually exclusive."

"What do you mean by that?"

"Where is Father Ravi?" I asked. "Where's your dad? It's not just Hari Lachan. I'd like to speak with him, too."

She shut her eyes and took a deep breath, like I was hopeless and she was exasperated with me. "My father is no longer with us."

"Dead?" I said.

"No," she said.

"Where is he?"

"Do you believe in God, Mr. Santana?"

"We had a thing when I was a kid. Why?"

"What do you believe in now?"

"Giving a guy an even break."

"Do you work out?"

"Work out? That's why God invented darkness."

"I thought you didn't believe in God."

"I'm moody."

"We would appreciate if your moods did not include snooping around here."

"Okay." I nodded. "But if you ever get an itch to see me again, and you will, instead of Tasers, how about next time you wanna talk we just have a cup of coffee? It's easier on my ego AND my pants. Dry cleaning is expensive."

I stood up one final time. "Tell me one thing," I said. "Are you honestly worried about Elvis Hernandez challenging you in any kind of race for anything?"

Mara Gupta looked at me and said, "Elvis and Chase were thrown out of the Amerasian movie theater for obscene behavior in public. The first time Elvis sent my sister Chase an e-mail, it was a picture of him naked. Do you know what Chase did?"

"Why don't you tell me?"

"She sent him a photo of herself naked," said Mara Gupta.

"So what?"

"Can you believe Elvis had enough memory on his hard drive for that?"

"I can't believe you just said that."

"Love means never having to say you're sorry," Mara Gupta said. "And nobody is worried about Elvis Hernandez or my sister Chase or any delusions they may be entertaining about their will to power. And Elvis Hernandez has bigger troubles now, right?"

"Funny how two people running against you for the presidency of this lemonade stand are now in trouble with the law."

"Hilarious," Mara Gupta said without so much as a grin.

She didn't even apologize for my Tasering.

"If you find Gabby or Joey before we do, I would be more than happy to have a cup of herbal tea and whatever else with you," said Mara Gupta, a seductive tone in her voice. "Until then, happy snooping *elsewhere*, Mr. Santana. We hope you do find Gabby. Until that time, feel free to stay out of any and all of our facilities and if I can be of any assistance in your search feel free to contact someone else. Shall I have you escorted out of the building?"

"No thanks," I said. "One electrocution per case."

She strolled to the door and said, "Try and have a powerful day, Private Investigator Chico Santana. And if you don't. Remember: It's your own fault."

"I knew that already," I said. "But thanks for the reminder. Every little bit helps."

"You're welcome," she said, throwing open the door. "Also, if you come near Hari Lachan or any of my sisters again, there will be much bad karma."

I nodded.

She pressed her hands together as if in prayer and gave me a little bow. *There will be much bad karma.*

I believed it.

I looked in her direction but not at her. I looked at what was *behind her* and it hit me. Another sculpture in the corner of the room. This sculpture was just like the sculpture spotlighted by the sun shining through the tall window in the conference room, six feet high: two figures, one with wings, wrestling.

Then it all came back to me: *"Beautiful. Isn't it?"*

"Yeah. Who did it?"

"He's no longer a member of TSP."

"What'd he do?" I said. "Tug on Superman's cape?"

"Worse."

ELEVEN

That day was our anniversary. Mine and Ramona's. I woke up again before dawn, cursing that pain in my side, in my guts, my lower back, passing through me like a breath of razor blades. I climbed out of bed and opened the window to smoke a cigarette before I realized that I had quit.

After Mimi arrived to watch Max, I took two aspirin, swallowed a pot of coffee, got dressed, threw on my Rockports and my Timex, and went out into the hot, wet August morning to pick up Kelly's fax at Kinkos, right off the Parkchester Oval, in weather that felt like a hundred degrees in the shade. Giovanni's background check was interesting:

ST. JAMES AND COMPANY
CONFIDENTIAL
CASE No. 2
Subject: *Giovanni Vaninni*

*Place of Birth: Rome, Italy . . . Hair: Blond . . . Eyes: Blue-Green . . .
Height: 6'2" . . . Complexion: Light . . . Weight: 190 pounds . . . Sex:
Male . . . Race: White . . . Occupations: Sculptor. Licensed
Welder . . . Nationality: Italian*

*Remarks: Vaninni may walk with an exaggerated erect posture and
his chest pushed out due to a lower back injury. Vaninni is also
known to smoke heavily. He has ties to anarchists in Italy, Germany,
France, and England. Graduated the University of Salerno. Father
was a professor of the history of Greek and Roman art at the University of Siena. Mother was a psychiatrist. Both deceased. Vaninni
was arrested a few times for altercations at several bars—mostly
assault. He obviously has a temper.*

*Vaninni operates out of Williamsburg on Kent Street where he
shared a work loft with Joey Valentin and Gabby Gupta.*

P.S. from Joy: "When are you coming in to say hola, Santooma?"

I felt like Boo when he would sniff at a spot on the sidewalk
for what seemed like hours. I found my spot on the sidewalk. Its
name was Giovanni Vaninni.

I called the number listed on Kelly Diaz's background check
for Giovanni of Williamsburg and told him that I was a private
investigator and friend of his old roommate Joey Valentin, and
was interested in having a chat. I promised Mimi that I would
be back by midnight to take over watching Max and her cat
Gizmo and walking Boo.

Giovanni Vaninni, Italian, sculptor, welder, artist, anarchist, violent or passionate, maybe both, I thought as I took the
stairs up to the Parkchester platform and my cell went off.

"Chico?" said Pablo Sanchez. "Joey called. TSP knows about
you. They've been following us, that's why he didn't show up at
my apartment."

"I know," I said. "Where's Joey?"

"He hung up before I even had a chance to tell him about
my mother."

"I'm going out to meet with a Giovanni Vaninni, today."

All I heard from Pablo was silence. "Relax, Pablo. I got this."

"Don't tell me to relax. You sound like my mother."

Then, "Giovanni isn't the one to see. You should be looking at somebody at TSP, not Giovanni. Giovanni's a good guy."

"The good, the bad, and the ugly," I said. "I have to check everybody out. What's the deal with Dr. Mara Gupta?"

"Mara Gupta," Pablo said. "She's not a real doctor. She got a PhD in economics. She used to work as an accountant for a computer magazine until she got laid off. Everybody just calls her doctor. She never corrects them."

"And Zena Gupta?"

"Why?"

"I got a feeling the sisters don't really agree on things," I said. "How does Chase Gupta get along with them?"

Silence.

Pablo's sense of loyalty to friends could get in my way. He had been sweating me like a poodle at a leg parade, and suddenly when I talk about Chase Gupta, he goes all Helen Keller on me.

"Why are you bothering Giovanni?" Pablo asked. "He's got enough problems."

"I gotta check every angle, every clue, even if it leads to a dead end."

Pablo paused. He sounded defeated. "I guess so."

"Is there something up with you and this Vaninni guy? Something I should know?"

"No," said Pablo. "No. He's a friend. Not really my friend. Mostly Joey's. Joey met him in art school and brought him into TSP."

"You know a girl named Kirsten at TSP?"

"She's nobody," Pablo said. "Like me."

"I'll pretend you didn't just say that."

"Would you," Pablo said. "Would you still go see Giovanni even if I told you that I think that's a bad idea? Even if I told you that I know for sure that Giovanni had nothing to do with Joey or Gabby's disappearance or my mother?"

"Yeah," I said. "Even if you swore on a stack of Bibles that this Giovanni burped rainbows, I'd have to go check him out."

"The police have a new suspect in my mother's murder."

"Do you know who?"

"No. Do you need my help with Giovanni?"

"No," I said. "You rest up. Your mission is accomplished for now. I'll talk at ya later."

"Wait!"

"What, Pablo?"

"I know Giovanni. He has a temper. He's not a little guy either. He drinks a lot of wine. Things could get rough. Maybe you could use a ride, maybe some backup?"

"Backup?"

"Yeah," Pablo said. "Somebody to watch your back."

"My back is fine, Pablo. I wash it myself and everything. I'm a big boy."

"I know," Pablo said. "But still. Can I come with you?"

"No."

"Please?"

"Pablo, I work alone."

"My mother is dead, Chico."

"I know. I'm sorry. I'm on this. I just need time. Time alone."

"Okay, fine."

The line went dead.

I thought that the Pablo drama was over for that day. It wasn't. When the L train landed at the Graham Avenue Station, three stops outside of Manhattan in Brooklyn, I walked outside and there he was; pudgy Pablo, in a vintage Batman and Robin T-shirt and red shorts, standing beside his raggedy Ford Fiesta, stuffing his face. What the hell did he think he was doing? I was doing my job. I was on the case. And what did I get in return? Amateur hour.

I shook my head but I understood. His mother was dead. Murdered. What *wouldn't* I do?

"What're you eating, Pablo?"

"Pizza."

"Is that ketchup?"

"Yeah," Pablo said. "It's my own invention. Wanna bite?"

He shoved the sweet-sour mess in my face. I pushed it away.

"No, thank you. I like ketchup as much as anybody. It's my favorite vegetable. But not on pizza."

"You sound like my mother," Pablo said, choked up, stuffing what remained of the slice into his mouth as quickly as he could, and pointed to his car.

"Drive or walk, boss?" Pablo asked.

"I'm walking," I said. "You're driving home, Pablo. Now."

Pablo Sanchez was a wannabe detective. I understood, but if I wasn't careful, the guy could get us both killed. I shook my head, and Pablo gave me a sad look like Boo did when I'd pull him back by his leash to stop him from eating garbage on the street. Pablo looked as if he was about to cry and said, "My mother, Chico. Somebody killed my mother," until all I could say was, "Walk."

Pablo looked at me like a geeky kid who just got his first microscope.

"You introduce me to Giovanni and then you step back and let me do my thing."

"You got it, Batman."

I winced. "Does Giovanni know about your mother?"

"I don't think so. I haven't seen him since Joey ran off."

I stared at Pablo, huffing and puffing along. There was red ketchup on his white shirt. I thought about Joey and his immaculate clothes, Joey ironing his shoelaces. I watched Pablo, picking his teeth, excited like he'd just heard the chime of an

ice cream truck, as we walked to an enormous converted warehouse on South 1st Street.

The clouds got dark above us.

Rain.

It's coming.

TWELVE

We went in through an open door, down a long spiral staircase to another door that led into the big hall of a windowless basement. It was hot as hell down there.

The muscular, long-haired blond and goateed man, with weird and exhausted gray eyes complete with dark sleepless circles under them named Giovanni Vaninni, stood bare-chested with a large golden crucifix around his neck before two parking-garage-sized doors marked LAVORI IN CORSO wearing pajama bottoms and sandals.

"Work in progress!" shouted Giovanni. "*Ciao,* Pablino. I didn't know you were coming, too!"

"I wanted to surprise you."

"Welcome to the gates of my inferno, *signore.*" Giovanni held up his beefy arms, a glass of red wine in one hand and a blowtorch in the other. "To enter, you must first pass the Vaninni test."

"If I knew there was gonna be a test," I said, "I woulda changed my underwear."

"Which is the greater masterpiece," Vaninni continued. "Rodin's *The Kiss* or Michelangelo's *David*?"

"*David*," I said, taking a guess based on who I remembered was considered the greater master in my Art Appreciation 101 class at John Jay (Ramona's idea), an elective that might come in handy now, along with my years of working security at the Met.

"You may enter," said Giovanni, dramatically throwing the garage doors open with a powerful ease that said the guy was not just possibly dangerous but strong.

Giovanni stood aside as Pablo and I passed.

"The rent is twelve hundred dollars plus utilities," said Vaninni. "You cannot beat that with a baseball bat."

A song from the Italian opera *Pagliacci* played. I recognized it. Ramona again. Giovanni's inferno was a huge, bright concrete loft space with thirty-foot ceilings and giant industrial fans blowing humid air. Dozens of dilapidated wooden dressers sat in every corner of the room, holding God knew what. There was a kitchenette with a dishwasher and three walls that probably hid two bedrooms and a toilet. In another corner were sinks full of dirty dishes and a hand-built shower stall made of tin with a garden hose for water. A NO SLEEPING sign hung over a cot, a NO SMOKING sign over an ashtray full of cigarette butts, and another sign read, "Art is a lie in the service of truth and TRUE ART IS NOT A CHOICE."

"Cigarette?" said Giovanni, offering one of his hand-rolled masterpieces.

"No thanks. I quit."

"That's like quitting life," Giovanni said. "Americans!"

"Thanks for the support," I said.

"*La vita*," said Giovanni, pointing, spanning his arm across the studio. Eighteen-inch molds of two figures wrestling were everywhere. These molds came to life as sculptures standing throughout the studio, repeated again and again with the same theme—two figures wrestling, made of wax, metal, plastic, bottle caps, comic-book paper, male and female wrestling, male and male wrestling, female and female wrestling, naked, and the faces anguished, fearful, and angry, gritted teeth, grimacing faces, hands clasped in a painful and eternal tug of war. It was a depressing sight, a tortured version of the sculptures I had seen at TSP. I didn't like it. I'm not saying it wasn't true. Maybe it was true, maybe life, *la vita*, was like that, or could be, but I didn't like it. Not one bit.

But the most unforgettable sight in Giovanni and Joey's inferno, standing spectacular in the middle of a mess of hammers and chisels and plaster, was an impossibly colossal hunk of untouched white marble, about nineteen feet tall. How Giovanni got it down there, I did not know—like Max's coin tricks, it was magic, and it was really something to see, like an undiscovered wonder of the world.

"So," Vaninni said, and slapped my shoulder. "How do you steal your money?"

"I like to think I earn my money."

"We all like to think that. That's what the banks think, too."

"I'm a private investigator," I said, "not a bank."

"Even so," said Giovanni, touching the collar of my shirt. "You do not look rich enough to buy my sculptures."

"How do rich people look?"

"Assholes."

"We just met," I said. "I haven't warmed up yet."

Giovanni laughed and slapped my shoulder again, all friendly-like.

"So you are looking into that *gruppo* we call as TSP."

"You don't approve of TSP?"

"No," he said. "Giovanni do not approve. They want only the money."

"You sell sculptures for money," I said. "I hope that doesn't make you feel like a hypocrite."

"*Roma non fu costruita in un giorno,*" said Giovanni, waving his hands. "Money is the tool that Giovanni will use to bring down this dirty house, this military-industrial state, this capitalism."

"Does that work with most of your customers?" I said.

"Some," Giovanni said, and laughed and slapped my back with an open hand. It was like being tapped by a Mack truck or a whale.

He felt my shirt again.

"What is? An antique?"

"Why do you hate TSP so much?" I asked.

"If TSP control New York City, give candy to children would be felony. No more Friday night, no more beer, no more cigarette, no more sex, no more *vino*. TSP can no accept the possibility that things in the world are not getting worse but better. They believe only in rules, money, power, the state, even worse than the Catholic church. They are *scientifico* only if you believe that to hate pleasure and freedom is science. That's what you are looking into, *signore.*"

He paused. "And much much more."

"Like what?"

Giovanni laughed. "You see. You must experience TSP first to believe."

"Joey. He was a friend of yours?"

Giovanni stopped, looked sadly at Pablo, took a drag on his cigarette, gulped his wine, and said, "Joey Valentin is dead."

"What?" said Pablo, obviously shaken. "When? Where?"

"I mean," said Giovanni, "Joey is dead . . . in a way."

Pablo let out a breath of air as if he'd been holding his breath for a year, relieved.

Giovanni sniffed at the air around me. Then he looked at me with one eye closed, shrugged, and said, "Go around the room, look at some of my old work and enjoy. I must finish some things now or go mad. I will only be a second."

Pablo and I went around the room, looking at stuff, as

Giovanni chiseled, rubbed, scraped, and cut at some sculptures with a metal string, running from project to project.

We were strolling through the enormous studio, looking at the sculptures, when I saw a knife marked *Michael Jordan's Steak House* and tiny scraps of tin foil, near a postcard picture I recognized as Michelangelo's *Sistine Chapel*, a book titled *Mussolini: A Biography*, another titled *God and the State* by Mikhail Bakunin, a black notebook marked *Notes of a Sculptor* and another marked *The Notebooks of Giovanni Vaninni*. Oh, the cat had dreams.

Then I saw that Giovanni had stopped darting around his studio and was standing, very still, staring at a particular sculpture of two wrestlers, both with wings, made of plaster.

"Is something wrong?" I said.

"*Essi*," said Giovanni. "She is no good. She is all wrong."

Before I could ask what was wrong with her, Giovanni Vaninni picked up a sledgehammer and began slamming at the helpless plaster sculpture until it crumbled into white dust. When the dust cleared, Giovanni said, "There. *Bene*. That's good. Much better."

Then he turned to us, massaging his lower back, and said, "*Spiacente*. You must excuse. I have no slept in almost a week."

"Just how much is this stuff worth?" I asked.

"Not much," Giovanni said, dramatic pause. "Not yet."

Giovanni went back to nervously darting about the room, not at ease while he was working, lit cigarette dangling from his lips.

I called out, "So you were good friends with Joey?"

Giovanni stopped moving, at last. He lit another hand-rolled, laughed, and said, "Joey and I, we meet at the School of Visual Arts. We make art. Why? Why are you so interest in Joey, *signore?* He is go."

"Joey was an old friend of mine," I said. "He was a good guy. A great artist when I knew him as a kid. I used to draw a little myself."

Giovanni looked at me with those sleepy gray eyes of his, laughed again, and said, "I do not know what you are, *signore*. But you are correct about Joey. Joey know how to make passion in persons. Joey make you feel he love you, you are his best friend, and there is no thing he would no do for you. That was how it was for me, and that was how it was for Pablino. Right, Pablino?"

Pablo nodded. "Joey was a great guy. I mean, Joey *is* a great guy."

"When I first meet Joey at the School of Visual Arts," said Giovanni, "I want nothing more than to stay indoor all day, read books, work as a art teacher, and sit on the café."

"Nice work if you can get it," I said.

"Joey take me away from all that," Giovanni said. "He give my first great original idea. My first great sculpture was inspire by his painting *La Battaglia*."

He pointed at the wrestling sculptures collected about the room. *"The Struggle,"* he said. "Yes. When I first meet Joey I was drawing the fruit."

I nodded.

"The difference between me and Joey in the end," Giovanni said, "was that Giovanni still belong to Giovanni."

Pablo went to open his mouth. I signaled for him to shut it.

This part of the investigation was easier than I thought. I wasn't sure why, but Giovanni Vaninni wanted to talk about Joey, maybe needed to talk about Joey, with me, with Pablo, with anyone. It was easy. Too easy.

"When I first meet Joey he was ocean of promise and possibility and dreams," Giovanni continued. "By the end, he was TSP, not artist."

"Unlike you?"

"Not like me," Giovanni said. "You. I don't know what you are, Chico. But Joey, he was . . . how do you say . . ."

"Magical?" Pablo said.

"Magical," Giovanni continued and glanced at Pablo. "To hell with TSP. Hypocrites. They throw you out, Pablino. After Joey go. Joey was not around to protect you. You could not go back, Pablino. It is a cult. Nothing but a bunch of Nazis and fascists with their blue and yellow and red uniforms, their weight and height, their rules, nothing but little Hitlers and Mussolini, all of them. From the top, all the way to the bottom."

"Is TSP really that bad?" I asked.

"Bad?" Giovanni laughed. "TSP says is not religion. TSP is not science. TSP is a cult. Confession circle. Physical. Measure this. Weigh that. Business workshop. Money lecture. Real estate lecture. *Abundance* is fancy word for greed at TSP. Buy. Power. Create. Buy. Make children. Buy. Make bread. Buy. Make money. Buy. Make art. Make bullshit. Preach bullshit. Buy, buy, buy. Go out and bring money. That is the TSP. They do not care about philosophy or history or art. They care about bling. Bling. Bling. Bling. *Bene,* Giovanni is not for sale like you, Chico."

"You think I'm for sale?" I said.

"Maybe you are," he said. "Just like the rest. Who knows?"

"So why would you agree to let me come here?"

Giovanni grinned at me. "I am an artist. The artist must keep himself open to all experience, always. You are experience Giovanni has never had. Now!"

Giovanni clapped his hands together again. "Who is this man called Chico Santana? Who are you really, *signore?*"

"Pablo thinks that Joey didn't have anything to do with Gabby disappearing," I said, ignoring his question.

"No," Giovanni said. "Pablo wants that Joey is innocent. It is not this way. Gabby was Joey Valentin's last painting. It was the truest thing he ever created. He lived a possibility but he died an artist."

"You say that like you admire him for possibly killing his wife."

"Who are you, Chico?"

"Me?" I said. "I'm just a little guy here trying to help find a missing girl."

Giovanni laughed. "But the answer you seek is not with me. The answer you and Pablo are looking for is not here, it is not with me."

I looked at Pablo and he shrugged.

"What do you know about Mara Gupta or Hari Lachan?" I asked.

"No more, *signore*," Giovanni said. "While I am Italian and I love a farce as much as anyone in *Roma*, my part in your play has ended. I must excuse myself. Go now from my beloved inferno."

"The marble," I said, pointing at the huge chunks in the middle of the room. "How much would that cost?"

"I'm not sure," he said. "I do not worry for money. Why?"

"Are you independently wealthy?"

Giovanni beamed. "I am God."

I looked up at the giant marble mountain. "That explains a lot."

Giovanni allowed me to see Joey's old bedroom before I left, a large space behind a separation wall. I found nothing but canvas and paintbrushes and overalls, a shelf stacked with plastic bottles of ginger, pepper, and saffron, and twelve rusty metal bookshelves filled with dusty art books and journals. Over the bed hung the painting of two brown-skinned females on a beach, one nude, one clothed, signed Joseph Valentin. The painting was an explosion of colors that made a rainbow look muddy: a Hindu deity, an elephant adorned with bright red rubies and gold bangles stood behind the brown nude, gazing at her, while she gazed out at us. Embedded in the painting was a quote: "Man is born free, and everywhere he is in chains."

I walked around the room, looking at things. I found a small pile of Superman comic books on the floor near the bed. There was an ancient, oversize comic featuring an unlikely Superman nemesis—Muhammad Ali. *Superman vs. Muhammad Ali* was a comic that every self-respecting comic-book collector at St. Mary's owned and treasured, a comic book where reality and fantasy came together.

Frankly, that comic book choked me up and broke my stupid heart.

Superman fighting Muhammad Ali?

Good vs. good.

Say it ain't so.

I never read it.

I didn't even crack the cover.

I couldn't.

It was my first protest.

One small vintage poster advertised P. T. BARNUM'S GRAND TRAVELING MUSEUM, MENAGERIE, CARAVAN & HIPPODROME and another from the 1920s advertised Houdini offering twenty thousand dollars to anyone who could prove telekinetic powers. They hung over a small stack of books: *Black Elk Speaks, Up from Slavery, The Diary of Anne Frank, The Wealth of Nations, The Communist Manifesto*.

I checked everything for clues.

Nothing.

Then I saw an old photo of basketballer Michael Jordan flying through the air.

Then I thought back to Joey's phone call and his business card sitting in Esther Sanchez's blood and Esther Sanchez being stabbed.

I went back out. I picked up the "interesting" Michael Jordan steak knife and asked Giovanni about it.

"I get from Joey," he said. "When Joey give up eating the meat. There were four knife."

Pablo nodded. "I got one, too."

"Who got the other two?"

"Gabby got one."

"The fourth?"

They didn't know.

I tossed the knife down.

Giovanni turned to Pablo, kissed him on both cheeks, and said, *"Ciao*, Pablino."

He turned to me and said, *"Ciao*, Santana. Parting is such sweet sorrow but part we must. *Ciao, amico."*

And with that, Giovanni Vaninni disappeared behind a separation wall, where I think he kept his toilet. Not exactly sure what his plan was, once he got back there, I looked at Pablo and said, "Let's get outta here."

On the humid streets of Williamsburg, Pablo and I walked past a construction site, chock-full of equipment and earth diggers and green temporary walls blanketed with movie posters and the latest news about whose hip-hop album was about to drop.

"I want you to search your apartment for that Michael Jordan steak knife Joey gave you."

I thought back to Joey's calling card.

"Check around your apartment and see if you find it."

"Why?"

I gave him a look.

His body went soft as pudding. "You think?"

"Look for it."

But why would Joey kill Esther when she was totally on his team? Because she knew too much about him and Gabby Gupta and he couldn't chance it? Why would Elvis kill Esther? Because he wanted her to support his presidential race and she wouldn't? She laughed at him?

No. I didn't think Elvis or Joey killed Esther Sanchez but I also once thought you could never lose money by investing in real estate so there it is. Maybe Gabby Gupta was someplace with sand in her mouth or maybe she was somewhere sipping on gin and juice, but I was gonna find out one way or another— if not for Joey's or Elvis's sake, for Pablo and Esther Sanchez.

"You think Joey did it?"

"Or maybe somebody wants us to think so."

Then I noticed that Pablo was looking back at something. I looked back too, and all I could see was a thin man in a white shirt and black slacks and a white panama hat run out of Giovanni's warehouse. It wasn't Giovanni. The man had his back to us. He was tall but leaner than Giovanni and he was hustling. I watched as Pablo twisted his head from side to side as if that would help him get a better look, as if he was trying to figure out what it was he was looking at. Then Pablo took off running in the opposite direction, away from me, toward the running man.

"Pablo!"

"Joey!" Pablo yelled. "C'mon!"

I ran. It was crazy, but I ran, past Pablo, toward the running man in the panama hat, across streets, zigzagging across avenues. I heard Pablo panting behind me, an echo, and when I finally looked back and saw Pablo holding up his belt, moving as fast as he could, he smiled and nodded and then went down, tripping into the gutter and bam!

"Keep going!" Pablo yelled.

I kept going. I chased the running question mark, chased it finally into an alley where it did a thing that put the fear of God into me. It floated. The mystery floated over a ten-foot fence like a bird. Well, didn't actually float, but jumped up on a garbage can, pushed off from the wall, held on to the topmost part of the fence with both hands, and leapt over to the other side. Then he landed on the other side of the fence and took off. I tried to scale the fence but I was too tired and it was too damn high and it was too damn hot.

I went out of the alley, exhausted, and tried to cross the street.

"Chico!"

Pablo came running, out of breath.

"Watch out!"

The party wasn't over. I turned and suddenly caught a glimpse of a red flash bearing down on me. I jumped and felt hard metal slam up against my back as I was flung over, wheels screeching, me drifting through the humid New York City air, worried that the connection between me and the world would snap, as soft flesh hit hard metal and then asphalt, a joyless tumble of blood-ied knee and hand and elbow. And as I rolled into the street like a ball of blood and fire, I wondered again about a change of pro-fession. I had always wanted to be a ventriloquist. And when I stopped rolling, I looked up from the gutter where I lay, and saw Zena Gupta, brown, tall, thin as a palm tree, in a yellow blouse and blue jeans. She looked down at me and said, "You came from nowhere . . ."

Later, I would tell anyone who would listen that the second time I saw Zena Gupta there were fireworks, and they would think that I was being romantic. The pain in my knee, my back, my gut, and my head was excruciating.

And that was only the beginning . . .

THIRTEEN

Pablo was gone and the sun was starting to set and I was alone with Zena Gupta. It wasn't wrong. She was connected to the case. Her older sister was missing. She could be a possible suspect. I had nothing to feel guilty about. I was only doing my . . . *You know better than that, baby. You don't eat where you* . . . Shut, up, Nicky!

Maybe it was beyond the call of duty. I confess.

But it was another unbearably humid New York City night, so Zena Gupta planned that we would drive back from Williamsburg in her red Mini Cooper, park, and sit on the concrete steps in Union Square's plaza with a couple of ice-cold fruit smoothies from a tin shack at the side of an overpriced hipster eatery called The Coffee Shop.

We purchased the smoothies and went and sat on the concrete steps about ten feet from a table where flyers were being handed out, with banners that said: *Support our troops. Bring them home!*

Zena Gupta kept going on about how she loved the English language and did her graduate degree in English Literature in London and how *bloody sorry* she was that she had nearly *bloody killed* me with her *bloody car* and wanted to make it up to me. She wouldn't let me go home to the Bronx until she was fully satisfied that she had made amends and had been totally and forever forgiven. The future, she said, her life in the next world, her *karma*, if the Hindus were correct, depended on my spending the rest of the evening with her. Karma's a bitch. What you put out comes back to you, she said. She also added that she knew I was a private investigator working for Pablo and would like to help me find her sister Gabby.

So there we were, alone together, while she explained what she was doing in Williamsburg.

"I was visiting Giovanni," she said. "I'm a painter's model. Giovanni uses me."

I raised an eyebrow.

"Not like that," she said and tapped me playfully on the chest. "Giovanni's not like that. Totally platonic."

"You model for extra money?"

"Not money," she said. "I'm an exhibitionist by nature. I'm the female wrestler in most of Giovanni's *Struggle* sculptures. Anyway, when I saw Pablo running like a madman through the streets of Williamsburg and I took off after him in the car, it wasn't because I was *thinking,* believe you me. I'm a total physical coward, the exact opposite of a female James Bond girl. It was nothing but reflex, I'm afraid. That ever happen to you? I feel awful smashing into you with my car. You came out of that bloody alley quite suddenly. I really am—"

"You already apologized. I forgive you."

"Mighty big of you, Santana."

"Tell you what," I said. "My most intimate friends call me Chico."

"Am I your intimate friend?"

"We can work on that."

"So," she asked. "Where is Joey? Do you know?"

"Not yet."

"I've been frantic ever since my big sister Gabby disappeared."

"You were close?"

"My sister Gabby is an artist and a saint. Gabby is the best human being I've ever known. She doesn't believe in villains. She doesn't believe anybody is bad."

"Doesn't read the papers?"

"You let your hair down," she said, "I'll let mine down. We'll trade information."

"Why?"

"We're both looking for the same thing."

"Your sister?"

"Of course," she said.

"Of course," I said.

"And I'm going to make it up to you for hitting you with my car. I am."

And I let her. I lied to myself that it was *just* part of getting to the bottom of the Joey Valentin case and possibly helping Elvis get out of his jam, beat the rap, if he was innocent. I lied to myself that I thought Zena Gupta might lead me even closer to the truth if I could only spend more time with her. That's all I was interested in. The truth. I was a sucker for the truth, that's all. I lied to myself. I could talk myself into anything, as they say, if I talked hard enough.

It's what I do.

I watched Zena watching a Mexican girl twirling two batons on fire.

"Only in New York," said Zena with wonder in her voice, taking a sip and letting out a tiny burp.

"Oh, dear me," she said, scolding herself. "That's not very ladylike, Ms. Gupta." I was staring at Zena's big hoop earrings when it hit me.

"Waitaminute," I said. "How old are you?"

"I'm twenty-five," she said.

"A little on the young side," I said.

"Young," she said. "I have a master's degree. You?"

"I once had a third degree," I said. "Burn, that is."

"You're silly."

"You're cute."

She stared at my face. "You have very nice eyelashes, Mr. Santana."

"Thanks."

"May I touch them?"

"Knock yourself out."

I closed my eyes as her hand approached. I could smell something sweet on her fingers soft against my cheek.

That smell. What was it?

"They're so bloody long," she said. "Like a girl's. I hate you."

"I'm getting that a lot lately," I said.

After drinking our fruit shakes and talking a lot about how easily we were connecting, and how it felt like we had known each other forever, I found myself promising Zena that I would spend the night with her and talk about her sister's case. I was to be her guest.

I would sleep in her bed and she would sleep on the floor, no ifs, ands, or buts. She would see to my every need and desire. I was helping to find her missing sister Gabby, she nearly killed me in the pursuit of my duties, she said, it was *the bloody least* she could do. She could help me in my investigation.

Everybody wanted to help Chico.

Besides, she was having a good time and she didn't want me to go home.

When I called Mimi and asked her if she could spend the night with Max and Gizmo and Boo in Parkchester, she moaned about having business *responsibilidades*. I told Mimi that she could take Max with her to the Cuchifrito. Gizmo the cat was safe in his box with the door closed and Boo (the potential Chihuahua killer of Gizmo the cat) could wait for his evening walk after she and Max got back home. Mimi stopped moaning, blessed me, and hung up. Then came the hard part.

That night, we walked to her five-story redbrick building on 25th Street and Madison.

Zena said, "My apartment belongs to TSP."

We walked quickly up the stairs, past the doorman, as she shook her head, breathing hard, with a small grin. "I don't want you to get the wrong idea about me, Chico. I'm still a member of TSP. TSP believes that sexual feelings are not important. They pass. So there's no need to get all batty about it. People get intoxicated because they want to forget their sadness they want to be happy but it's a desperate way to go about it. They scream, they laugh, they howl in drunken merriment, this semblance of happiness is but a tepid form of despair. Smoking and drinking and having mindless sex are things I choose not to do anymore, because of what TSP has given me, and people who do these things are in denial of the truth. I say that without judgment. I don't drink. I don't smoke. I don't do sex. I don't eat meat. So don't get any ideas. I'm just lonely for my sister Gabby and confused about Elvis and full of a need for answers. Are you lonely, too?"

"I'm not but I can learn."

Zena had a big swanky loft with open spaces and exposed brick walls and a staircase and two floors filled with tall windows and sunlight and red and blue furniture that looked like it was bought five minutes ago in a showroom and never sat on and original art (all nudes) that hung on walls and went from the floor to the ceiling.

There was also an altar full of stones, colorful flags, gems, rocks, oils, and incense. Over the altar was a large painting of a male nude.

In the painting, the muscled nude was surrounded by Hindu

gods and goddesses that she described to me as Ganesh, Shiva, Krishna, Durga, Saraswati, and Hanuman. The painting was signed Gabby Gupta.

To the right of the painting was a cuckoo clock.

She pointed at a spotless marble fireplace: "I can't keep a fire going in that thing during the winter. I think I'm doing everything bloody right, newspaper, kindling, logs, nice and dry. The logs catch, but when they burn, they smolder without a flame. It's a pretty good metaphor for my currently loveless life. Any advice?"

"Try a sweater," I said.

She took my Rockports and brought me a pair of sandals.

"Hara!" said Zena. "Here's my pretty boy!"

Hara was a fat tortoiseshell cat with greenish eyes. Unlike Max's cat Gizmo, Hara had four brown and black legs. Some cats have all the karma.

She picked Hara up and began kissing him, threw him over her shoulders and began dancing about the room. Hara ate it up, purring all the way. I wasn't too unhappy myself. On a long red coffee table, I spotted a picture of a white woman surrounded by four dark-skinned Asian Indian children, all girls, before the gates of what looked like an English castle.

"Who is that woman?" I asked.

"That's me mummy," Zena said, and put Hara down. "My mother was white . . . British . . . and Jewish."

"I didn't know they made those."

"They do," she said. "Jews have been in England longer than Shakespeare."

"She looks nice."

"She was who she was," Zena said.

"Where is she now?"

"She passed," Zena said. "She was ill. I gave her injections of morphine almost every day in the end. She's dead. You're nosy."

"Curious," I said.

"Please come up to my office, Curious," said Zena.

I walked up to the second floor to her bedroom. I followed her cue and lay on the giant canopy bed with rainbow sheets and rainbow pillows flanked by two shelves, fat with hardcover novels—mostly Jane Austen, Emily Brontë, and E. M. Forster. I remembered Ramona having to read those guys, too.

On the wall before Zena's bed was a colorful painting of another nude by Gabby Gupta. Embedded in the painting was a greeting card with a list in childish crayon titled *How to Be an Artist*. One of the requirements was, *invite someone dangerous to lunch*.

I pointed at the painting.

"Am I just part of your to-do list?"

Zena looked up. "Silly," she said. "Don't be daft. It's way past lunchtime."

"Silly me."

"Remember," she said. "You can stay here in my humble flat. But just talking about Gabby and then sleeping. No hanky-panky."

"I've never hanked a panky in my life, senorita."

"You and I, we are a rare breed indeed, Chico," she said. "Not looking for some sordid hook-up, just looking for a cool hand, just looking for a little sugar in our tea. We're confused and looking for answers, for someone to fill the void."

"I will gladly fill your void," I said.

"That's naughty," she said and smiled wickedly.

"That ain't right at all."

Zena exited to one of her four bathrooms, not ashamed, but with a goofy smile. When she came back, minutes later, she was wearing a red nightie. She sat on the edge of the bed and didn't look at me. "I hope you're honestly interested in finding my sister. I hope you didn't just come here so I could play with your thing."

Shocked by her directness, I said only, "That dirty thought never crossed my mind. I was raised Catholic."

"That would be very Kryptonic," she said, looking down at the wood floor, and added, "I'm a good girl."

I swallowed deep. "I was counting on that," I said.

"I'm not looking for sex," she said. "Or any Kryptonic behavior. No alcohol, no drugs, no cigarettes, no promiscuous sex."

"No meat," I said. "I know."

"I just want some sincerity and some answers. Get it?"

"Got it."

"TSP teaches that love is something sacred, beautiful, and holy, and that you should share your love only when your feelings are pure. You have to wait for that special moment when you know, and then when you know, you give yourself to The Superman and only The Superman."

"I'll keep an eye open for 'im."

"I was once too much in *Maya*," she explained. "Meaning that my pride distracted me from my search for truth."

"And what is the truth?"

"The way I lived before I accepted TSP as the true way was untruth," Zena said. "I've never, never been stronger and more convinced than now."

I nodded.

"The point is that everything now is going to be different, is going to be clearer," Zena said. "Everything, even if I'm not prepared for it, Chico. I want it. Do you want it, too?"

"Oh," I said, looking at her shapely brown silhouette under the red nightie. "I want it."

"What's the object of suffering?" she asked, and answered, "I don't know. But will the average person know any better than I do, when they're crushed by hardship and weakness, an old sick person staring into the dark? What will they have to show for having lived?"

"Stretch marks?"

"Stop joking," she said. "I like it ever so bloody much better when you listen. Have you ever seen any Satyajit Ray films?"

"Who?"

"Satyajit Ray. He's a famous Indian filmmaker."

"Not in the Bronx he's not."

"Before you leave here in the morning," she said, "I am going to give you the gift of Satyajit Ray."

So all night long she talked about growing up Gupta and what she knew about Joey and Gabby's relationship and how the sisters were divided over everything that was happening at TSP and how she felt they were all keeping secrets from each other. She talked and cooked vegetarian Indian dishes. We not only talked about Joey and Gabby but looked at books on Indian folklore and Indian folktales, exchanged body and foot rubs, did yoga, and belly danced and ate more vegetarian food: mixed vegetables, potatoes and cauliflower cooked with spices and yogurt sauce, cottage cheese cooked with spinach, eggplant, onion, green peas, rice, lentils, fritters, stuffed bread with garlic, green salad, rice pudding. Something called *barfi* fudge and *gulab jamun* and fried dumplings in syrup and *jalebis,* fried rings batter dipped in syrup, and melons and rice milk and washed it all down with something called mango lassi.

And Saturday morning, as the sun came up, I yawned and she gave me a massage for extracting negative energy and read my chakras and insisted we watch that Satyajit Ray film from her big rainbow canopy bed. *The World of Apu,* about a frustrated Indian poet, was her favorite. She said it reminded her of her cousin Arjuna who died in the war. And not once, even though Zena wore only a skimpy red nightie, did sex ever take place.

Nothing.

Not even a kiss.

Superman?

Maybe there was something to it.

Then she said, "My sister Chase and I are going up to TSP's Utopia Farms to grab some stuff before they sell it. Would you care to join us? Gabby used to keep an art studio up there. You could private investigate. We have llamas and alpacas."

"You had me at llama," I said. "Yes."

I had to go, I told myself, I had just wasted an entire night with no clues, no evidence, nothing, and I finally got a bite. It was my duty, as a professional private investigator, to go with Zena wherever she needed me to go.

Later, washing up, I opened up Zena's medicine cabinet and in the cabinet, along with Excedrin, coconut massage oil, and vegetable shampoo, I found a familiar little sliver of folded tin foil. Too familiar.

I left the bathroom, my hands shaking. Zena, wrapped in a red bath towel and ready for a shower, sat by an open window, apparently sleepy, nodding, watching the morning traffic dribble by.

"Can I have some more rice milk?" I said, wanting to take a peak in her refrigerator.

"You can have anything you want so long as it's not Kryptonic, darling."

Darling.

Man, she played rough, I thought.

Zena went into the bathroom, and I walked to her large silver kitchen and to her large silver refrigerator with a magnet that read, *Do no harm.*

I found small bottles of orange liquid hid behind the piles of green vegetables and fresh fruit and soy milk. I thought back to the bits of foil at Giovanni's and what Zena had told me about her mother: *"I gave her injections of morphine."*

Being who I was, and considering who my father was, this was almost funny. But I wasn't laughing.

I grew up with those little orange bottles. My father had them in the refrigerator in our apartment on Brook and in his medical office, and when I'd ask what they were, he'd say, "They're for the sick people. People in pain."

I thought about the little scraps of tin foil in Giovanni's studio.

Zena and Giovanni had more in common than art.

Pain.

Painkiller, like marble, costs money.

Where the hell was Giovanni getting his money for the marble and the painkiller?

I grabbed some rice milk and closed the refrigerator, then sat at the massive silver kitchen table, sipping, petting Hara the cat. It was a big place for one girl.

Even if her dad was Father Ravi.

When Zena came out wrapped in wet towels, I didn't ask about the orange bottles and tin foil. Everything had been so perfect. In that swanky nude-filled apartment, everything was magic, like the coin tricks Max performed, like Giovanni's nineteen-foot piece of white marble, only more real. So I said nothing. I didn't want to push too much and scare her off. Not now. Not yet, I told myself.

I dressed, wished Zena good morning, and went out into the hall.

"I'm glad you came." There was no trace of regret in her voice.

"Me, too," I said.

"Don't forget our trip to the farm," she said, closing her front door. "I *will* hunt you down."

It was only five flights to get myself out of Zena's building, but suddenly I was getting that awful rip in my gut so I pressed for the elevator. If I had known what was coming next, I mighta taken the stairs, I mighta prolonged the magic just a bit longer. But it wasn't meant to be.

When the elevator arrived, the doors opened and I saw Hari Lachan in his silver wheelchair. Even his legs, though unmoving, looked powerful.

"You must be Chico," he said with a very soft and calm voice.

"Yes. You're—"

"I'm Hari Lachan. Zena's husband."

"Zena's husband?" I said.

Silence.

"Oh."

"Didn't she tell you?" Hari asked with a pained look.

She didn't tell me. Nobody told me. They were all keeping secrets from each other and from me.

"Yeah," I lied. "She told me."

"And what are you doing here?" he asked timidly with no sign of suspicion or hostility, just curiosity.

"Interviewing your wife about her missing sister Gabby."

"Oh," he said and smiled. "Mara didn't scare you off?"

"Not yet," I said.

He laughed. "Give her some time."

He put out his big hand and we shook.

He nodded. "I want you to know that I don't agree with my sister-in-law Mara and that anything you're doing to help find our dearest Gabby is very important. I don't know if anyone at TSP has thanked you yet."

He teared up. The big guy actually teared up about his wife's missing sister. This was Chase Gupta's dangerous man? The mastermind behind Esther Sanchez's murder?

"Thank you," he said. "Excuse me."

I stepped aside and he wheeled past me, away toward Zena's door. I remembered the cuckoo clock. HIS door. I got on the elevator.

Hari Lachan. I wanted to hate him. I really did. I couldn't. I thought that the Joey Valentin investigation was going pretty good, as far as I was concerned; it had taken turns I didn't expect. But anything I did felt even more personal now. It was no longer just about Joey or Gabby or poor Esther Sanchez.

It was about Zena, too. I wanted to hate her. I didn't. I couldn't. I thought about our night together.

Never.

But that pain in my belly got worse and worse as the elevator went down. As if I was being stabbed. The pain came sharp and without rest. When I got off the elevator on the first floor,

I was nearly doubled over. As I went for the front door, past the doorman, the pain began racing a million stabs an hour. Jesus.

I made it outside Zena's building to Madison.

"Psst!"

I looked across the street. Pablo was standing there, holding a chocolate doughnut and iced coffee.

I grabbed my belly and sat down on the curb and moaned in pain.

Pablo dropped his iced coffee and doughnut and came running over.

"What're you doing here, Pablo?" I said, through gritted teeth.

"You were right about the Michael Jordan steak knife," Pablo said. "It's gone. I looked everywhere. I called in and had somebody take my morning shift at the comic shop. I went to the Bronx, you weren't there. I thought you might be here since the last time I saw you was with Zena. I wanted to talk to you. Are you okay? What did he do to you?"

"Who?"

"Hari. I saw him go up. What did he do to you?"

"Nothing. It wasn't him," I said, trying to catch my breath. "Why didn't you tell me about Hari and Zena being married?"

"You didn't ask," Pablo said. "I didn't know it was important. Are you okay?"

"No. I'm not okay," I said, bent over, holding my belly. "Do I look like a man who is okay?"

"What's wrong?"

"I don't bloody know," I said.

"My mother's memorial is tomorrow," Pablo said, handing me an invitation.

"I'll see what I can do," I said through gritted teeth.

I tried to straighten up and stand, and down I went on Madison Avenue, like a folding chair, hand on my lower belly, in horrible pain, the filthy curb beneath me. I was being carved out by some unseen blade, feeling a pain that I had never felt before, worse than spraining a leg while trying to skateboard down a flight of stairs in the Bronx, worse than a spinning firecracker burning a hole through your shoe and then through your skin and down to the bone of your foot on Brook Avenue, worse than the sharp tip of fence metal puncturing a hole the size of a dollar coin through your right leg, worse than a letter opener slicing across your chin. Worse than being Tasered. It was a mythological pain, radiating from my back, down my flank, and into my groin, so bad I thought that I couldn't possibly survive it.

Then it hit me. I've been poisoned! But why? What did Zena know about her sister's disappearance, about Joey Valentin? Why had Hari Lachan shown up so suddenly and where was he all night, and what was she really doing in Williamsburg, how exactly did Giovanni Vaninni *USE* Zena? Who, what, where, why, and how could I have been so stupid!

Jesus, the pain! I'm dying, I thought as Pablo, worried, almost near tears, yelled, *"Manito,* stop it, you're really freaking me out!"

I'm dying . . . It's almost as if I was born to be murdered . . . It was only a matter of time . . . this is it . . . not yet, not yet, not yet . . .

FOURTEEN

Poison." Ramona shook her head, new reddish dreadlocks flying this way and that. "You're lucky hypochondria isn't fatal. What happened?"

"I fall down and go boom," I said.

It was nighttime and Ramona, all hazel eyes, was standing at the edge of my gurney in the Emergency Room of Beth Israel Hospital, on 16th Street and First Avenue. Men and women in white lab coats rushed past.

"Kidney stones." Ramona shook her finger at me. "And something called gastric reflux and fatty liver and the doctor said you have the cholesterol level of a pig."

"Is that a good thing?"

"Only if you're a pig. You're too young for this mess, *nene*."

In the belief that I was spending my final hours on earth I had called Officer Samantha Rodriguez and told her that her brothers in blue might want to keep their eyes open for a Michael

Jordan's Steak House knife in the Esther Sanchez case, possible murder weapon.

Then I hung up and called Ramona to say that I was being driven to the Emergency Room at Beth Israel Hospital; and there she was, getting her shame on.

"Shame, shame, shame," Ramona said. "Be nicer to yourself, Chico. Self-mutilation isn't cute. And stop trying to be so tough. You have a human heart, just like everybody else."

"Did you call Mimi about staying with Max and walking Boo?"

"*Oui.*"

"How did she react?"

"She danced a mambo. What do you think? She said you were *malcriado.*"

"Badly raised. Sounds about right."

I leaned forward and took her lovely brown hand. She pulled it away. "*Non.*"

"I have kidney stones, Mrs. Chico. Have you no pity?"

"You don't need pity. You need a life coach."

"Does that come with a sauce?"

Ramona smiled and patted my face. "You start taking care of yourself better, or I'm going to brain you."

"You better stand in line."

Ramona's dark brown shoulders were exposed. Her thick brown arms were tight, and her dark skin seemed wrinkle-proof, ageless.

"You didn't call me Mr. Ramona," I said. "The divorce papers aren't signed yet, you know?"

Silence.

"Chico," she said. "Maybe you should lean back."

"I think I'll sit up for now."

More silence.

"I met somebody."

I leaned back. Yeah, my life was really picking up since I opened my own office.

"That's okay. I'm happy for you. What's his name?"

"Chris," she said. "French. A theater and film director. Directing *Waiting for Godot*. Wants to meet you."

"You're kidding?"

"Chris is waiting outside."

"Aw, man."

"I know," she said. "Try not to look too shocked when you meet Chris."

"Don't tell me," I said. "Chris is a gonny-goo-goo?"

"Worse."

"A Pentecostal?"

Ramona gave me a guilty look. "I'll be back. Don't go anywhere."

"Funny."

Ramona blew me a kiss and went out through the exit, under the prominent EMERGENCY sign.

The doctors and nurses strode quickly past patients suffering from broken bones, head traumas, and heart attacks. I had already been through the X-rays and diagnosis. Kidney stones. I just had to pass them and all would be well again. Easy.

Another ripping pain shot through my gut.

"Nurse?"

Was that a whimper, Santana?

"Nurse?"

The nurses zipped by, ignoring me. I wasn't an emergency, even in the emergency room.

"Nurse!" I said. "Excuse me. More, medicine, please. It hurts like hell."

"I'll be right with you."

"Now!"

"Excuse me?" she said, a defiant hand on her generous hip.

"Please."

After the nurse gave me my medicine, I started to worry that since I had left St. James and Company, I had no health insurance.

I looked at the list that the nurse had handed me of things not to consume to avoid hospitalization in the future. Seven things on the list stood out: cigarettes, alcohol, milk, chocolate, spinach, aspirin, and caffeine.

I wasn't too broken up about the spinach. Milk I could also do without, maybe chocolate, maybe fried food, but not coffee, no way. Coffee, first thing in the morning, for at least ten minutes, makes you think you're happy. I wasn't about to give up those happy ten minutes for any stupid old kidney. No way. *Pull it out, Doc. Gotta go, gotta go!* I thought when another pain blew through my side like a spiked cannonball. I was re-assessing my coffee habit when I looked up and saw Chris on a cell phone—dark brown hair, small green eyes, and a big, almost cartoonish nose, wearing a tight green short-sleeved soccer shirt, with yellow stripes, sneakers, and jeans—sauntering into the Emergency Room behind Ramona.

Chris.

Ramona met someone.

Chris.

Chris was white.

Not only that.

Chris was a woman.

What happened to wanting a husband and children?

Chris smiled big at me.

"Bon," said Chris, putting her cell away.

"Very pleased to meet you," I said.

"Oui," she said. "And the universe was created ten thousand years ago."

She laughed with that big stupid nose of hers.

"Chris is directing *Godot* on the Lower East Side with female actors as a play against female circumcision in Africa and the Middle East," Ramona said.

"Cheerful," I said.

"Not bad for the daughter of a plumber," said Chris.

Ramona swallowed and put out her hand and there was a

silver band on her wedding ring finger and it wasn't the one I had given her. Then she said it. "Chris is my fiancée, Chico. We're going to Massachusetts. We're getting married."

Ramona was marrying some white girl, a *blanquita* from France with a big cartoon nose.

I felt the room spin and the lights go dim.

Chris stood there smiling proudly.

"Let's go home, Chris," said Ramona. "I don't think Chico likes me right now."

Ramona patted my leg. "We'll talk some other time, *mon ami*."

So that was it. It was totally and finally and truly over with Ramona. No more Harlem and 135th Street, red rocking chair, African masks, rugs, red bookshelf, Zora Neale Hurston, Virginia Woolf, Nella Larsen, Marguerite Duras, Earth, Wind, and Fire. No more B. B. King. No more competing with Arturo A. Schomburg, black Puerto Rican scholar, deceased—as if I ever could. No more Nina Simone, Miles Davis prints, green houseplants, colorful yarn, knitting needles, *New Yorker* magazines. No more Siamese cats, fleshy legs, homemade corn bread, Columbia sweatshirts, and Samuel Adams beer. No more Metropolitan Museum, the African Art wing, reading *The Lover* in French. No more. She was Ramona Guzman Balaguer. The Dominican Republic. Haiti. The Public Library. She was her first book, *Driving Lessons*; her second book, *The Detective*; and her new lover Chris. No more Mrs. Chico. No more Ramona.

I closed my eyes and thought about Zena. The thought of her dark cinnamon-colored neck, that scent she wore, the sight of her fresh out of the shower, whispering, talking, listening to Hara the cat purr and the morning birds sing.

My cell phone rang. It was Samantha.

"They found the knife that killed Esther Sanchez. You were right. It's a *Michael Jordan*."

"I'll call you back," I said.

I nodded and hung up and sank, worn out, into my hospital gurney and closed my eyes.

And when I opened my eyes again, it was morning, and she was there again, smiling cheerfully down on me, holding a bouquet of flowers and some walnuts, and I felt it, her compassion, as I looked up at her sunburned face, smiling wide and eager like a blessing.

I did not hesitate. I jumped out of that gurney and out into her waiting Mini Cooper, and we drove off.

"Washington Heights," I said.

The truth is, I didn't care where. All I knew was that I was going and I wanted to go, wherever Zena was. I wanted to be with her, to protect her, because she needed protection from what was coming. Or was that me?

FIFTEEN

Washington Heights. 166th Street and Riverside Drive. Community Center lunchroom. Esther Sanchez was loved. People lined the walls again to remember her. And again, so many turned up that people had to take turns going in and out of the Community Center.

Zena had dropped me off and excused herself. She just wanted to make sure that I was okay. But a memorial for Esther Sanchez was all too bloody much.

I watched the Dominican teenagers, students at George Washington High School and members of the Washington Heights Comic Book Club (originally founded by Pablo and Elvis Hernandez when they were in high school), dressed in superhero costumes. Pablo's idea.

The usual suspects. Aquaman held hands with Elektra. I'd never seen anything like it outside of Halloween. The kids were a smattering of awkward boys and girls, so quiet and shy, no one, except teachers and bullies, ever took notice, with glasses and backpacks full of comic books. They were there to pay homage to their friend and neighbor.

A Dominican female, dark-skinned, and a taller, pale-skinned Dominican male were arguing.

"Superman can't be black! Why would you want a black Superman?"

"Because I'm black," said the female.

"You are not black," said the male. "You are Dominican."

"No. You're white Dominican and I'm black Dominican."

"*Que-ba-he-na!*" said the male.

"*It's v-aina with a V!* Meaning sheath for a knife. Or a woman's thing. Not *b-aina* with a b. There's no such word as *b-aina.*"

"*Chopa!*"

"I'm a Dominican American if anything."

"I'm European," said the pale young man.

"What!" yelled the crowd of teens.

"The Spanish conquered Santo Domingo. The Spanish are European. I am European."

"Well, I'm Taino Indian," someone else chimed in.

"The Arawaks were mostly killed off by the Spanish conquistadors in the Dominican Republic, in Haiti, in Cuba, in Puerto Rico. You probably don't have any Indian blood. You have white Spanish blood. And I have black African blood. That's why I look like me and you look like you."

"Look, Sandra," said the pale young man. "You can be a Duyorcian, African, or a black whatever. I'm still European no matter what you say!"

"*Chopa.*"

"I'm a snob?" said the male. "And what're you, a sugar-cane cutter?"

"Maybe I'm educated, but I'm no Doreo."

"What the hell is a Doreo?"

"Dominican on the outside and white in the middle."

"Now," said the pale young man, "you're just making shit up!"

"You're both wrong," said a younger Dominican girl with braces. "All Superman has to be is willing to lay down his life or sacrifice his powers for good, help the community. Superman is modest and humble. He catches his foes. He spends his life helping others and doing good. White or black."

"Yeah," said one boy in glasses. "We're all Superman. Or none of us are."

"Shut up!" everyone yelled in unison.

The memorial began. Everyone stood along the walls or sat in small rows on red plastic chairs. Pablo, slicked black hair, decked out in his cheap blue suit, yellow polyester shirt, red polyester tie, and red polyester handkerchief again, was trembling before the red, white, and blue flower arrangement and a large photo of Esther Sanchez. In the photo, Esther was wearing a long dark brown leather jacket with a big silver buckle and dark sunglasses. Her hair was long and dark. She was healthy and plump and looked to be in her early forties.

Pablo read his memorial speech from a piece of white lined notebook paper without ever taking his eyes off the document: "My mother Esther Sanchez was one of the most beautiful people. In the ghettos, all over the world, no matter where, life is not cheap, just more fragile. And when you live in these places you learn, as those before you learned, that you do not dwell on tragedy, you put away the sick and the dead as quickly as possible and you sweep the tragedy under the rug and you try not to look under that rug, because it's dark in there. You try to forget, to go on, past the dirty old man and his trash bags, because if you stopped too long to think and maybe even feel sorry for the old man or, God forbid, yourself, it's over, you're done, all that would be left was ordering the marble and the flowers. Whatever was chasing you, whatever had caught up to that old man, would catch up to you. So you have to walk past the old man, that's what you're taught; you have to make him invisible, or you, like him, would not make it. My mother

143

was one of those people who refused to walk past the old man and his trash bags. To ignore the need, the poverty, the pain. My mother would stop and talk to the homeless on the street and hand them money and offer to find them shelter. This was a woman with no experience in social work, no degrees in law, no college degrees of any kind. But caring doesn't need a degree. The heart and the mind don't need degrees to do something to help make the world a better place. Some would even say my mother was naïve. But hope is always naïve. My mother was hope. If people who believe in God and the afterlife are correct, this is not my mother's last voyage, and for my sake and yours, I hope that's true."

Pablo stopped speaking, looked up from his paper for the first time, tears welling up in his eyes. He asked the audience for a minute of silence in remembrance of Esther Sanchez.

Everyone applauded the gentle-voiced Pablo after the moment of silence. Then came a few more testimonies.

"Esther was a great friend of our Comic Book Club and always fed us when we'd have meetings at her house, yucca and rice and pork chops. We can't read a comic book from now on without remembering her and talking about her," said a boy named Jarrife.

"I came here to pay tribute to one of the sweetest and most tough ladies I ever met," said a girl named Barbra.

"From heaven, you will continue to be an example of true sweetness," said a kid who identified himself only as Frank. Between shouts of *Que vaina que vaina*, and tears, he left the stage.

A singing duo called Justice and Judge ended the memorial service with a rendition of the Celia Cruz song "Yo Viviré." *I will live.*

"I'm dying of thirst," a voice said.

I looked up and saw Pablo.

"Can we talk?" said Pablo.

I followed him into an office full of dodgeballs, volleyballs, basketballs, soccer balls, board games, folding chairs and folding tables, blue floor mats, ESL and GED workbooks, and musical instruments.

He closed the door, wiping his tears, and said, "Thank you for coming, Chico."

The door opened again.

A young man peeked in. I recognized him. It was the same young man (about five-foot eleven, 117 pounds, about eighteen) that I saw wandering Washington Heights in rags, weeping and pulling a shopping cart and skinny pit bull on the street. He had cleaned himself up, washed his dark face, blew out his Afro, even shaved, and was wearing a green suit that almost fit his long limbs, for Esther Sanchez's memorial.

"Can I help you, Yayo?" Pablo said.

Yayo stared at Pablo as if pleading for a moment alone, shook his head sadly, and sulked out of the room.

"Yayo is completely helpless," said Pablo. "I don't know what happened to him. He was a great artist once. In high school. Better than Elvis. Maybe even better than Joey. That kid was legend."

"What happened?"

"Drugs."

"He looks good today."

"Today," said Pablo. "Tomorrow is another day. Everybody's pretty much given up on Yayo. Except my mother. My mother treated him like he was related to us, like he was one of her sons."

"She was good people, huh?"

"She was a sucker," Pablo Sanchez said, wiping more tears. "She couldn't just save herself. It's a family thing."

Then Pablo Sanchez smiled, remembering the imaginary golden past where everything was simpler in the musty air of the Community Center office. "My mother used to play Bingo at the Audubon Ballroom. Go see movies at the San Juan Spanish movie theater on 166th. Did you know that Freddie Prinze— the father, not the son—grew up on 155th Street?"

"No."

"He was Puerto Rican like you, and Hungarian. Tiny Tim grew up here, too."

As a rule, I am allergic to trips down memory lane. All that talk about the *good old days* leaves me cold. It always has. But Pablo was in pain over the death of his mother.

"And Henry Kissinger, and Harry Belafonte, and Alan Greenspan, and Manny Ramírez, the baseball player, they all went to George Washington High School, right in this neighborhood. My mother would tell me stories about Nelson's Deli at 170th and Broadway, Tasty Pastry Bakery on Broadway, Greenspan's Luggage, Merit Farms. She grew up here before all the Italians and Irish and Jews started moving away. In those days, she said, somebody might chase you down the street after school with a knife, or cut your coat, or beat you if you didn't want to join their gang. But they wouldn't kill you, shoot you with a gun, the way these bastards do now."

"Ah," I said. "The golden age."

"Don't mock me, Chico."

"Sorry," I said. "It's a reflex."

"I didn't get involved with drugs and stuff like Yayo when I was a kid," said Pablo proudly. "I could have. I was too independent."

"Did you hear from Joey?"

Pablo got out his asthma pump. "No."

I heard a commotion coming from outside, someone yelling, "Police!"

I ran out of the office, Pablo on my tail.

SIXTEEN

The NYPD had found the murder weapon, a bloody knife marked *Michael Jordan's Steak House*, in Yayo's shopping cart and arrested him for the murder of Esther Sanchez. His old gray New Balance sneaker footprints matched the prints found at the crime scene. There were two sets of bloody footprints. One set belonged to Elvis. The other set belonged to Yayo. Yayo did it. Killed a kindhearted woman who offered him shelter, food, and pocket money in the past. For drug money.

Yayo told the police only that he had been in the apartment, had found Esther, had taken the knife out of her back because he felt terrible, realized she was dead and what he had done by touching a murder weapon, and left the apartment taking the murder weapon and a cell phone with him to buy drugs, but swore up and down that he was not the killer of Esther Sanchez.

Samantha even got me a quick interview with Yayo at Rikers: "You're not lying to me, are you?"

"I swear by my dead mother and my dead sister," Yayo said. "The front door was open. I found her like like that. I didn't do it."

Yayo's mother and sister died six months apart from one another. Yayo took to drinking and then drugs, lost his job as a computer graphics designer, then his apartment, and then he took to walking the street. But everybody in the Heights was saying how he was a good, smart kid, trying to get off the street with Esther Sanchez's help. Word on the street was that Yayo couldn't have done it and the real killer was out there free.

No matter.

Elvis got sprung.

Yayo got jailed.

Them's the breaks.

But Gabby Gupta was still missing and so I still wanted to take a look at Utopia Farms where she kept an art studio. It was hot outside. Zena was tense and sitting in the driver's seat of her Mini Cooper, blasting the air conditioner. Aretha Franklin's "Chain of Fools" played on the car radio.

"For five long years, I thought you were my man . . ."

Zena was wearing a white blouse, bell-bottom jeans, and brown sandals, her flamboyant nest of black hair draped across her beautiful shoulders.

But don't get me wrong. I wasn't in love. I was still working a case.

Sure, I was almost happy for the moment looking out the car window at the bright lights of New York City at night, my head full of the possibility of Zena, not thinking of Joey Valentin or of murder, but dreaming of a happy ending. The only thing that made me nervous was that I had just found the fourth knife. The fourth knife marked *Michael Jordan's Steak House* in Zena's glove compartment with a bunch of other junk. She also kept a packed suitcase in the backseat of her car, as she said, for the last year because she had thoughts of leaving poor Hari once and for all.

Other than that, nothing suspicious at all.

Maybe it was nothing.

Maybe.

Right.

But when Zena pressed my hand, looking at her heart-shaped lips, every doubt about her almost flowed from me like river water into a vast ocean of sweet forget.

I wanted to forget.

Who was I kidding?

"You're married, Zena," I finally said. "What the hell are you doing?"

"Looking for my sister."

"I'm talking about your husband," I said. "Hari."

"He told me he saw you at the apartment."

"Yeah," I said. "Awkward."

"I thought he was going to be at Utopia Farms for the weekend, packing stuff up."

"That's no excuse."

"The English," Zena said, "have this thing, an arrangement really, called companionate marriage, which is not based on passion and sex but on two people who love and care for each other and love each other's company. They make a nice, quiet life together. That's what Hari and I have. If you believe, as my father preaches, that marriage is a long conversation, Hari and I just don't speak the same language. And after his accident, things became physically *impossible* between me and Hari. But neither of us liked the idea of divorce. And my father was dead set against it. Hari made me promise that if I ever did anything, it wouldn't be with an artist. No unemployed writers, actors, dancers. Just an ordinary TSP member. And then you walk into TSP. I saw you with that wanker Kirsten, staring at me. I saw how she looked at you, and how you looked at me. Maybe I just wanted to take you away from that blabbermouth. Hari's not my husband in the traditional sense."

"Why did you marry him?"

"My father thought it was a good idea that I marry an older man. My sister Gabby introduced us. Everyone at TSP thought it was a good idea. They thought that Hari would be good for me, calm me down. I used to be a little bit wild. Kryptonic."

"Now?"

"Less," she said, and bit into her lower lip.

"You married Hari because your father and TSP thought it was a good idea?"

"My father is Indian, Chico. Indians still practice arranged marriage. Yes, the idea is considered crazy in this country, but the divorce rate here is over fifty percent. So who is the crazy one? Romance is an invention of the thirteenth and fourteenth centuries that didn't catch on until the nineteenth and twentieth centuries, really. And Romeo and Juliet died in that play by William Shakespeare."

"What's your point?"

"My bloody point is that American women who think men have changed for the worse forget that marriage was once about livestock and property, women were owned by men. In India, not so long ago, when a man died, his wife was killed and buried with him. So we've come a long way. But I know that I must make the rules for the kind of life I want. The old models are dead with wool suits and girdles, and good riddance. I'm no bloody romantic."

"You contradict yourself a lot," I said. "One minute you believe in faith and giving yourself *only* to The Superman and the next—"

"I contradict myself." Zena grinned. "Problem?"

"That's a kind of consistency, I guess."

"Or not," said Zena and looked out the car window. "There they are."

When I next looked out of the car window, I spotted Elvis Hernandez standing on the corner of Broadway and 163rd Street, outside of a bodega marked *Hernandez Grocery Center*.

Chase and Elvis were arguing.

As we pulled closer to the bodega, I saw that Chase Gupta, holding a take-out bag that said *Punta Cana Restaurant*, was wearing her fifty shades of eye shadow, still short, still brown, still lovely and fat. Elvis was holding a green cooler. He was a man transformed, in a loose-fitting red linen suit with no collar, no socks, and blue leather sandals. As we pulled up he yelled, "The Buddha of *El Barrio*, baby!"

Chase wore another short skirt wrapped around her enormous legs, gold sandals, one gold ring, under a new short black leather jacket.

It was a humid eighty degrees that night.

"Welcome to Washington Heights," said Elvis, jumping into the backseat. I noticed that he was wearing Chase's diamond-encrusted watch. "My name is Elvis. I protect those who come here."

"What's in the cooler?" I asked.

"*Cerveza*," Elvis said. "You can't go investigating without beer."

"We don't allow beer at the farm, Elvis," said Zena. "You'll never become TSP president doing that."

"I'm a Budweiser man," said Elvis. "Baby steps."

As Chase squeezed into the backseat of the car, she yelled, "Elvis, I'm warning you. You're the love of my life, but you have low standards. You'd better stop kissing that lousy filthy Jew's ass."

Zena shook her head and said, "What are you going on about now, Chase?"

"That stupid slag of a lawyer. That Jewish bitch who keeps calling Elvis on his cell phone."

Zena sighed, looked at me, and said wearily, "When you go off like that about Jews, Chase, people get the wrong impression. You sound like an anti-Semite."

"How can I be an anti-Semite?" Chase barked. "My mother was Jewish. She was an English Jew, not a low-class Polish Jew like that slag of a lawyer from Park Slope. That stupid, aggressive, obnoxious, always-in-your-face bitch. In India she would be a farmer or an Untouchable."

Chase turned to me and said, "Zena doesn't like understand that there's two kinds of people in the world: farmers and merchants. Farmer types act in a low-class way, like those Pakistani dot heads in Queens wearing kurtas and *chappals*, saris and *churidars*, who give modern *desis* a bad name. Merchants tend to act in higher-class ways. When I talk about that Jewish slag of a public defender that was helping Elvis while he was in jail, I'm talking about a certain type of Jew. The kind my mother always warned us about."

"Well," said Zena, "I don't care. I don't like stereotypes."

"Stereotypes are like so true, Zena," said Chase. "Irish people are drunks. Italians are Mafia. Black people steal. Puerto Ricans bring cockroaches."

Elvis looked at me and smiled and winked as Chase went on. "Indians stink. Jews are cheap. Polish people are stupid. Chinese are sneaky. Not everybody. Not all of them. But like a lot. I mean, I'm Indian and I don't stink but a lot of them do. You can't argue with the truth."

Zena rolled her eyes.

Chase held up a brown cigarette and said, "Anybody mind the smell of cloves?"

Zena looked at her, disappointed. "You're still smoking those Djarums?"

"I know," Chase said. "Disgusting habit. Illegal. The worst. Anybody mind?"

"No," said Elvis. "Light up."

Elvis tapped a Newport cigarette out of a crumpled pack and offered me one.

"No thanks," I said.

"Elvis," Zena scolded. "Smoking is Kryptonic behavior."

"Give it a rest, little sister," said Chase, as if she were more than just a year older than Zena, cracking the window a bit.

"You'll never make it back into the program at this rate, Elvis," said Zena. "I'm taking notes."

Chase opened her mouth wide, as if to say something.

Elvis put an arm around Chase, kissed her.

"Elvis is like my little merchant in training, Chico," said Chase, easing up. "My little Superman and I love him. Zena's just jealous." Then she and Elvis went into a long, passionate round of sloppy tongue kissing that sounded like my dog Boo lapping up water, while Zena made a disgusted face. Somewhere over the George Washington Bridge, I heard: "Where do you live, Chico?"

I looked back at Chase. "I live in the Bronx on Parkchester with a little girl, a Chihuahua named Boo, and a three-legged cat called Gizmo."

"A three-legged cat?" yelled Chase. "Like ewww!"

"I kept a wounded pigeon once," Zena said and patted my hand sweetly.

"Are you going to kill it?" said Chase.

"What?"

"Kill it," Chase said. "Put that three-legged cat like out of its misery. It's the right thing to do."

Zena shook her head furiously.

"I'm like serious," Chase said, looking at me. "Life is for the strong. Life should be worth living. That's what my father, I mean, Father Ravi or whatever teaches, no?"

Zena stopped the car suddenly and we screeched along the highway. The car came to a slow halt as horns blared and car lights zoomed past. Zena turned on her younger sister.

"Who are you to decide what's worth living?"

"Zena?" Chase pleaded, putting up her hands in surrender. "It's like just a cat. Take it easy."

Zena stared at Chase. "You know what your problem is, Chase?"

"What, Zena the wise child?"

"You don't know what's good, Chase."

Chase frowned, folded her arms under her enormous breasts, and leaned against Elvis, who put a lanky arm around as much of her as he could.

"Enough, little Zena," said Chase.

Zena glanced at Elvis and smirked. "The beginning of wisdom, Chase, is knowing what is and isn't necessary. The house of wisdom is a tall house with long, winding halls, and most of us are dead before we even reach the doorknob."

"What's your point?"

"My point is that you don't even care if the doorknob exists."

"Now who sounds like her control-freak mother, little sister?" Chase said.

"I'm wasting my breath," said Zena.

"Exactly," said Chase. "But it never seems to stop you or Mara."

Zena looked at me. "Is that cat happy, Chico?"

"He seems happy to me," I said.

"Good. Is that all right with you, Chase? Can we let Gizmo the cat live? Even if he only has three legs? Even if he is a cripple? Is that okay with you?"

"A cripple," Chase said almost in a whisper, and bowed her head, as if realizing what was behind Zena's sudden fury. "Aw, Zena. I didn't mean Hari. What're you like saying? What kind of person do you think I am? I was just philosophizing. I would never actually kill a living creature."

Then she got angry. "I can't believe you would even like suggest that I'm talking about Hari."

Then she yelled, "Apologize, Zena!"

I signaled for Elvis, who was just watching the exchange between the Gupta sisters with a quiet smirk on his face. Elvis leaned in front of Chase to stop anything from going down. Chase allowed him to do so; if she had wanted to, I think she could have easily bowled Elvis over, passed through me, and snapped her little sister Zena like a twig in the jaws of a rhino.

"Zena," said Elvis, holding down Chase's massive arms. "Let's not fight. We're all on the same side here, *mamá*."

"Very bloody well," Zena said, sitting very still and facing the road now, talking real slow, like a warning. "I accept you, Chase, the way I accepted Mother, in a very unconditional way. And I love my sisters, the way I loved her. But sometimes you say stupid things. I'm not interested in your daft ideas about types of Jews or Hindus or Muslims or Untouchables or any of your petty little prejudices. I'm going up to Utopia Farms to help find Gabby, to help Chico, and to breathe fresh bloody country air for two minutes. But if you keep spewing your nonsense, I swear to God we'll turn back to New York City and drop you off on the nearest corner, I'm serious."

"I see," Chase said, and sat back, with a quiet but vicious look on her dark face.

There was a vengeance in her silence.

SEVENTEEN

Montague, New Jersey. Utopia Farms. Utopia Farms was once a working farm that TSP members shared in operating. It occupied acres and acres of fenced green land and included an enormous three-story, twenty-eight-room, multimillion-dollar lodge.

Utopia Farms was up for sale now, on the market with no bids since last August, all but abandoned.

Dense woods surrounded organic gardens and pastures once used for the llamas and alpacas whose luxurious fur hides represented a high-priced cash crop for TSP. Zena said that the TSP members who usually tended the gardens and canned and packaged the farm-grown vegetables and fruits, mostly the wives and children of stockbrokers and money managers, who would prepare meals and relax with nature, picnicking, hiking, bird-watching, swimming, and boating on the property's twenty-acre lake, would not be back for financial reasons. The married couple who lived on the property and cared for the animals had divorced and left the lodge.

We parked and stepped out of the car, as Chase and Elvis, drunk on beer already and full of takeout from Punta Cana, guided us, laughing and chopping needlessly at the forest with a machete, through the great green property.

I was just about to play my *tell-me-everything-you-know* card when I heard Chase scream, "Get away from me!" I turned and saw Pablo Sanchez waving a small ring and grabbing at Chase Gupta.

"I love you!" Pablo yelled. "Elvis doesn't love you! This is all his fault!"

"Why is it always blame with you, Pablo?"

"Pablo?" I said and ran over and reached out for his arm. He whipped around and said, "I didn't know it, Chico. I never saw Yayo coming but who knew I had to be twice as careful with Elvis. He runs another man down. He takes my work. He takes my girl. He takes what's sacred. He's just as much of a killer as Yayo. Maybe even more."

"No," Chase said. "You're all mixed up, Pablo."

"I guess it's that easy nowadays," Pablo said. "Love is like changing a shirt."

"Go home, Pablo," I said.

Pablo screamed, "Fool! What a fool I am! How stupid! How could I have been so wrong about you, Chase! This is how it's all done, you trade, you move on, you forget! It makes me sick!"

"Let her go," I whispered.

"Fool!" Pablo shouted and released Chase.

"Go home, *manito*," Elvis said, not without sympathy.

"Go home, *manito*?" said Pablo, charging at Elvis. "Go home, *manito*? You swindler! You have debts to pay! You make a profession of stealing the work and women of other men! You sickening, rotten, petrified so-called friend! While the real man, the true man, the honest man, The Superman, gets nothing!"

"I don't want any more trouble," said Elvis, backing away,

almost near tears again. "I loved your mother. I loved Esther like she was my own. This isn't a comic book, bro. We're friends."

"Do you think it's that easy, God damn it? You drop a fake tear and all is forgiven? It's not! One of these days somebody's going to break your legs, Elvis. And you will *crawl* away on your belly like the snake you are!"

Pablo charged again and flailed and threw punches at the air just inches from Elvis's pretty face and Elvis didn't fight back but just kept dodging and moving and peddling away beyond fat Pablo's rage, almost laughing and crying at the same time.

I grabbed Pablo. Zena came running, too. She stepped in front of Pablo and stopped him in his tracks.

"Listen to me, Pablo," Zena said in a soothing but stern voice, and grabbed Pablo's face. "She doesn't bloody love you, Pablo. Here is the truth. Chase doesn't belong to you. She's not your girlfriend. She never was. Your friendship was just that, a friendship. A platonic thing. Don't blame Elvis. It's not Elvis's fault or your fault or even Chase's. There are these accidents we call love. The accident of meeting someone and then choosing that someone over all others for an indefinite period of time. Sometimes an hour, a week, a day, sometimes, rarely, hardly ever, almost never, no matter what they say, a lifetime. There are lots of things we can control, Pablo. But we can't control that. We can't control who loves us and who doesn't and for how long. I used to believe that love was something I could control. But I don't anymore. What's most offensive to you is not your delusion. You can always forgive delusions. What's most offensive to you is that you have been bloody deluded and now, even though you know the truth, you still worship your delusion. You were wrong, Pablo. Forgive yourself for being wrong. It's over. Let her go."

Pablo relaxed. "She's right," he said as I released him, tears in his eyes. "I'm through with you, Chase."

"Go home, Pablo," Zena whispered.

"I don't love you anymore, Chase!" Pablo yelled, moving past us, back in the direction from which we came.

"Go home, Pablo," I agreed, as I saw him go in the direction of the parked Mini Cooper. "Go home."

EIGHTEEN

We went into the empty lodge, through the wide wooden doors to the living room, bookshelves stocked with philosophy, six large plush sofas and matching love seats that sat under the shade of tall potted plants, through the huge kitchen where everything still sparkled and shone like liquid mercury, down a hall with five lavish bedrooms, each equipped with its own Jacuzzi and sauna, up a long wooden staircase, to the second floor, to the art studio marked GABBY GUPTA in gold. And all I could think was, if this is the spiritual life, bring it on.

Elvis and I went in and searched the contents of the large open area filled with Gabby Gupta's nudes while Zena and Chase picked at Gabby's old art supply storage room on the top floor. I stared at the poem by Elizabeth Bishop, tacked to a dusty window:

*so many things seem filled with the intent to
be lost that their loss is no disaster*

"This is great, *papá*," said Elvis, while searching. "After you find Gabby, you should join TSP. Zena could help you get into the *Superklatura*. As a member of the *Superklatura*, you can do anything you want, Chico. You get to skip levels at TSP. You don't have to follow what the other members do. And I wanna thank you for what you did for me. I don't have many friends I trust. All of my old good friends are either dead, in jail, or they left town. Pablo trusts you. I trust Pablo even if he's too stupid to see what a good friend I am. You're Puerto Rican like me. I trust you. I guess, you could say you sorta inherited me."

"I feel lucky."

Elvis put his fingers under my nose and said, "Smell that."

I slapped his hand away.

"You don't like the smell of pussy?" Elvis asked.

"Charming."

"I'm kidding." He laughed. "I washed my hands."

He moved closer to me by a stack of piled blank canvas. "It's not Chase," Elvis said, sniffing his fingers. "I went to this bachelor party with that public defender chick that Chase was complaining about. It was on Central Park West in this penthouse. They hired strippers. Get this, over the television is a portrait of the last supper by some downtown artist. Playing on the TV below it, pornography!"

"Adorable."

But Elvis continued. "We all sat in this circle, right? While these strippers dance and kiss and rub themselves. Then the groom, he got pulled to the middle of the room, stripped naked, and the strippers they touch the guy! Right there in front of us! And, get this, no matter how much the girls rub the guy, the groom won't grow. We all start to laugh and laugh and laugh. The groom, right, he looks up and around the room, everybody laughing, even the strippers, even this lawyer chick, and he laughs too. He's laughing and we're all laughing and the strippers are laughing then suddenly he begins to cry!"

"Why?"

"I don't know, this guy, he's a rich computer geek, he just balls up like a baby, in the middle of this fancy living room and he cries. He cries like a little bitch in front of everybody."

"Maybe he's allergic to strippers."

"What's not to enjoy!" Elvis said. "These bitches were fine. It was like Gabby and Zena times two. Two girls, one white with blond hair, one black with red hair, bikinis, thongs, big fake tits. I slept with the white one and my lawyer. Married. Two kids. Husband's a pothead loser works for the MTA, managing tunnels or some shit, and she's a total undercover freak. I can still smell her. Smell my fingers."

"No thank you," I said. "I'll wait for the movie."

Elvis sniffed his own fingers and shrugged.

"Well," said Elvis. "Thanks for not telling Zena or Chase about that night."

"What night?"

"That night at Pablo's," he said, as if he didn't want to get too deep into the details. "I wasn't exactly keeping it together."

"Oh," I said. "The crying."

"Well," Elvis said, "it wasn't *exactly* crying."

"No?"

"No," he repeated. "It was more like anxiety, like stress or anger, you know? It was more like angry crying, you know? About what was happening. Like why me, why now, you know?"

"Yeah."

"We gotta take over, you and me," Elvis said, resuming his search. "We're both working the same angle, Chico. You and me, we're alike. I can tell. We're not guys who end up living with our mothers, working some dead-end job. These Dominican kids like Pablo, they don't get it. No business sense. They work dead-end jobs or sell street drugs and think it's gonna get them somewhere. You, you're Puerto Rican like me. My father was a professional wrestler and he fought and saved enough money to buy a bodega and that bodega's practically mine, so I understand you. You're a businessman like my father. But that's not enough, *papá*. You're restless. I can tell. I'm good that way. I can read people. My mother was a *Santera* and she had the gift, too. One minute, you're working for Pablo, the next minute, boom-bam-ala-kazam, you're running around with the boss's daughter and making moves in Jersey. You got plans, *papá*. Like me. There's no shame in your game. We gotta build a partnership. You and me, with Chase and Zena, we could run TSP. I'm talking millions. Selling this property alone. We could go places. Places our folks only dreamed about."

Elvis angling to get me to go in with him on some kind of hostile takeover of TSP made me wonder if any of these people ever talked to each other.

"I guess so," I said. "Maybe we *should* sit down and have a meeting."

"*Vaya*," said Elvis, slapping my back.

"I'll tell you a secret," I said, getting closer to Elvis, drawing him into my web. "I sometimes dream about the rotten foster home where I grew up and sometimes I imagine myself trampled by anonymity, an avalanche of nobody-ness."

"I understand. That's my nightmare, too. Pablo don't understand. Forgive us, Pablo, if the only thing we see worth doing now is being rich."

"So your goal is to be rich, too?"

"I'm gonna be the next president of TSP, you'll see."

"I thought they tossed you out because of the Esther Sanchez thing?"

"I'm working on that."

"What about Hari Lachan?"

"He's in a wheelchair. Superman? C'mon. Think about it."

"Yeah," I said. "I guess. How did he get in that wheelchair?"

"He got hit by a car on Eight Avenue right outside TSP, last

September. I heard the bone was sticking out of his leg and everything."

"Mara might still make trouble."

"I can take care of Mara in the long run. I see the way she looks at me."

"What about Zena?"

"Zena will come around once I get Mara," said Elvis. "Are you cool?"

"Yeah," I said. "I'm cool."

"I knew it! I took a chance on you, brother, and I won. Birds of a feather. You work your side of the street with Zena. I'll work mine. We'll find Gabby. I'll meet you in the middle."

"Sounds good, brother. I wanna run with the winners."

We shook hands. Then I remembered that "smell my fingers" line of his and took it back as quickly as I could.

"You help me," Elvis said, "and I will make your dreams come true. If what me and Chase know and are planning works out, you'll be set. Pablo can stay living like a loser. Stupid jerk doesn't know a gold mine when he sees one."

"What're you planning?" I asked.

"Soon, *papá*," he said. "Soon."

Then he looked at me and asked finally, "You think that kid Yayo killed Pablo's mother?"

"No," I said. "I don't."

Then Wagner began blasting through the halls of the lodge. I heard scuffling outside Gabby's studio, and then a man screaming, and more scuffling, and then silence.

"What the hell?" I jumped out of the room into the hall.

Zena came running down from the top floor.

"I'll go down," I whispered.

"No," Zena said. "We're not supposed to be here. Don't go."

"It sounds like somebody's in trouble."

"It might be Hari."

"I thought you said you had an arrangement?"

"No need to shove it down his throat."

164

"We haven't done anything, Zena."

"Do you really believe that?" she asked, looking into my eyes.

"No."

A loud BANG!

I ran past her, down the stairs to the living room on the first floor.

Nothing.

Dark. Silent. Empty.

I ran into the kitchen and caught a glimpse of a door closing that looked like it went down into a lower level. I leapt for the door but it slammed shut as I just about reached the doorknob. I tried the knob. It was an automatic lock. I put my ear to the door. It was thick and apparently soundproof. I heard nothing.

"What are you doing here?"

I turned and saw Mara Gupta, shaking her head.

"I'm going to have you arrested for trespassing," she said, flipping open her cell phone.

Zena came down, walked past her older sister Mara over to me, put her car keys in my hand, and said, "Go back to the city with Elvis, Chico."

"I'm not going anywhere until I see what's down in that basement," I said.

"Ah-hem," I heard from behind me.

I turned and saw the blocks of steel called Doyle, Lieblich, and Big Man.

As I followed Elvis out of the lodge, past a row of photographs of members, the next to last photo was a photo of Gabby Gupta, blond Kirsten, the TSP GUIDE, at some kind of picnic in Peace Corps T-shirts flanked by the mysterious S of the possibly African accent and L of the interminable "man."

There was a fourth person there.

The person implied but never seen.

The person taking the photo.

Joey.

NINETEEN

Returning to Manhattan with the moon beaming in through the Mini Cooper window, Zena in my head, naked under a thin red nightie, hardly touching, frustrated, not feeling like a Superman at all, I knew that Zena knew more than she was saying and I felt like a puppet with somebody's hand up my butt. I just had to find out whose hand it was and why.

I casually questioned Elvis and he told me that Kirsten Smith, an old friend from Gabby Gupta's Peace Corps days, had been Gabby's personal assistant, and Kirsten Smith had a brother—a kid named Larry. Kirsten Smith was also in charge of locking up the TSP building.

By the time we reached NYC, I knew that no one could be trusted, not even Zena, that the truth was being twisted, and that one more good thing was gone.

After I dropped Elvis off on 163rd, I drove to the TSP building on 47th Street, Kirsten was alone, working on some data entry at the reception desk drinking a Coke from Mc-Donald's.

There was one guard doing the rounds, she said.

Doyle and his goons were up at Utopia Farms.

It was closing time.

I went to work.

"What're you doing back here?" she asked.

"I missed you," I said. "Being a private investigator makes you work up an appetite."

"Hmmm." She smiled.

While I leaned against the desk making with the gaga eyes, she spooned into her story, how unhappy she was without a boyfriend, how her old boyfriend was a gambler and a chain smoker and not passionate enough, how she hated her father back in Arkansas.

"We get married young in the South. That's why I left," she said.

She reminisced again about the lover she had left behind, a professor, how she loved intelligent men, artists, how she really saw herself as some kind of artist, maybe a writer, and believed she was wasting herself here at TSP as a secretary really, how she was thinking of going back to school and becoming a social worker or even going back to the Peace Corps.

Kirsten unbuttoned the top button of her blouse. "Is it hot in here or is it me?"

"You were in the Peace Corps?"

She nodded. "Right before the Peace Corps," she said, "I was living and going to school in Arkansas where I met my ex-boyfriend on a bus from San Francisco. He told me that he was a feminist and a Marxist and I became a feminist and a Marxist."

"Is that what you are?" I asked.

"Not anymore." She laughed. "I like expensive French restaurants too much."

I said nothing and leaned closer.

"May I ask you a question, beautiful?"

"Sure," Kirsten said, breathing audibly now, standing up, and leaning into me.

"Are you a Superman?"

"Oh, no," she whispered. "I'm just an ordinary member but I'm working toward it. It's not as easy as you may think. There are steps."

She touched my face.

"How many steps are there?" I said. "Are we talking Chrysler Building or Empire State?"

"Empire State. Definitely Empire State. But it's worth the walk. You probably have real strong legs."

Concentrate, Santana.

"How do you know being a Superman is so great if you've never been one?"

"Oh," she whispered and leaned closer, almost touching my chin with her lips. "I read the literature. I listen to the stories told by members who have reached The Superman stage. The success, both financial and personal, is amazing. The program guarantees happiness, health, and wealth."

"And if it doesn't work?"

"If it doesn't work, it's not the Project. It's you."

"What do I have to do to speed this process along?"

"All you must do is," she said, taking my hand, "is follow the calling. Follow Father Ravi's guidance."

She placed my hand against her breast. "Do you feel my heart beating?"

"Yeah."

"That's biology. That's science. TSP is not a religion; it's science like the beat of my heart. Father Ravi teaches that no matter can be created, therefore no matter can be destroyed; that's the first principle of The Superman theory. You are eternal. Isn't that great news?"

"Wonderful," I said, my hand against her chest. "With that much time on my hands, maybe I can finally learn how to play the accordion."

"Aw, sweetie," said Kirsten and brushed my face with her pale hand. "In TSP, we believe that anyone with the right attitude, the right support, and perhaps most importantly a sense of hope for the future of mankind can learn and succeed at anything. We see it every day."

"Well," I said, taking my hand back, "I will try not to let you down."

"How does working again with joy and having a healthy and happy social life and successful career sound like to you?"

"Not too shabby. I could use some of that."

"You'll get some of that," Kirsten said and batted her blue eyes and played with her long blond locks. "And more. You'll sing and dance and fall in love and make more money and buy an apartment and meet some financially secure friends and do whatever you please."

"Whatever I please?"

"Well," she cooed, "as long as it ain't . . . isn't Kryptonic. But anything goes in a committed relationship."

"Anything?"

"Anything," she said and leaned into me again.

"Maybe we can work on that."

"You remind me of a boy I fell in love with once," she said. "I like your face."

She pinched my cheek again.

"Yours ain't too shabby, either," I said and pinched her back.

"So," Kirsten said. We were alone. At the desk. Breathing. Heavy.

"So," I whispered. "What's next?"

She leaned a long way over the reception desk, her lips open and beckoning, and that's when I kissed her.

I stared into Kirsten's pale blue eyes. I kissed her again a long time.

It's a dirty job but somebody's gotta do it.

"Kryptonic," she said, and pulled back. "But nice. I wish I could take you home to Queens with me."

"Me, too," I said as she came from behind the desk and pushed me gently toward the door.

"Maybe we could go upstairs?" I whispered. "Maybe we could find some room?"

"For brokenhearted lovers?" She smiled.

"To cry away our gloom," I whispered. "I get so lonely, baby."

"Mmm," she moaned.

She went in for another kiss, eyes closed, lips puckered.

"No!" she said, pushing me away. "Not here, bad boy. I'll call you tomorrow. Good night, bubba."

Improvise, Santana!

She shoved me toward the closed green entrance door and forced herself to turn and walk away from me. I did not exit. I watched her back as she went past the cuckoo clock and I tiptoed, sneaking quickly up the red-carpeted spiral staircase.

I waited on the second floor for the elevator.

Within minutes somebody was in it and heading down to the basement.

I took the stairs.

I opened the door to the basement and as I got into the hall, from behind me, I heard: "*Hola*, pal."

I turned and couldn't believe my eyes, though I knew it was true and had almost been expecting him. He wore blue jeans and his upper torso was so muscled that his pectorals bulged through his blue button-down shirt. His jet-black hair was long but perfectly cut, not in a barbershop way but expertly manicured by a hairstylist.

"Hello, Joey."

"You've met my associates," Joey said, grinning. "Kirsten, Solange, and Larry."

S of the African accent.

Solange.

I nodded at Solange the African, Kirsten of Arkansas, and her brother Larry of the interminable "man," who stood beside

Joey. The whole gang was there. Kirsten looked at me apologetically.

"Why the hide-and-seek?" I asked him.

"It's more like a game of tag," said Joey. "I tagged you and Pablo and a few other friends to go places and see people I couldn't get near but I don't always know who's on my side so I have to be careful who I tag and when."

"You can't put all your tags in one basket, man," said Larry Smith.

"Until you know for sure who can be trusted, brother," said Solange.

Kirsten Smith just nodded.

"Sorry about the lack of confidence," Joey said. "We had to know for sure that you were on our side and staying on our side."

"What makes you think I'm staying on your side?" I said.

"I'll take it from here," Joey said and pulled me down a white corridor.

Larry Smith smiled and jumped clumsily onto the elevator with the others. Solange nodded. Kirsten pressed the close door button and blew me a silent kiss and said, as the elevator door closed, "Sorry."

I nodded. Kirsten of Arkansas and her brother Larry and their friend Solange the African were helping Joey, just like Pablo. They all were, I thought, friends, true friends, as me and Joey walked through an endless maze of pipes and wires and vents to a small office marked JANITOR, and in smaller letters, Pablo Sanchez.

Joey opened the door and flicked on the light switch. The room was full of comic-book posters.

Joey threw down the keys. "Somebody's trying to frame me."

"You think?"

"It feels like I'm not getting any closer."

"Where's your wife?"

"I don't know."

"Who killed Esther Sanchez?"

"Some kid named Yayo, right?"

"That night with Esther. You were scheduled to hide out in Pablo's apartment. You called. I answered the phone. That was you, but before that, play it back for me."

"The night Esther was killed, I was supposed to show up there, like you said. Pablo was going to hide me. I never showed up because I got word that Doyle and his boys were asking questions in Washington Heights. Pablo's a good friend. I'm only sorry the confusion caused by my plan on going there might have gotten his mother's killer off and that poor sap Elvis doing some other guy's time. Do you think I wanted to start this whole mess? Send Pablo to you? Gotten you and Kirsten and Larry and Solange involved?"

"Why me?"

"I saw your ad in the paper, months ago. Just a coincidence. I clipped and kept it. Then when everything went down, I had a hunch."

"Which was?"

"That you were still the kid I knew growing up at St. Mary's with Nicky and the other boys. And if you were, you would help me."

"How have you stayed free so long?"

"I call friends I trust. I meet them at a designated place sometimes. Sometimes. They let me crash or give me money for a flop or some food. I never stay too long. I try not to call on anybody more than twice. I keep moving."

"How long did you think you could keep that up?"

"Until I ran out of friends. As long as it took." He smiled that brilliant smile. "I have a lot of friends."

Something wasn't right. Something was missing.

"Did you do anything to harm your wife?"

"What do you think I am, Chico? It's me, bro. It's Joey."

He grabbed me by the shoulders, looked sincerely and hopefully into my eyes, and shook me a bit and whispered, "'Member?" I remembered, all the way back to St. Mary's. Bronx rooftops and junkyards and water balloons and comic books and movies and stickball games and soda pop, skelsies and basketball and football on concrete, and playing the dozens-your mama so poor-your mama so dumb-your mama so-karate and boxing and telling jokes until we almost pissed ourselves, and I knew he was innocent. I just knew it.

Didn't I?

"Help me out a little bit, Joe," I said. "Ever since this started, my brain's been getting banged around like a white heavyweight. Where is your wife?"

"I don't know," Joey repeated.

He stopped talking, and he seemed genuinely shook up.

"Tell me all of it, Joey," I said.

"Gabby and I fought about another woman that I was seeing," Joey said. "The day she ran away, Gabby slapped me. She had never slapped me before. We never hit each other. We destroyed things, we cried, we screamed, we meditated, we prayed but we were never physically violent, never. I slapped her back."

"You slapped her?"

"I slapped Gabby *back*," said Joey. "It was a reflex. I didn't mean to. I've never hit a woman a day in my life before that. I shouldn't have. But I did. Don't you think I regret it?"

"What happened then?"

"Gabby went berserk. Started throwing things at me, breaking things against my back, kicked me, kicked me so hard I thought she broke my leg. I didn't fight back. I went down. Can you imagine what she would've done if she wasn't a vegetarian and a pacifist?"

"Then what happened?"

"By the time I got up off the floor she was gone. She just ran out of the apartment and I haven't seen her since."

I nodded skeptically.

"You've got to believe me, Chico. The cops took me down for questioning. Forty-eight hours later, I'm in my office, surrounded by Mara Gupta and some board members with hatchet faces. Asking what I've done with Gabby. I get told that I've been suspended from TSP. Hari suggests that I should cooperate with authorities. I'm no *bobo*. I get up slow, calm, say I just want to go home to Williamsburg early and make art and relax. I go home and I run out of there. I pack stuff together and get my ass out of Williamsburg before anybody can blink. By the time I got to Brook Avenue, heading for St. Mary's, I don't know why, but I realized that I couldn't go back."

"Why did you run?"

"If you had seen the way Mara and Hari looked at me. I thought these were my people, my family and friends, but they had me guilty. What would you do?"

I shrugged.

"Gabby was missing, and I was being blamed."

"So why didn't you *stay* missing?"

"I got to thinking about it," said Joey. "I got to thinking about spending the rest of my life on the run for something I didn't do. I believed in Father Ravi because he believed in me, as an artist and as a human being. He was like a real father to me. He was smart, an artist himself, a writer, a spiritual leader, older, wiser. I thought that the fact that I could help Father Ravi grow TSP and have new people actually believe and follow us was something special, something powerfully spiritual. I sincerely believed that the creation of The Superman Project was going to save the world."

"What went wrong?"

"Father Ravi and I finally wrote down the Twelve Steps to Power and the Twelve Personality Defects. Before I got here no steps or principles were written down; everything was in Father Ravi's head. It was all based on some German philosophy and some Hinduism and some Buddhism with a splash of Christianity and Islam, and I added a bit of comic-book mythology and created the Artist's League of TSP with Gabby and Giovanni Vaninni. Then everything snowballed; we recruited fresh, new, young, energetic, and artistic members, then came generous donations and members and fellow travelers with money and more money. Then we inherited the mansion and the farm from a wealthy old couple, members who had no children, and we moved out of our dilapidated building across the street from the mansion."

"How did you meet Gabby Gupta?"

"Gabby and I met in the Peace Corps but only started a relationship and married after I joined TSP."

"Mara Gupta and Hari Lachan," I said.

"It was Gabby's younger sister, Mara," said Joey, "who finally contacted the police about Gabby's disappearance, Hari who suspended me from TSP, and fearing that I was slowly being framed and fearing that I would shortly be jailed, I ran. Even without a body, I feared that the circumstantial evidence could send me to jail if something has happened to Gabby. But Gabby is still alive, I swear, Chico, and the scratches on my face and domestic violence calls were caused by attacks *from* Gabby when she found out I had been cheating."

"Scratches?"

"I'm not proud of my cheating," Joey said. "I was going to step away from TSP before Gabby disappeared and they suspended me, but I have no intention of spending any time, like my father before me, in a jail cell."

"Mara Gupta and Hari Lachan," I said, "are taking advantage of your wife running off to take over TSP. Father Ravi is old and sick. You're out. Discredited. Accused. Suspended. Wanted by the law. TSP needs somebody."

Joey nodded. "The next man in line. That's Mara and Hari."

"Mara's not a man."

"Says who?" said Joey.

"Maybe your wife Gabby is cooperating with Mara and/or Hari, with or without their knowledge, by staying out of sight.

Out of revenge for your infidelity. And once Mara or Hari becomes president and your *career* and reputation and everything you've worked to help build are destroyed, Gabby appears again, or not, because she's so angry with you."

"How do you do it, pal?"

"That's why they pay me the small bucks," I said. "Let's go."

"Where?" asked Joey, calmly.

"Police station in Astoria eventually," I said. "You're gonna turn yourself in to a friend of mine. Her name's Samantha Rodriguez."

"You sound like you think I'm guilty of doing something to hurt my wife."

"Nah," I said. "I just think I can help you more if you stop with the Speedy Gonzalez routine."

The truth?

Joey told a nice story.

Nice and neat.

But it had more holes in it than the socks I was wearing.

TWENTY

The Bronx. Joey and I played a final and quick game of one-on-one basketball on Sedgwick Avenue and quit just before I sprained an ankle. I wouldn't say Joey Valentin slaughtered me in the game, but I wouldn't advertise the score either. Let's just say I put up a valiant fight. After the slaughter, the wanted fugitive, wearing a Yankee baseball cap, sat at a stool next to me, exhausted, bathed in the neon lights in Mimi's Cuchifrito, for one last meal before I handed him over to Officer Samantha Rodriguez.

James Brown sang, *"This is a man's world . . . "*

"Remember you wanted to be a priest?" said Joey.

"I did not."

"You forgot."

"I'm no priest."

"Once a Catholic, always a Catholic."

"That's cute," I said. "Now tell me about the bunny rabbits."

"Fedco is gone," said Joey, glancing out at the Bronx. "Alexander's. Gone. The old Yankee Stadium. Gone. Teatro Puerto Rico is a church now or something. Remember Reggie Jackson?"

"I think he's still alive."

"How is Nicky? You two still in touch?"

"Yeah. He's in Atlanta."

"Good old Nick!" said Joey, grabbing his coffee cup with a massive hand. "I wonder who benches more?"

"My money's on Nicky," I said. "No offense. Do you think that any of the Gupta sisters besides Mara Gupta could be behind your wife's disappearance?"

"No," Joey said.

"Chase Gupta?"

"No."

"Zena?"

Joey gave me a look.

"What's the look?" I asked.

"You said *Mara Gupta* and then you said *Chase Gupta* and then you just said *Zena*."

I nodded real slow because he was right. But—

"I'll be playing the part of the detective tonight," I said. "Thank you very much."

"Don't tell me," said Joey, not letting go, like Boo on a chicken bone. "You got something going with Zena?"

I ignored the question.

Joey nodded and looked at himself in the window glass.

"Look at what they've done to me, Chico. How long, how far I've come. I've suffered and survived. And now this. And my poor Gabby. I loved her, Chico. I really did."

I noted that he said I *loved* her, not I *love* her.

Who's the detective now?

Joey took a deep breath and let it out slowly. "Aw, Gabby. Ever since she disappeared my teeth hurt. My head hurts. Help me make it stop, Chico."

"I'm trying, but you have to cooperate," I said. "Stand still. No more running."

"You trust me, right?" Joey asked and looked at me.

"Sure," I said. "Sure. You trust me, right?"

"All night long, baby," he said.

Mimi came in from the kitchen, hauling a large plate piled with white rice, yucca, and fat red beans (no meat because Joey was a vegetarian now) and set it down before Joey.

Joey looked at me and said, "Is it morning already?"

I looked out into the dark night. "What do you mean?"

Joey looked at Mimi and said, "I just saw the sun come up."

Mimi giggled, leaned over the counter, and kissed Joey's forehead. "*El mismo*, Joey."

Same old Joey.

Yeah.

Mimi went into the pocket of her blue apron and handed me back my Yankee baseball. "Dolores says it's not real."

"Not real?"

"Fake," said Mimi. Mimi told me that Dolores reported her sister Maria had asked her boss Ray, who did autograph authentication, and he said that my ball was *not* an official major league baseball and the signature was a fake. "One more *café*, Chico?"

"No, thanks," I said, examining the phony Roberto Clemente autographed ball.

"You need a new shirt," Mimi said, pulling at my collar. "I saw a shirt on Westchester. Black. Short sleeves. It would look nice on you."

"You got me a shirt last month, remember?"

"A man cannot have too many good shirts, or shoes, or watches."

She glanced at my Timex.

"Don't even think about it," I said.

She laughed, sniffed at me, slapped her fleshy thigh, and

scolded me with her red-polished fingernail, "Are you smoking again?"

"No."

Max came scampering out of the kitchen, holding Boo in her arms, wearing a long white shirt, shorts, a red towel cape, and a black tie.

"Didn't I tell you to stay in the *cocina* with that Chihuahua?" Mimi scolded. "You want to get me *arrestado*?"

"Is that my tie?" I asked, pointing at Max.

Mimi laughed. "She would not come if she could not wear it."

"I got a new superhero name," Max said and held Boo up for Joey to get a better look at and vice versa. "I'm Black Cherokee and this Chihuahua is my partner, Agent Moon Willow. Wanna see my penknife?"

"I'll take your word for it, sweetheart," said Joey.

"Am I too fat to be a superhero?"

"No, you're the right size," Joey said. "Perfect."

"I'm not a dope. I'm good at spelling, reading, writing. I have the highest reading score in my school in Detriot."

"What about math?" Joey said.

Silence.

"I'm not gonna lie to you," Max said. "I'm not so good in math."

"No worries," Joey said, tugging on her/my black tie. "There's still time. But maybe you should concentrate on getting through elementary school?"

"Good idea," said Max. "Brilliant!"

Joey laughed and held out his cheek and pointed.

On cue, Max, on tiptoe, planted a kiss on Joey's cheek.

When charmers meet.

"*Hurry,*" said Mimi, ushering Max back into the kitchen area, away from the wanted man known as Joseph Valentin.

I turned to Joey and said, "How are you feeling?"

"Tired," he said softly and ate his food and squinted at me, as if pained by the white glare of the countertop.

"Why did you get involved with TSP?"

"To do good," he said and pointed into the dark. "There are things out there that are not right, Chico. We're too attached to material things and the need to be famous and have that as the idea of success. I didn't make it to Tahiti, you know? I decided to go west. I met a girl on a bus in Reno. She took me home to Arkansas."

"Kirsten Smith?"

Joey nodded.

"Since when were you ever a Marxist Feminist?"

Joey smiled like a new day. "We were kids," he said. "We lived in an attic in her parents' house. We were in love. I made art. We went to college. I played in a band with her brother Larry. We joined the Peace Corps together. I met Gabby and Solange. After the Peace Corps, Kirsten and I broke up and I came back to New York from Africa and got a job in an art supply store and went to classes at the School of Visual Arts where I was lost and confused and bumming around with Giovanni Vaninni until I reconnected with Gabby and Kirsten and they introduced me to Hari and Mara and Father Ravi and TSP and I found a new ambition. I decided that as a human being, as an artist, as a citizen, as an American, I had to stay involved. I needed to stop being scared and alone and make a difference. TSP made me feel empowered and unafraid. I didn't want to hurt anybody. I was trying to bring awareness to people. Now, the NYPD is trying to pin Gabby's missing on me. They need one person to pin it on and I'm the first contestant. People can't imagine something existing like a conspiracy. They need somebody to pin all this stuff on. That's my role. You know how we grew up. You know the pressures. Unemployment, guns, crime, violence. You know how hard it was to keep our noses clean. I just want to find Gabby and run away to India and make my paintings and forget TSP. To just be a man. To just be alive. To take my lumps and survive and do my work. Maybe that's enough."

He took off his Yankee cap and his long black hair fell down around his broad shoulders.

"The Superman movement as I knew it has changed, Chico. Giovanni was right. It's an experiment gone wrong. When it started, it was a revolutionary model of spirituality. The original plan was for it to become a worldwide human rights movement. It would offer the power of community and transform the lives of people suffering everywhere. It isn't that anymore."

"What is it?"

"A monster," Joey said. "A mutation. A betrayal of what it once was and was meant to be. It is a debilitating escapist program, and a money cow for a select few at the very top called the *Superklatura*."

He ran his fingers through his long black hair.

"I didn't kill Gabby. I didn't hurt her. I didn't do anything. She ran off. You believe me, don't you?"

"Eat your beans," I said.

He ate a forkful of rice, avocado, and beans, chewed, then looked into my eyes. "Make it stop, Chico," he said. "You can make it stop. You can make the world make sense again. It's clearer to me tonight than it's ever been since Gabby disappeared. You're the one. Esther Sanchez is dead. No one trusts anybody. Not at TSP. The left doesn't know what the right is doing. You're the only one who can help me make the world make sense again."

"I'll do my best, Joe," I said. "When Samantha gets here we'll get down to the precinct and get you checked in and lawyered up and we'll start sorting everything out. I believe you, Joe. I'm gonna go hit Mara Gupta and Hari Lachan hard and low as soon as we have you settled."

He nodded.

I felt bad watching him eat, head down, wide back and massive arms from lifting weights but he looked like a kid to me. He looked fourteen. He really did.

My cell phone rang.

"Let me take a wiz before your friend gets here," Joey said, swallowing his last bite.

"Cool."

Joey headed into the kitchen where Mimi and Max and Boo were shelling green beans.

My cell phone rang. I picked up.

"Hello, Yankee."

"Hey?" I said. "How's Madrid?"

"Great," Willow said. "On the way here I got accused of stealing a melon. A group of friendly young men surrounded me and an Arab girlfriend in a nightclub and said really interesting things about our mothers, and a little Spanish boy stopped me on the street in Madrid to tell me how much he hated Americans and how much he hated black people even more. You?"

"About the same," I said.

"Do you miss me?"

I remembered our kiss. It was a nice kiss. "To be honest, Willow," I confessed, "I think I've met someone."

"You bastard!" Willow said. "You give me false hope and then before we even start, get our groove on as Max would say, you cheat on me while my back is turned? What's this heifer's name?"

"Zena."

"You dropped me for a warrior princess?"

"You don't want my drama."

"What makes her so deserving of your drama?"

"She's in trouble. Maybe."

"You love the damsel in distress, don't you?"

"It's a living."

"Nicky was right."

"He's one to talk. Anyway, I'm at Mimi's with a friend. He's a fugitive from the law."

"Oh," she said. "You're making all the right moves as usual."

"It's a curse."

"The reason I'm calling," she said. Pause. "I might not be coming back to New York."

"What? What about Max?"

"I already called my sister in Detroit. She's agreed to come and pick Max up at the end of September."

"The end of September? Jesus."

"Max loves you."

"I love me, too. That's why I said Jesus."

"Is she being a pest?"

"Nah," I said. "She's a doll. She's a superhero with a sidekick now."

"What?"

"Long story."

"I'm sending you some cash through the mail."

"Don't send cash through the mail. The mailman will steal it."

"The mailman has no time to worry about silly things like cash; he's too busy plotting who he's going to kill if he can get his hands on a machine gun."

"True dat."

"I have translations to finish; I'll call you again. Kisses."

"Right back at ya." I hung up.

Joey still wasn't back.

I checked my Timex.

I waited five more minutes.

No!

I rushed out, behind the counter and into the bathroom at the rear of the kitchen, past Mimi and Max on short wooden stools, shelling green beans, Boo chewing on the discarded green shells and growling like they were alive and resisting and he was taking them down. I threw the bathroom door open. The small window above the toilet was open and I looked out and there was an alley and a fence and rows of Brook Avenue tenements but no Joey. On the windowsill was chipped paint and cracked wood chips and a note scribbled in red marker on a white hand towel.

HELP ME

Then I heard sirens and rushed outside. I ran out of the Cuchifrito, signaling for Mimi to hold on to Max. I was met by a swarm of men in bulletproof vests jumping out of three unmarked cars and a van. One of them rushed up and shoved a gun in my ribs.

"Don't move!" he said.

I put my hands up, hard metal promising cessation of all toil and trouble, poking my third rib, remembering that I never did ask Joey about that comic book and said, "Don't worry."

TWENTY-ONE

Same night. Parkchester. Turns out that the police had been following Pablo Sanchez, who had followed me to the Bronx, and when the cops finally figured out who the big guy was they called for backup and I almost got a bellyful of lead for my troubles. It took every string Samantha could pull to keep me out of a holding cell.

"Thanks, Sam," I said into my cell phone when I heard breaking glass and a high-pitched scream. "I gotta go."

I ran down the hall to the bedroom again and flung open the door, ready to let the kid have it. But the room was empty and the air conditioner was running and the window was broken.

And Max was gone.

I had fifty-two heart attacks and ran to the window.

I saw her in the backyard, looking up at me with frightened eyes, in a pile of glass and that red towel tied around her neck.

There was some blood running from a cut below her chin. I jumped out the window and picked her up.

"I don't feel good," Max said.

I ran her back inside, to her room, sat her on the bed, and ran and applied a clean towel and alcohol and a Band-Aid to her bleeding chin.

It was just a small cut, luckily.

"What happened?"

Max reported that she was jumping from the dresser in her bedroom to the bed, trying to fly. She would jump, hit the bed, then go back to the dresser and repeat the jump, again and again.

It was fun, she said, like Superman, like flying.

Then things went terribly wrong.

She jumped.

She bounced.

She bounced right out the window.

Backward.

Luckily we were on the first floor and she bounced out the window into the grassy area outside in the yard on her backside.

"I almost died, Uncle Chico," she said dramatically.

I sat down on the edge of her bed. "Listen," I said. "It's okay to play, Max, playing is good, but from now on, I don't want you opening windows and trying to fly or jumping on anything and trying to fly. No flying, this is a no-fly zone, understand?"

"I wasn't—"

"No flying unless you're on a plane or a helicopter, understand? And if you're gonna go out a window, I'm gonna be the one throwing you out, understand?"

She chuckled. "Yeah. Or maybe I'll throw you out the window."

"I wanna see you try."

She came over and tried to lift me up. I stood up on my toes and said, "You're stronger than you look."

She nodded. "I'm real strong. Feel my muscle."

I did. "Now you," she said.

I made a muscle. She squeezed and I pretended that she was killing me.

"Suffer, baby, suffer!" She laughed. Then she shook her head and said, "Uncle Chico, there ain't no God is there?"

Long pause. What the hell do you say to that, Santana? "Depends on who you ask, honey."

"What do you think?"

"I try not to think about it."

I put Max into bed with those *Black Falcon* comic books and went back out.

When the sun came up, I was waiting impatiently for Mimi, still pacing inside the Parkchester apartment with Boo. It was past our bedtime. I needed answers. I dialed Zena. (I still had her Mini Cooper.) Nothing. I dialed Giovanni. Nothing.

I didn't wanna do it, but I did, I dialed Pablo. "Have you seen Giovanni?"

"He's in the hospital," said Pablo. "Bellevue. He's in a locked ward. The only way to get in is if you're crazy or suicidal."

I paused.

"What're you thinking, Chico?"

"Nothing," I said. "Is Giovanni crazy?"

"Nah," said Pablo. "He's an artist. He goes for days and sometimes a week at a time without sleep and works and gets ideas. He calls them visions. He thinks it'll make him a great artist. Joey was always on him to get more sleep and stop drinking and stuff. TSP even has its own rehab program. Giovanni wouldn't listen. He's been to Bellevue lots before, it's like his vacation place, when he gets too worried or stressed out, he breaks down, says he feels safe there. They know 'im at Bellevue."

"Gotta go, Pablo."

"What's up, Chico?" Pablo asked. "What's the plan? I'll pick you up!"

"Look, Pablo," I said. "I'm sorry for your loss but I'm tired of humoring you. Listen. Joey probably killed his wife. Then he ran away. Your mother was murdered by Yayo for drug money and I start connecting things that aren't connected. Jesus. I actually thought I had been poisoned the other day. It's over, Pablo. I like you. You're a good man with a good heart. A loyal friend. And I'm sorry about your mom and Joey. But you gotta stop following me, bro. You need help. Go see a doctor. Take care of whatever this thing is that's got you obsessed over Joey. But don't call me unless you wanna catch a movie or go bowling. Otherwise, this Joey case is a dead end, closed. I don't care about that comic book or the money. You can get on with your life. It's over, Pablo. Gotta go."

Did I believe that? No way. But I didn't need Pablo mucking things up anymore.

Sometimes luck finds you, as Nicky Brown loves to say, and sometimes you make your own luck.

Bellevue Hospital. First Avenue and 27th Street. The blissfully air-conditioned ground floor—Psychiatric Department.

I sat in the waiting area, a strip of floor between an intake window and a row of plastic chairs lining the wall, scanning Father Ravi's Superman and waiting for the male nurse to get back to me about Giovanni.

Joy called.

I answered my cell, and I said, "You won't believe where I am."

"Disneyland?"

"Close," I said. "Bellevue."

"Doesn't surprise me," she said. "You're nuts."

"Good morning," I said.

"Nicky," said Joy. "He lost your cell number. He called here. Left a message no number to call back."

"Sounds like Nicky."

"He's coming back to New York. He's looking for you."

I thanked Joy and she cursed me and I hung up and walked to the window as soon as the nurse came back.

"Giovanni Vaninni is not available for visitors," said the Filipina nurse; she looked about thirty, with glasses and black hair, perfectly protected from me behind a glass partition.

"I have to talk to him," I said. "I haven't slept all night. It's a matter of life and death."

The Filipina nurse arched an eyebrow and leaned over her desk to make sure that the cop and his gun were still seated at the doorway. She leaned back and said, "Are you okay, sir?"

I checked her ring finger.

No ring.

I pressed a worried face close to the glass partition and said conspiratorially, "I need your help."

I slid my card through the slot.

"One day," I said. "You might need a friend. Call me."

She screwed up her face and said, looking me up and down with a suspicious eye, "You are a private investigator?"

"That's what they wrote on the card."

She examined me from top to bottom. "Your shoes are from hell and you need a nicer shirt, that one's nasty and disintegrated."

"I'll try harder," I said.

"And better pants," she said. "Those are disgusting."

"I'm taking notes."

"It's obvious you're not married," she said. "A good woman would make you shave and look neat. You are not terrible-looking but you wear bad stuff like a bum."

I thanked her for her fashion tips and added, "Maybe we could help each other."

A smile played at the corner of her lips. She casually removed her glasses.

"Chico," I said.

I noted that she was wearing a rose pendant and rose earrings.

I took a shot. "Rose?"

"Rosie." She smiled big.

"Beautiful name. It fits you."

"Hold on."

I watched Rosie the nurse as she unlocked and opened the bolted ward door. I slid through the door, and Rosie locked the door behind me.

Going into the ward, I thought that being in a psych ward must be a lot like being in prison or going on a blind date. Strangers introduce themselves by their first names and what they do—or what they did wrong that brought them there.

I heard the creak of a metal door and a bolt slide shut and the world go away as I followed behind Nurse Rosie.

Giovanni was in the day-room area, stripped of his shoelaces, his belt, his clothes, his keys, and his wallet, behind the bolted door to the wonderland of doctors and nurses and patients and pills known as the Bellevue psychiatric ward.

I looked over my shoulder at the police officer at the bathroom door and looked back at a patient swallowing pink horse pills and drinking water from a small paper cup, patients watching the evening news, some dazed and confused, most just bored and doped up. Giovanni, looking at a spot on the wall, turned as I approached, smiled big, nodded. He tugged nervously at his long blond hair and scratched at his hands and knuckles. He was handcuffed to a wheelchair, a paperback novel in his lap, at the front of the row of patients in chairs facing the TV, and he whispered as I approached, with a listless voice now, like he had cobwebs covering his brain, "Amico."

My friend Giovanni was wearing the standard blue hospital gown. He looked like the only non-black, non-Spanish speaking patient in the joint so far. His one free and nervous pawlike hand fiddled about his forehead, arranging and rearranging his mass of tangled blond locks.

We shook hands. His were trembling.

"Hey," I said softly and nodded and looked at him sympathetically.

"I saw you outside reading," he said and pointed at Father Ravi's book.

"Yeah," I said. "Reading. Nasty habit. I tried to kick it by smoking more but that didn't work out."

"You and I are working together," Giovanni said, looking over at a dude in a blood-spotted nightgown who was sedated and handcuffed to a wheelchair. "People are crazy in here."

"That's the rumor," I said.

"I wasn't always a patient here," Giovanni mumbled. "I had a life. I do not even know why I am here and now they won't let me out."

"You checked yourself in. Just check yourself out."

"Well, I did not exactly check myself in. They forced me."

"What?"

"Yes."

"Jesus."

"What, *amico*?"

"If they take you involuntarily," I said, "they can keep you in the hospital for observation for as long as they want."

"I do not care of this," he mumbled. "But I have had enough. I would like to go home today."

"No," I said. "You're involuntary."

"So what is this mean?"

"Means," I said, "that you go home when doctor says."

"How long? A week?"

"It could be months."

"Months?" He laughed. "No. Giovanni am leaving here today."

"How? What're you gonna do? Escape?"

Silence.

"How'd you get here?" I said.

"The police take me away."

"Why?"

He shrugged innocently. "I was listening to Mozart and drinking Merlot."

"That all?"

He looked away. "I was naked."

"That's it?"

"Oh," he said, as if remembering. "I was in Times Square."

"That would do it."

He told me that he had decided it was a good idea to get naked in Times Square as an art experiment. The police were called. He told me that there was a misunderstanding. A female doctor in a white lab coat came out, and he gave her a hard time about checking him in and the cop handcuffed him to that wheelchair. He also discovered there wasn't much to do in a mental ward except watch TV, or watch other patients pace or sit, some in handcuffs. The screamers would be told to calm down, and if they didn't, they'd be taken into a bright room with an open door, where orderlies would hold them down and a doctor would tranquilize them with a shot in the arm—as an example to the rest. He found a novel in the tiny room that they had installed him in. Then he told me that he was God.

"Why do you keep saying that?"

He smiled like a child. "Because I am God."

"A child of God?"

"No." He smiled. "I am THE GOD."

"God-God?" I said.

"Yes," he smiled.

"Did you tell the police and the doctors that?"

"Yes," he said. "I tell everybody."

"How's that working out for you?"

He lifted his handcuffed paw and laughed a bit. "Not too good."

"Maybe you shouldn't tell people you're God."

"No," he said. "They like it. It make them happy. They smile when I say I am God. They feel good. I like to make people feel good. I am God."

I nodded. "You're crazy."

"That's what they tell me." He laughed.

I had gone in to see Giovanni about the case. I didn't ask him anything, though. I couldn't. I thought about Joey. He had been Joey's best friend and I felt sorry for the guy. Anyway, what kind of relevant information could you get out of a medicated dude who tells you he's God? I'm no doctor but what I knew from people was that I could press Giovanni and maybe make matters psychologically worse for him. Some private dicks would still press a guy. I'm not that kind of dick. Not yet anyway. I'd wait a bit until Giovanni's mind and feet were back on planet Earth.

"As soon as you get out of here, you come see me and we'll talk."

We shook on it.

"Remember," mumbled Giovanni. "You are not dead. You are alive. Don't forget, Chico. As long as there is the life, there is a chance to do things different, to live different and have life. After I get out, we must make choices that will not lead down this road. Despair. Death will win in the end, but today, even if it does not look like it, I am winning."

"Sure," I said, rising. "Sure."

"Mr. Vaninni!" yelled Rosie the Filipina nurse, coming over; she had three huge black orderlies beside her. "There's an actor here. Kirk Atlas. He wants to talk to you."

Kirk Atlas?

No way.

"To me?" asked Giovanni. "Why?"

"He's doing research for a part in a movie. He needs someone articulate. I told him about your background."

"Send Silverman."

"No," said Rosie. "He would like to talk to the Italian from Williamsburg."

"No," said Giovanni.

"Be nice."

"I am not the nice."

"Pretend."

"I will pretend I am Napoleon for you. I will pretend I like the Lebanese boy bands. But I will no pretend to be the nice."

"He's in Dr. B's office, if you change your mind. Anyway, it's time to go up, honey."

"Home?" Giovanni smiled.

"Maybe next week," said Nurse Rosie. "The doctor will say."

"That's what you say last night."

"We'll see. Feeling better?"

"Yes, thank you," said Giovanni. "Much better. Home now."

Rosie laughed. "We'll see what Dr. B. says."

"*Buono*," he said, standing up. "Where is he?"

"No," said Rosie. "Not now. Giovanni, sit down!"

Giovanni said he was going home that day whether Rosie or the doctors liked it or not.

"Vaninni!" said Rosie again, forcefully.

The three black orderlies flexed and prepared to launch.

"Sit down! You're not going home today!" yelled Rosie.

"I am God!" said Giovanni, coming to life again.

I was asked to step back.

I stepped back.

"Let's go, sweetie," said Nurse Rosie.

"Wait," Giovanni said, hulking before the wheelchair. "There has been a mistake!"

"No mistake, buddy," said the equally hulking orderly, grabbing him by the arm. "Stay in the chair!"

"I need to speak with the doctor!"

Rosie the nurse soon had a magic needle readied in her small brown hand.

"Relax," said Rosie the nurse. "Stay in the wheelchair so we can take you upstairs. I can give you a mild sedative if you'd like."

"No!" Giovanni protested. "My name is Giovanni. I am not crazy. There has been a mistake. I do not belong here."

"Sure," said Nurse Rosie. "Nobody does. Yes, honey. We just need you to relax."

"I can no relax."

"Don't you want to be cured, sweetheart?"

"I am cured," Giovanni said. "I just need the sleep, some time to think, to figure this thing. And I have work waiting for me in Williamsburg. I have my work. I have responsibilities. I want to go home now!"

"Don't you want to have a life like normal people?" asked Nurse Rosie, calmly now.

"No!" said Giovanni.

"But we can help you," said Nurse Rosie. "Stay in the chair. Go upstairs. Do it for me."

Nurse Rosie said that they were merely going to push him through the long white corridors past men and women in white lab coats into an elevator going up.

"Giovanni," I said. "Relax."

"No!"

I was asked to step back farther.

Knowing when to fold and not being a big fan of straight-jackets or needles, I stepped back farther.

A cop was called in and he placed his hand on his gun, and the female doctor politely suggested that Giovanni sit and come with her. Giovanni glanced at the cop's gun and the three order-lies and sat back down. Ah, politeness and a gun; they worked on him like a charm.

But as they wheeled him past the glass partition at the nurses' station Giovanni began banging on it.

He was told to pipe down, didn't, screamed, "Chico, now!" jumped up and was restrained by the three massive orderlies, the cop, the doctor, *and* Nurse Rosie and was dragged into a bright room and needled into serenity.

Then a small man with dead eyes and a red Jewish Afro

shuffled down the hall yelling, "Arabs! Kill them all! If we don't fight them in Iraq, we'll have to fight them in Boston!"

"Silverman!"

Silverman was also told to pipe down, didn't, and was restrained by the three orderlies, screaming, and wheeled into the bright room and needled into serenity.

I don't think Giovanni would remember much about the struggle when he was discharged or how many people were involved in dragging him to the bright room. But I do know that the last things he probably saw were Silverman with the red Jewish Afro mumbling something about "Fucking terrorists" and me at the open doorway as he whispered, "I think you're right about the God thing, Chico," as the needle pricked his arm again and before the world went slack and his eyes closed.

I saw Giovanni lifted up and placed in the wheelchair again and soon he looked like he was feeling *mucho* relaxed after taking the second injection they gave him to calm down.

Giovanni was a dead end after all, I thought, then I looked over and to my shock I saw, laughing with a cop, the thin man, the one who ran from me and Pablo outside Giovanni's studio in Williamsburg. He was tall, thin, in a white shirt and slacks, a young black man in a panama hat!

He saw me, shook the cop's hand, and made it out of there as quick as he could.

"Rosie!" I went to the bolted door and yelled for the nurse. "Rosie!"

TWENTY-TWO

Little India in Jackson Heights, Queens, was a hothouse of Asian Indian grocery stores, clothing stores, restaurants, jewelry stores, glass, steel, and concrete. I felt like an Eskimo who took a wrong turn.

The city was melting and an old Asian Indian man stood outside the 99 Cent Dream King, watering the sidewalk. He was a tall old man in his eighties with a potbelly, dyed black hair slicked back, wearing a brown suit jacket, white shirt, and tie in the oppressive heat of August like he was immune. His sweaty brown skin glistened. He was smoking a cigarette, gripping an Indian newspaper under his arm, and proudly admiring a brand-new silver Mercedes parked outside the store.

I had followed the thin young black man in the panama hat in Zena's Mini Cooper as he rode his Vespa motor scooter into Queens. Was Giovanni just playing crazy? And who the hell was this guy in the panama hat, riding the scooter? What was he doing in Williamsburg? Why was he visiting Giovanni in Bellevue? Why did he run?

"Excuse me," I said, knocking the old Asian Indian man out of his daydream. "Are you familiar with Giovanni Vaninni?"

"Why?" he said gruffly, turning to me. "What is your business? How may I help you?"

"My name is Chico."

"Chicken?"

"Chico."

"I thought you said chicken."

"Why?" I asked. "You got any?"

He looked at me curiously. "Why would I have chicken?"

"How would I know," I said. "You're the one who brought it up."

"You are a strange young man."

"I'm also a friend of Giovanni Vaninni's and a private investigator."

"Ah," he said. "You're not what I expected a private investigator to look like."

"Imagine how my parents feel," I said. "What did you expect?"

"I expected a white man."

"I gave that up last year."

"Obviously," he said, "you are a black man."

"Obviously," I said. "May I ask you your name, sir?"

"Sir?" he said and smiled. "Manners at last. I like that. My name is Edgar Gupta."

"Are you familiar with Gabby Gupta?"

"She is my niece."

"You're Father Ravi's brother?"

"Yes," said Edgar Gupta. "I am William Gupta's brother. I was. But he's not my business now."

This was the first time I'd heard of Edgar Gupta. Nobody had mentioned that Father Ravi had a brother. Maybe the people I'd talked to so far believed Edgar Gupta's existence wasn't my business either. Edgar Gupta was either an irrelevant detail or a secret. Well, I don't believe in irrelevant details and I don't like secrets.

"Could I ask you a few questions?"

Mr. Edgar Gupta took a long drag on his cigarette, dropped his water hose, and snapped his fingers for me to follow him into the store. "Come inside!"

Inside, the young black man from Bellevue in the panama hat was stocking laundry detergent. An African girl stood behind the tall counter. I knew her.

S of the African accent.

Solange.

What the hell was she doing here?

On the wall behind Solange was an American flag. She was ringing up some plastic bottles of Coca-Cola, slowly eating away at the short line of bargain-hunting customers.

Solange looked at me. She saw me. She knew me. She looked away, wished me away, sang me away, as Edgar Gupta proudly went around the store pointing out his wonderful and affordable items, blank notebooks, telephones, seasonings, cookies, toys, wrapping paper, cans of sardines. A small crew of African men, also in white shirts, ties, and black slacks rushed around the store stocking shelves.

"I do not allow stealing in my store," said Mr. Gupta. "No theft."

"I kinda assumed that."

"I'm not kidding. I will not hesitate to call the authorities. And no drugs."

"What about coffee and cigarettes?"

"That's between you and your God. I am talking about the illegal kind. Are you on drugs?"

"Not at the moment."

"Are you an alcoholic?"

"I used to be but only when I drank too much."

"Ah," said Mr. Gupta, squinting at me. "I see. You are like my cousin Pasha. You think you are funny. You are a smart-ass."

"Not really," I said. "I'm exhausted and a long way from the Bronx and I really just want to have a few words with you and one of your men."

"Who?"

I pointed out the young African I had seen running outside Giovanni's studio and then at Bellevue.

Edgar Gupta looked away from me and yelled, "Kenyangi! Your detective friend is here!"

Kenyangi was a tall, thin African man, dark skin, early twenties, neatly cut Afro, large round eyes, smiling with big, spotless, enviable African teeth. Kenyangi laughed, removed his panama hat, and greeted me like a buddy.

"Welcome, my friend!" said Kenyangi with a big smile. "How did you happen to find me?"

"I was running by and saw you in the window."

"You are a very fast runner." He smiled.

Edgar Gupta pushed Kenyangi away and pulled me by my arm.

"Give me your business card," he demanded.

I handed him my card.

Edgar Gupta shook his head at my card and said, "Now, go away, *dabbawaalah*, unless I call for you. I have work to do and you bother me."

With that, he snapped his fingers again, walked away, and yelled out, "Boys! Help this gentleman to the door!"

The young African workers stopped their stacking and came toward me in a bunch.

I backed out. "Thanks, fellas. I know the way."

TWENTY-THREE

That same night, I stood on the corner waiting for him. After pulling down and locking the gates to the 99 Cent Dream King, Kenyangi sat on the sidewalk, removed his shoes, and rubbed his feet.

I made my move.

"You like, my friend?" Kenyangi whispered as I approached and pointed at Solange's plentiful behind, at the other end of the street as she disappeared around a corner.

Before I could respond, a skinny African man, approaching, angry, all puffed up and aggressive, said, "What is wrong with you, Kenyangi?"

"What?" said Kenyangi, still seated calmly on the sidewalk.

"You got a big mouth," the skinny African man said.

"Why are you being mean to me, brother?" Kenyangi said.

"You told Gupta on me, that's why."

"I'm just trying to do a good job, brother. A good manager reports the truth."

"We don't need any more *managers* like you," the skinny African said. "What did I ever do to you, Kenyangi?"

"You come in five minutes late when you know that Gupta will not be here. I warned you before, brother."

"I live far away."

"Move, brother."

"Gupta took a day's pay from me," said the African. "I have three children."

"I would have taken two days' pay from you, brother. I did not make your children. That's none of my concern."

"You will not get away with this, Kenyangi."

"Are you threatening me, brother?"

Kenyangi stood up and took what I recognized as a kicking stance. He was a good six feet, lanky and athletic. The other man backed off.

"Go home, John," Kenyangi said. "Next time, when I tell you to do something, you do it. I am good to you, and all you do is complain. If you want to keep your job, you'll show me more respect. When Gupta is not here, you come in on time. You respect me."

"I didn't mean to disrespect you," said African John and bowed his head. "I thought we were friends."

"At work I have no friends."

"Yes, Kenyangi," said deflated John.

"And from now on," said Kenyangi, "when we are at work, you will also call me sir, like everyone else. I've been too good to you, John."

"Yes, sir," said John, and looked at his feet. "Sir."

"I am your boss," Kenyangi said. "Now you know the truth. When we are at work I am your boss. Outside of work we can be friends. But not at work. Can I help you with anything else, John?"

John shook his head.

"Why are you still standing here, John?" said Kenyangi. "Go home, John."

"Yes, sir." African John bowed and walked out into the street, going back home, wherever that was.

"Don't feel sorry for him," Kenyangi said to me. "John and me, we came to America together. I am like father to his children. I've known him all my life. We grew up together in Kampala."

"He really is your friend?"

"He's my best friend," Kenyangi said. "But he is a lazy, stupid cockroach."

"I'd like to talk to you," I said. "About Giovanni."

He stood there squinting at me.

"If you're scared," I said, "I understand."

"Kenyangi fears nothing and no one."

"So can we talk?" I handed him a hundred-dollar bill.

Kenyangi smiled and pocketed the hundred bucks, grabbed his shoes and started walking down the street.

"Follow me, shamus," he said. "Follow me."

TWENTY-FOUR

Kenyangi and I walked up a street, past a steady trickle of Asian Indians, to Edgar Gupta's house. Kenyangi spoke of Uganda, of Kampala, Lake Victoria, tea bushes, coffee plants, berries, cane fields, white butterflies, hippos, crocodiles, the Nile, and witches. One minute Kenyangi was a student in Uganda; then he was a scientist, then a hunter, a bartender, teacher, tutor, poet, school guard, newspaper salesman, shoe salesman, waiter, messenger, social worker, and finally a journalist. Kenyangi, according to Kenyangi, had more jobs than a Korean on Red Bull; he had played more parts than Bette Davis in a good year, fought off lions and tigers and cannibals with his bare hands, saw killings, fought in three wars, fought off curfew police with machine guns armed only with a homemade spear. As a child, he spat in the eye of Idi Amin and lived to tell about it.

"Here," Kenyangi said, "I am a stock and errand boy. In Uganda, I am a prince."

"A prince?"

"I come here because I believe in democracy," said Kenyangi. "My family and I had a row. In Uganda, I have a palace at the foot of green volcanoes. I am a writer, a scholar, and a painter. Also an elephant killer. I shot many elephants in Africa. We would hunt. Do you know Hemingway? I met him. My great-uncle is the man he calls Juma in 'An African Story.'"

"Sounds like you're the one telling the African story." I smiled.

Kenyangi laughed so loud that a couple of people crossed the street, a car stopped, and a squirrel fell from a tree.

"Jesus," I said. "You always laugh like that?"

"Like what?"

"You know, like a hyena with a bullhorn."

"Like a hyena with a bullhorn!" Kenyangi said, laughing even louder.

"Keep it down," I said. "There are astronauts sleeping near the moon."

"Welcome to Hotel Gupta!" said Kenyangi, pointing. I couldn't believe my eyes. The grand house of William Gupta was a bright white marble behemoth construction with two tall Greek-style columns out front, white marble window frames, a white marble porch, a white marble domed roof, surrounded by an enormous dead garden. The size and grandeur of the house was almost an insult to the tiny two-family aluminum-sided structures that dominated the block, a gob of spit in the eye of lousy urban planning.

"Truth," said Kenyangi. "That is why I am glad to help you. For truth."

"You wanna give me back the hundred?"

"Maybe not." Kenyangi laughed. "But Edgar Gupta is a good man. You will see that. He is not the man you want. Father Ravi is the man you seek."

"Does Edgar Gupta pay you much to be a manager?"

"Not just a manager," said Kenyangi. "He gives me many side jobs."

"What kind of side jobs?"

Kenyangi's eyes went cold. "Who are you investigating?" said Kenyangi. "TSP or me, brother?"

"Just trying to get to know the man who's helping me."

"It is better for you to concentrate on Father Ravi. He is the elephant. Not me. Okay, brother?"

Kenyangi slapped me on the back and grinned wide.

"Let the hunt continue," he said as we crossed the street toward the house.

"Where are we going?" I said, following him.

"Paradise," said Kenyangi. "Paradise. Where you will tell me of your adventures as a private investigator and I shall tell you of my life with Gupta."

Inside, Gupta's house was an unfinished shell of tile, wood, and marble, filled with saws, hammers, ladders, cement, marble dust, music, yelling, and happy noises. Africans overflowed a large unfinished living room, shouting, laughing, eating, sitting on milk crates and windowsills and rickety chairs and old car seats. One tall, dark, skinny man played bongos, his back pressed up against a half-painted blue wall. There was no furniture, but someone had set a wooden plank across a rusted bathtub in the corner of the room to use as a table for the beer, wine, meat, fish, yams, and salads.

"What's going on?"

"Party," said Kenyangi. "For Mr. Gupta's employees."

"How many stores does he own?"

"Three."

An effeminate man in a pink T-shirt and green pants pointed at me, marched over, and said, "Gupta!"

Everyone in the room turned and stared at me.

"No! He is not Gupta!" said Kenyangi, putting his arm on my shoulder. "Back, cockroach!"

"You are Gupta!"

"No," I said. "I am Chico."

The exasperated man put a hand on his hip and called a friend over to inspect me. The friend, dressed in a suit and mirrored sunglasses, looked at me, nodded, and agreed, "Gupta! Yes!"

"No," I said. "I'm not Gupta. I'm Chico from the Bronx."

"He is lying!"

"He is Gupta!"

"Muhindi!"

"No," said Kenyangi. "He is no Muhindi! He is not Gupta! He is my friend! He is Porto Reecan! Bronx! He is Chico!"

"Ahhh!" A wave of recognition and an explosion of laughter went around the room.

"Welcome," said a thick, pretty woman in a bright green wrap. She handed me a bottle of soda. *"Bienvenue!"*

Kenyangi showed me around the house. There were rented rooms on the second floor, all locked. We went to Kenyangi's rented room. It was small, hot, damp, and cell-like, with one tall window and a cot.

"This is where you sleep?" I said.

"This is home," Kenyangi said. "Intellectuals do not need a lot of room."

"What about oxygen and sunlight?"

"Overrated."

"Where does Edgar Gupta sleep?"

"In the basement."

"Edgar Gupta owns three stores, drives a Mercedes, and lives in a basement?"

"It is a beautiful basement," said Kenyangi. "I saw it once. He has a pool table, a stereo, and a big television. He drinks and smokes alone. No one is allowed down there. No one bothers him down there. They never see him. I collect the rents. They hardly know what he looks like."

I heard a buzzer go off. Kenyangi said, "That's Solange."

"Solange," I said. I must have said her name with too much feeling, because Kenyangi said, "Beware of Solange. She thinks too much for a woman and takes the fun out of everything. And these African girls, they will take advantage. They want a baby. They want a green card. They want money."

"I don't have any money," I said.

"You are an American," said Kenyangi. "You have more than you know."

Kenyangi grabbed a drum and we went back downstairs and saw Solange. She was carrying a guitar case. Kenyangi kissed her on both cheeks, and she kissed him back. She kissed me, too, like she had just met me. We went silently into the living room and moved to the bathtub table. Solange set down a bottle of cheap red wine with her long, thin African fingers.

"What are you doing here?" I whispered.

She shook her head and said, "Do you like music?"

"I love music," I said. "I need to talk to you."

Solange ignored my request and removed her guitar from its black case and stood with Kenyangi and two others with drums before the bathtub. Kenyangi ordered everyone to be quiet, sit, and gather round her. I sat on a rickety chair and waited for my chance to question Solange after I got through with Kenyangi.

I felt Solange's music wrap around me. Everyone listened without talking while three men danced, heads and arms flailing, and as for me, I couldn't see anyone but Solange. I found myself gripping the arms of my chair as she played her guitar and sang. Solange was playing and singing and I was over on my seat, eyes closed, wanting more. I never wanted her to stop singing. I never wanted to go back to Parkchester. I wanted to forget about Zena and her husband Hari Lachan. I wanted to be left alone here; to sit still and listen to Solange. I wanted to sink and rise on the notes of Solange's music, among the Africans, pushing away the almost unbearable new life I was leading before Solange kissed me with her playing and singing. As the singing went on, I wanted never to be haunted by the impulse to be off somewhere else trying to solve a missing persons case or a murder. I felt happy. And several times I tried to rise from my seat to applaud or dance, in my way, but I couldn't. Too many sleepless nights maybe or maybe just too much murder and lies and confusion for one week, and my body, like my soul and my feet, was too tired and had had enough.

Solange played and sang and the drums beat as three African men danced, flailed their heads, jumped, twirled, forward and back, left, right, until midnight; Solange, sweaty and exhausted but singing, which finally worked on me like a sweet lullaby.

Later, when I awoke, I was in one of those rented rooms in Edgar Gupta's house.

There was just enough room on the windowsill for Solange's books. Solange sat on the floor, reading, as the night traffic dribbled by, and said, *"Parlez-vous français?"*

"Oui," I said.

Solange launched into a tirade of perfect French.

"Whoa," I said. "I speak a little college French, and I speak it so badly I'm not even allowed to *visit* France."

Solange frowned and a piece of plaster fell loose from the ceiling.

"We pay too much in this crumbling house," she said, picking up the plaster.

"You live here, too?"

"I exist here. I survive here. I wait here. I am here."

"You do a lot here," I said. "So you're also from Uganda?"

"No," she said, "I am from Rwanda."

I don't keep up much with current events, but I knew that, some years ago, in Rwanda over eight hundred thousand people had been killed in a couple of months, mostly a group called Tutsis, killed by other Africans, a group called Hutus, all approved and instigated and financed by the Hutu government of Rwanda. Nothing so evil had happened since Hitler tried to exterminate the Jews, that's what Ramona and the papers had been saying. It was hard to avoid, even for me.

"Are you Tutsi or Hutu?" I said.

"Both," she said. "My father was Hutu. My mother was Tutsi. I am a country divided."

I didn't ask her about her mother or father or her family. I couldn't.

"I guess you're never going back to Rwanda," I said.

Solange nodded her head. "I must go back. Home is home. Have you read Chinua Achebe?"

"No."

"Do you like reading?"

I shrugged. "My ex-wife is a writer and a librarian."

She walked over and touched my face. "What are you exactly?"

"What do you mean?"

"You are white? You are black? What are you?"

"Cockerdoodle," I said. "Half cocker spaniel. Half poodle."

"You are black or white?" she said, annoyed. "You are Muzungu?"

"No," I said. "I am Mofongo."

"What is Mofongo?"

"It's a dish made with plaintains," I said. "And just as delicious as I am. My turn. How long have you known Kenyangi?"

"Kenyangi is a distant cousin."

"Are you a princess?"

"Excuse me?"

"Kenyangi told me that he was a prince."

Solange laughed. "Kenyangi's family worked in the fields in Uganda. Their job was to set fire to the bush to help the crops grow. Kenyangi tells lies, but they are interesting lies. But don't believe anything he tells you."

"What about you?"

"I am just an innocent girl from the bush," she said. "You have nothing to fear from Solange."

"What's your relationship to Edgar Gupta?"

"I bathe him."

"Is that slang for 'I sucker him for cash'?"

"No," she said. "He has trouble washing. I work in the store. I cook his food. I spy on him for Joey. I wash him."

I tried my best to look unaffected.

"Let me tell you how this is gonna go," I said. "It seems I'm not gonna get anything from Kenyangi except praise for Edgar Gupta and it's obvious to me from your behavior at the store that you don't want Edgar Gupta knowing that we've met. So you start singing or I tell Gupta that we're part of a ring that's been shoplifting Vitamin Water from his store."

Solange's face went darker. "I thought you were Joey's friend?"

"What's your relationship to Joey?" I asked, ignoring her question.

"We are friends," she said. "Gabby Gupta helped me get this job years ago when I came to America when Edgar Gupta was still her beloved uncle. I work in the store. I cook his food. I wash him."

"Rewind the tape for me," I said. "Take me back."

"There was a time when," said Solange, "The Superman Project was in debt and all but dead. Father Ravi accepted one hundred thousand dollars from his brother Edgar to save the project, and signed a silly contract on the back of a napkin that gave Edgar ownership of all TSP assets, including those accrued in the future, so long as the Project lived. It not only lived but thrived. Then one day Edgar Gupta called, after a couple of years of not speaking to his brother."

"He wanted the hundred thousand."

"No," said Solange. "He wanted everything. The farm. The TSP mansion. Everything. He had that contract on a paper napkin."

"Maybe Edgar Gupta had something to do with his niece Gabby Gupta disappearing. Maybe he did it or he hired someone to do it. Giovanni. Kenyangi."

"I don't know," she said.

"Edgar Gupta hates his brother," I said, daring her with a stern look to deny it.

"Edgar Gupta hates his brother," she conceded. "Father Ravi convinced Edgar Gupta's only child Arjuna to enlist in the military in 2001. He told Arjuna that it was his duty as a Superman. The boy was killed. He was twenty. After that, Father Ravi and his brother never spoke again."

"That's not all of it," I said.

"No," she said. "Edgar Gupta, like his brother, was married to a much younger woman, a beautiful *desi* girl named Anu. Father Ravi had his brother agree that they would take part in an experiment."

"Experiment?"

"An experiment, swapping their wives," said Solange. "Edgar got nowhere with Ravi's wife. She was one of the so-called sex-haters Ravi preached against in those days before he developed The Superman philosophy. But Ravi and Anu spent many hours together. Father Ravi was old but still impulsive, self-indulgent, vain, naïve, and sexually frustrated with his young wife. He told his brother Edgar everything. And it was Ravi's idea, but Edgar did go along with it. In the end, after his son Arjuna was killed in the Iraq war to topple Saddam Hussein and save the United States from nuclear obliteration with weapons that did not exist, Anu left Edgar Gupta. Edgar blamed Father Ravi. Edgar and Ravi stopped speaking. But, a year ago, Edgar contacted Father Ravi again: with a lawsuit claiming ownership of all TSP funds and property. The case was dismissed out of court six weeks ago. Not long after that Gabby Gupta disappeared. But Edgar Gupta's dropped the lawsuit."

"Why?"

"Giovanni," she said. "Giovanni found out from someone on the inside that TSP is bankrupt."

"What do you mean?"

"TSP has more bills than income."

Solange added that Edgar Gupta and Father Ravi Gupta had been very close. They were brothers and best friends. They had a plan. They were going to become millionaires in America. In India and then Uganda and then Britain, the lines were clear, and it seemed as though nothing could separate the brothers then.

Solange said she didn't know if a man could be a muse. But if a man could be, Edgar Gupta was Ravi's muse. Edgar was the cheerleader, saying, "You can do it, Ravi. You're just as good as any of them. Start your Superman Project. I'll loan you the money."

And then, one day, all the love, brotherhood, and trust was all over, dead and gone, stomped, crushed like a dry leaf, lost and blown away.

"Poor Arjuna and Anu were casualties of Father Ravi's growth," Solange said.

Solange also told me that the construction of Mr. Gupta's house had been frozen, interrupted by the unexpected flight of Mrs. Edgar Gupta. Without Anu Gupta, Mr. Gupta's house was the Taj Mahal without its beloved Mumtaz.

"Tough luck," I said.

"Arjuna," said Solange, "was born in the United States. He was a quiet boy, not a bully, a poet. A poet is the very opposite of a bully."

"I wouldn't know about that," I said. "But go on."

"Arjuna had all kinds of friends," Solange said. "Indian, Trinidadian, Guyanese, Italian, Irish, Africans. I loved that boy. Everybody loved Arjuna. Arjuna was too young to be killed in that war. Father Ravi killed that boy."

I nodded. "So Edgar Gupta felt he lost his son AND his wife because of Father Ravi's Superman experiments. After the court case was thrown out, maybe he thought that Ravi should lose some people, too."

Solange nodded.

"The disappearance of one of Father Ravi's children may be

the only thing that could satisfy Edgar Gupta after he finally lost his lawsuit."

Solange nodded.

"And Giovanni is working for Edgar Gupta?" I confirmed.

"Yes," said Solange. "They both share one thing in common. They both *hate* The Superman Project. Giovanni was Edgar Gupta's spy at TSP, the way I'm Joey's spy here."

"Does Joey know all this?"

"Yes."

"Why didn't he tell me?"

"Joey doesn't tell everything to any one person," said Solange. "I don't think he really trusts anybody. Not even me. Would you, if you were innocent and in his position and felt that the people you loved were either double-crossing you or out to get you?"

I watched the smooth trek of a cockroach, crawling slowly up the wall.

"No," I said.

My cell phone rang. I picked up.

"I know where you are," she said.

TWENTY-FIVE

Threatening clouds flooded the sky. I heard a clap of thunder as I watched Mara Gupta from inside the president's office at TSP. A door connected to a short hall, which in turn led to a library. In the library, Mara was conducting a workshop called "Reeling in The Superman: A Woman's Perspective," and I peeked in through the open door. Mara looked cold and unblinking in her glasses, her mouth tight and unsmiling, all clipboard and red pen, all business. She made female politicians look like schoolgirls on spring break.

A thin, attractive blond woman in blue jeans said, desperately, pleading, tears in her eyes: "Dr. Mara, I don't even know where to start. I feel unloved."

The blond woman called Jessica straightened her back a bit more. "I'm a very giving person. I love love. I do sweet things for my friends and family. But the things that SHOULD be happening for me are not happening. Look at me. I'm twenty, pretty, college educated, intelligent, fun-loving, the kind of girl most guys would want to date. I shouldn't even be here complaining like this. I know I'm supposed to be a Superman, but I can't deal with my problems alone."

"You are not alone!" said Mara. "The Superman is within you." Then came the smack down, the tough love, the bitter pill. Mara shook her dark head and crossed her legs, the perfect crease of her designer slacks almost accusing the blond woman. She pointed her red pen and said, "Now for some truth. Your main problem, Jessica, is that you are asleep. It is possible to find a man who is *serious* about his career, and about having children and being happy. It is possible to find your Superman. But first you must stop trying to find a copy of the little man you have in your old reptile mind. You must start working from your Supermind."

The women around the room nodded in agreement.

"So what do you think the problem is?" Mara said, and bit down on the cap of her red pen.

"I don't know. I just feel needy, unappreciated, and uncared for. My friends say I deserve more."

"Do you think you deserve more, Jessica?"

"I deserve more." There were nods, and a small burst of applause went around the room.

"Have you read Father Ravi's pamphlet 'Letting Go of the Grundies'?"

"Yes," said Jessica. "I love that one."

"Many so-called men today don't want children," said Mara, almost jumping from her chair. "They don't believe in marriage. They just want to work and enjoy themselves after work without any *real* responsibility, commitment, and maturity. These are the Grundies. So if you're looking for a man who wants to marry you, cross those Grundies who don't want children, don't want to marry, off your Superlist. They are not the One, The Superman. The Superman can hold a job, support a wife and children, take out the trash, ask you about your day, and turn off the football

217

game to talk about his feelings. Demand a Superman, expect a Superman, and you will get one." The women applauded wildly. I stepped back.

"Next up," said Mara. "Brenda will share her experience and hope in the Project."

The only black woman in the room, wearing a silk purple sari, stood up and said, "I had a vision of what the ideal man should be. I wanted someone whose income combined with mine could afford us a family, an apartment, a car, and all the travel, luxury, and fun we could possibly tolerate. I wanted a Superman."

Brenda patted her slightly bulging tummy and said, "I have that now. And more. Thanks to the Project. And baby makes three." With tears in her eyes, she said, "I'm happy. I'm really, really happy. And it's all thanks to Father Ravi and this Project."

The women exploded in applause. Brenda sat back down.

"Wonderful, wonderful," said Mara, looking around at the ecstatic faces, slapping the sides of her chair. "If you're new here and want to find a Superman to whisk you off your expensively heeled feet and show you a good time and the good life, read this new manual." Mara held up a booklet titled *Metamorphosis of the Supermind*.

"This manual will heal not only your purse but also your heart. It will help you focus your Supermind. Do you want, one day, to wear a beautiful wedding dress, eat wedding cake with the man of your dreams and the future father of your children? You must not only ask for certain things, you must *demand* them. Take it slow at first. Get in touch with your Supermind. Get closer to the Superman. Then everything you ever dreamed of becomes possible."

Mara got to her feet, closed her eyes, bowed her head, and began: "I am . . ."

The women, taking their cue from Mara, also stood up,

bowed their heads, closed their eyes, held hands, and chanted with Mara: "I am. You are. We are. The Superman."

After a bit of silence, they all opened their eyes, released hands, applauded, hugged, whistled, and wept. The thin blonde in blue jeans wept the most. Three other women formed a circle around her, and put their arms around her neck and shoulders, and hugged her tight.

Mara smiled triumphantly and shook hands with the other women who approached her. After the tears and fervor died down, Mara dismissed them with a wave of her hand and they all went out in a neat and orderly mob, laughing, telling jokes, wiping tears.

"You can come in now, Mr. Santana," Mara said and signaled me to enter the room. "How'd you like the show?"

"Coulda used more butter," I said. "Other than that, interesting. How can I help you?"

"I'm looking for Giovanni," she said. "As you probably already know, Giovanni was working for me."

I tried not to look surprised. "Giovanni was also working for your uncle Edgar Gupta."

Now she looked like she was the one trying not to look surprised.

Giovanni was working for Mara Gupta and Edgar Gupta. It was some kind of double cross. Giovanni was playing everybody. That meant he knew more about this whole mess than anybody else and he was gonna talk.

"Where is he?"

"Question of the day."

"My men saw you meeting with Giovanni at Bellevue before he escaped."

"I didn't know Giovanni escaped from Bellevue."

"His art studio is completely empty and he's disappeared. My men also saw you in the Bronx with Joey Valentin. They followed Pablo Sanchez there. Where are they?"

"I don't know where Giovanni is," I said. "I don't know where Joey is. You called the wrong P.I."

"Do you even understand what we're trying to do here?"

"Waste my time?"

"Massive overpopulation," said Mara Gupta, looking out into the night. "Environmental degradation, extensive poverty, ethnic and religious strife. The Superman Project will eliminate these troubles, unite all nations. There will be no more threes. There will only be one."

"You believe?"

"I believe." Mara Gupta raised her eyebrows and said, "And more."

"Sorta like a spiritual Swiss Army pocketknife?"

Mara smiled for the first time. "Humor is good. The Buddha was a laughing Buddha, you know? And Christ loved to laugh."

"Yeah," I said. "Jesus was a prankster. Raising Lazarus. Walking on water. That devil in the desert thing. Jesus knew comedy."

Mara stopped me in my cynical tracks. "An earthquake took thousands of lives in Haiti, and The Superman Project gathered collections and sent relief. What did you do, brother? Don't be sorry. It's the same for all of us. We want to help, but we don't know how or where to start. The original Americans killed millions of Native Indians. Europe's African slavery killed countless millions. The German Nazis killed six million Jews. Stalin killed forty million Russian souls or so. The French killed thousands or a million in Algeria, depending on who you ask. In Uganda, Idi Amin was responsible for the deaths of three hundred thousand human beings. The guerrilla war under Obote killed at least a hundred thousand. The killing continues. If the Superman Project had been in place, these horrors would never have happened. Those people would have lived."

"You believe that?"

"I know," said Mara Gupta. "The way I know that subatomic

reality is just as real as this table." She slapped the table with a flat hand. "The Superman Project will do away with the old ways, the old caste systems."

"What about your height and weight requirements? Sounds like a new kind of caste system."

"We must have standards," said Mara Gupta. "The Superman Project will not do away with all rules and laws. But we will give everyone an opportunity to be happy. Isn't that what America is about? Not the guarantee of happiness, but an equal opportunity for all to pursue happiness?"

I nodded. "Uh-huh."

"Hand me your cell phone, Chico," she said, like a mother talking to a naughty child.

"What?"

"Go into your pocket," she said, real slow, like it was my first time behind the wheel of a car or at the foot of an escalator. "Pull out your cell phone and hand it to me."

I shook my head. "I don't think so, lady."

I went toward the door.

I opened it.

I looked around for guards with Tasers.

Nobody there.

"Chico?"

I turned to glance at Mara Gupta.

I had my back to the open door.

Mara Gupta held her clipboard to her chest, looked at me, and said, "Where are you going, Chico?"

"Home," I said.

Mara looked at her clipboard and checked something. "That's a mistake. You're not going home."

"What do you mean?"

"Where is the comic book? The first Superman comic book."

"Joey's comic book?"

"That comic book was bequeathed to Joseph Valentin because he held a position of honor at TSP, without TSP he would never have inherited it. That comic book is TSP's property as far as we're concerned."

"So take him to court," I said.

"Do you have the comic book, Chico?"

I thought back to the nonsale of Utopia Farms and what Solange had told me: *"Giovanni found out from someone on the inside that TSP is bankrupt"* and *"TSP has more bills than income."*

"If I didn't know any better," I said, turning to get a good look at the TSP accountant, "I'd think you were hard up for cash and more interested in getting your hands on that three- or five-hundred-thousand-dollar comic book than you are in finding your missing sister."

"Is that what Zena tells you?" she said, without missing a beat. "Does my baby sister still talk in her sleep?"

I just looked at her. "I don't think I like you, Mara Gupta," I said.

"Why not?"

"You don't play well with others."

"Poor Hari," she continued. "First, Joey and Zena and now—"

Joey and Zena?

She looked at my face. My stupid telltale face. A smirk appeared on hers.

"Oh." She smiled. "Didn't you know?"

Joey and Zena?

No, I didn't know.

I thought about what Joey had said about him and Gabby fighting over other women.

Joey and Zena.

No.

I didn't know that.

Joey and Zena.

They suckered Gabby and Pablo and they suckered you. You were wrong about them, and it stings like hell. You don't like to be wrong about people, about your friends, about the people you love or loved or were in danger of loving, do you, Santana?

You're wrong, like Zena said; suck it up, baby.

Mara inhaled and exhaled deeply and turned her head away. "Zena doesn't know where Joey is. I thought she did. And now I'm convinced she doesn't. And I suspect that you and Giovanni do, Chico."

She looked at me again. "You don't think Zena's been using you to find out where Joey could be? You don't think Zena could actually be in love with Joey?"

Zena and Joey.

That's all I was thinking about when I heard a quick rush of footsteps behind me. Before I could turn, I felt a terrible weight on my back and then a massive bicep suddenly around my neck, slowly cutting off my air supply . . .

I tried a . . .

Too late, Chico, too late . . .

Lights out, Chico . . .

Hello, darkness.

Nighty nite, Chico, nighty nite . . .

TWENTY-SIX

As I ran through the crowd at the Brook Avenue train station, pushing and shoving, finally running along the wrong side of the orange danger line painted on the platform, I felt a hand, felt the push, the shove, and fell, my Zippo lighter flying, my life, saw the train lights, heard the screeching wheels, the screams, felt my head smack against metal, saw the train, now before me, roaring and rolling like a demonic beast made of steel, and turning my head I saw my father's dead body beside me, and Esther Sanchez's dead body beside his, and then another and another and it was only a matter of seconds before the train was on me, seconds before the pain and shattering, the breaking and rupturing and more pain, blood, the red and the black, and then darkness, my father's darkness, Esther Sanchez's darkness, rolling over me and just as the white light of the oncoming train drowned me the last thing I saw as I looked up were Joey and Zena on the train platform, laughing before a wall with the words THE SUPERMAN PROJECT *painted in red, as the train passed over . . .*

When I regained consciousness, came out of it, fog in my head, ears ringing, room spinning, startled, I found myself lying on my back in the dark on a flimsy cot, still dazed, head hurting, teeth hurting, chest hurting, expecting to find Mimi and Max asleep on the floor like campers. Instead, I found myself in a locked and dark room. It was cold and it smelled faintly of vomit and piss and sweat.

Good morning.

Zena and Joey?

Giovanni?

What the hell?

I was being played.

Santana, you are being played, I thought as I tried to forget the lousy nightmare and looked around the room with no windows. There was only a cot in the room and a yellow line marking a safety zone before the door.

The last thing I remembered was Big Man applying the brakes to my windpipe with his bicep.

From this point on, I would trust no one—not Zena, not Joey, especially not myself, no one.

I jumped up off the single cot.

I felt the walls.

They were padded.

I checked for my cell phone.

It was gone.

I went to the door.

It was steel and bolted from the outside.

Mara Gupta thought I was in contact and cahoots with Joey and Giovanni, had taken my cell phone and was holding me prisoner.

I looked around the room with no windows.

I sat back down on the cot.

I didn't know how I would escape. But I knew an opportunity would present itself, and when it did, I would have to be ready. I remembered how Nicky once had everyone in the Dirty Dozen read something called *Zen in the Art of Archery*. I thought about that book now. I would move like a cocked arrow and shoot out of that bright room with the padded walls. Any hesitation on my part would land me right back in.

First I had to get past the bolted steel door, then Big Man, and God knows how many TSP guards were waiting once I got outside that room.

I heard keys and lay back down on my cot and closed my eyes, cracking them just enough to see what was coming at me.

The lights snapped on and the overhead lighting hit my eyes like an ice pick.

"Hello?" said the girl in the red uniform, carrying a ring of keys and a clipboard, looking at me as she walked in cautiously. "Are you awake?"

I pretended to still be unconscious.

I peeked over her shoulder at the open steel door as she entered, locked it behind her, checking her clipboard. She looked confused. No sign of Big Man; not even one living soul on the floor.

"Hello?" she asked in a concerned voice. "Are you going home today?"

I didn't respond.

"Did you eat yet?"

I didn't respond.

She went back toward the steel door, keys and clipboard in her hands. Her eyes were on her clipboard, not mine. My eyes were on her as she slowly unlocked the steel door.

This was my moment.

I didn't know what was beyond the area outside my door. Guards? Guns? Dogs? Gates? But it didn't matter. This was my chance.

The girl, her eyes on her clipboard, didn't notice as I slowly moved beyond the yellow line marking the safety zone before the door. But then, as if she had eyes on the back of her head, she turned and saw me, and she bolted the door again.

"Hey!" she said. "Step behind the yellow line!"

I stood behind the yellow line, and the girl, God bless her, did the sweetest, dumbest, and most wonderful thing, she turned the key to the metal door and started to open it again. I sprang. Screams and "Stop him! Stop him!" But it was too late. I pushed past her, trying my best not to knock her over.

"Stop him!" she yelled, feebly lifting her hands before her, only to drop them and jump back as I roared like a wounded animal, "NO!"

I ran down a long, well-lit but empty hall, with a thousand elevator banks leading God knows where. I pressed every button, then hid around a corner and waited. When I heard a ding, I jumped blind and hopeful into an empty car going down.

I went and slouched at the back of the car.

People exited and entered as my escape elevator hit different floors.

At one floor, the elevator filled with passengers, people with VISITOR tags talking about the evening news, some dazed and confused, most just looking bored and hungry. A blond girl nodded at me as she was wheeled past by a woman in a green gown. She closed her eyes. One man smiled, nodded, but didn't say anything. He tugged nervously at his red Afro and scratched at his hands and knuckles and soon I heard the voices of Big Man and the young girl in the red uniform, standing by the elevator door, their backs to me, talking excitedly.

"He just ran out?" said Big Man, not without admiration.

"He just ran," she said. "I'm sorry. I just started my shift. Nobody told me that room was filled and it wasn't on my chart. I thought it was a mistake. He had no gown and his street clothes on. I thought he was a discharge who had fallen asleep or something."

"Not your fault," said Big Man.

"What was his problem?"

"Heroin," said Big Man.

"Ah," said the young girl. "Makes sense. How long was he a member?"

"Long time," Big Man lied. "But TSP can't help nobody that don't wanna get better."

"Nope."

From the sound of it, I had been held in some kind of drug withdrawal room for TSP members.

"Well he's long gone."

"Yeah," said the girl. "I'm so sorry. He's long gone."

When the girl said this, Big Man clenched his large fist. I crouched down and hid behind other passengers until the elevator landed on the first floor, and everyone got off. Like a leopard returning to the jungle after being caged, I walked briskly for the street, hiding in the crowd. I was about fifty feet from the exit when I saw the girl in red and Big Man again. They had spotted me, and my heart began to beat like a small fish on the deck of the *Titanic*. It's over. They got you, Santana.

For a frozen moment, Big Man stood there, rubbing his hands and looking at me, confidence overcoming him, a hunter with his prey in sight. Then, confident, he stalked me slowly, on tiptoe, and I almost laughed, because there's nothing funnier than a huge man walking on tiptoe.

I moved toward the door, getting closer and closer. I imagined Big Man beating me with his fists, his hard knuckles beating into my face, his professional rage becoming more and more terrible. And I, as many before me, was crushed like an insect beneath the arms of steel and kicked about the halls of agony by the Mean Machine of TSP.

You've lost, said my heart. But I ran out through the door into the wan light of the empty street. I heard the rumble of traffic and taxis and trucks, and it was still as humid as the night they choked me in. Big Man ran too, faster and faster behind me, gaining ground in the night. There was a matter of professional pride in his chase. I saw traffic ahead. I thought about making a sudden stop and using Big Man's weight against him, tossing him headfirst into the cars ahead of me. But that might kill him, and he's just a worker trying to do his job, I thought, when another man, even bigger than Big Man, jumped off a concrete stoop as I ran past.

"Stop him!" Big Man yelled. But the other man didn't even try to slow me down. I glanced back and saw him do something I didn't expect. As Big Man ran past him, he threw out a muscled arm and caught Big Man under the chin, and Big Man's legs went flying forward, and he slammed onto his back with a sound like a redwood falling.

Nicky Brown! I shot faster along the street, hearing Nicky's pounding feet following me, until I could finally see that I was on the corner of 47th and 8th Avenue. I looked across the street and saw the closed doors of TSP directly opposite what looked like an abandoned building on the outside—the building I had escaped from.

Nicky, carrying a large green duffel bag, rushed with me to the corner of 47th Street, asked a white lady to hail a cab for us, then we jammed in the back.

"Williamsburg," I said.

Before the cabbie could protest, Nicky said, "Drive!"

"I prefer not to."

"I didn't ask you your preferences," Nicky said, stuffing forty bucks into the money slot dangling from the partition window, flipping it from the passenger side to the driver.

I tried, with Nicky, to find Giovanni in Williamsburg again. No luck.

"Harlem," I said, jumping back into the cab, closing my eyes, and shaking my head.

TWENTY-SEVEN

Harlem. Nicky dropped me off at 124th and I entered the three-story brownstone that housed St. James and Company, dark oak walls, through the electronic door, went past and flirted with Kelly Diaz, office manager, Sugar Hill, kid, husband, twenty-five, big-boned, big-breasted, Colombian, short purple hair, through her living-room office and up to Joy's office with the glass desk, two chairs, file cabinet, and fresh flowers.

Somebody was playing me like a bongo drum. It was hot and humid and it looked like the sun and the dark rain clouds above me were in a fight and I was caught in their shadow with no umbrella. Typical.

How I hated New York that morning. Maybe everyone hates the place they were born at a time like that. But New York seemed to deserve a little extra dose of loathing, felt like walking through a putrid mouth full of eight million rotten teeth.

Joy entered, hair cut short and tight to her perfectly round head and dark Benin mask of a face, tall, beautiful and stylish always, in a charcoal-gray blouse and pants with short black boots. "Where do you think this Giovanni got all that money for that marble in Williamsburg, Chicklet?"

"Mara Gupta and Edgar Gupta," I said.

Hank lumbered in, red-faced, behind his wife Joy, also tall but with remnants of an egg breakfast on the salmon-colored shirt and tie draped tightly on his chunky frame, carrying a file under his arm. Tossing me a doughnut, he bit into the one he was holding and nodded his head. "Delish."

Joy slapped the doughnut out of Hank's hand and kicked it across the room.

Hank looked at me in shock. "She totally caught me off guard on that one."

"When I want to be a widow," said Joy, "I'll feed you those doughnuts, intravenously if I have to. Or you can leave me for a woman who doesn't care about you and eat all the Bow Ties and Boston creams you want."

Hank laughed, picked up the doughnut, and put it in the trash. "I thought you had my back, Chico? Why didn't you warn me, buddy?"

"How was Ireland?" I asked, biting into my doughnut.

"Beautiful," Hank said, passing a hand across his thinning brown hair. "The beer is warm and the land is green and my family tree is full of nuts."

"Congrats," I said. "Okay, before you bust out the vacation slides what about Giovanni Vaninni?"

Hank pulled the file from under his arm and read, "Giovanni's father was a failed artist and an anarchist. He lived on a very small pension from a university job in Siena. He's dead. His mother was also a professor. Also dead. Kelly checked it out.

Giovanni inherited nothing except a grandfather who was a member of the Italian Fascist party. His grandfather was hung by his fellow townspeople in front of Giovanni's father as a boy."

"With that kind of history," I said, "I could understand how Giovanni's father could maybe grow up hating authority, and how he could have passed that on to Giovanni like a gold watch and how Giovanni would be a perfect suspect in terms of Gabby Gupta's disappearance. Tell me about the statue."

Hank sounded off: "Michelangelo's *David* weighs between six and nine tons, that's without the pedestal."

"Giovanni told me he wanted to sculpt *two* wrestling figures, David and Goliath. Let's say that's twenty tons of marble. Where does a starving artist get the money for twenty tons of marble? Not even counting the shipping charges."

"Plus," said Joy. "He didn't get that marble in the U.S. He had it shipped from Italy. A place called Carrara, same spot Michelangelo got his rock for the *David* sculpture and Edgar Gupta got the marble for his house. Your hunch was right."

"Giovanni was tired of being the starving artist. Hunger, I understand. I know what that's like. Giovanni's got expensive marble, a bad back, and a need for painkiller. With money from Mara Gupta for keeping an eye out for Joey and Edgar Gupta for digging up dirt on TSP, he could finish his statue. That's all artists want, isn't it?"

Hank nodded. "To finish their masterpiece."

I added, "Also, I thought maybe Giovanni got rid of Gabby Gupta to frame Joey and help Edgar Gupta fulfill his dream of destroying TSP by dividing it. Or maybe Giovanni got rid of Gabby to frame Joey and help Mara Gupta fulfill her dream of becoming president. Maybe he got rid of Gabby for both of them and they *all* gave him a bit of extra money for his sculpture. But then a funny thing happens."

"What?" said Joy.

"Esther Sanchez got murdered."

"I thought they caught the guy who did that?"

"What's the connection?" asked Hank.

"That's what I'm going to find out," I said.

Outside, I pulled out that pack of Djarum cigarettes that I had gotten from Chase Gupta and had been sitting brown in my pocket like a bad penny, lit up, sucked the dark burning clove smoke into my lungs and let the punishment begin. I heard once that clove cigarettes made your lungs bleed. Sounds good. Maybe it was just an urban legend. Sure. Just one. One pack never killed anybody. Or maybe it did. But who cares, right?

The smoke was sweet and it burned and my sides hurt and my gut hurt. But they have not killed you, Santana. Not yet. Joey and Zena. You stupid sucker. Find Giovanni, I thought.

Desperate times call for desperate . . .

I picked up my phone.

I dialed.

I heard: "Puerto Rico!"

"Elvis," I said.

"It's Elvis, *papá*. The freakin' Porto Reakin from El Barrio, baby. What's up?"

"Not much," I said. "I need to meet up with you. Ask you a few questions about Zena Gupta and Joey and what you know about Giovanni Vaninni. I think that that Yayo kid from Washington Heights may be innocent of having anything to do with Esther Sanchez's death. We need to team up, like you said."

"Can Pedro Sanchez come along?"

"Pedro Sanchez?"

"Pedro is Pablo's older brother. Pedro's a badass. Black sheep. All that shit. He just flew into town from D.R. He's mad. I told him what you said about how you didn't think Yayo killed his mother. He's got a gun and he's confused."

"Great," I said.

I didn't know Pablo had a brother. Maybe Pablo didn't think his brother, like Father Ravi's brother, was my business either. Pedro was just another irrelevant detail. Did I mention how I felt about irrelevant details?

"Don't tell Pablo or your girlfriend Chase. You and this Pedro meet me tonight."

"Gonzalez y Gonzalez on Broadway," said Elvis. "I'm Johnnie Walker Black. What's your poison?"

"Aspirin."

"Say what?"

"White Russians."

"You got it."

TWENTY-EIGHT

That night, in Gonzalez y Gonzalez, I walked past the black Porsche toward bouncers in black T-shirts and black pants checking IDs; pretty, bejeweled, and overly made-up women in skimpy clothes, butts and boobs a-poppin'; and their macho dates, who looked around proudly and sneaked glances at the dates of other macho men, careful not to stare too hard at the wrong man's woman. Reggaeton music blasted as though the human ear drum were its mortal enemy.

Go get those beers to start. Go past the happy pink drunk waving hello outside the bar. Hello, pal. Go into the dark room. Good. Whitney Houston sings *"Learning to love yourself it is the greatest love of all."* Order. Samuel Adams. Slam 'em back, Chico. One. Two. Good. Look at your shadow on the red walls. Like Nicky says, as long as you cast a shadow, baby, there's hope, you may live and die happy yet.

Your teeth hurt. Your head hurts. Your guts hurt. Heart? You have no heart, Santana.

I slammed back my third beer and looked up and saw Elvis at the bar talking to a pretty hostess dressed in black, his arm around her thin exposed waist.

I also saw that Chase Gupta was sitting at the bar sipping from a cold bottle of Corona, a delicate diamond bracelet dangling from her thick brown wrist. She wore jeans and a tight blue blouse; her breasts spilled over the top like brown balloons. Her heavy makeup, blue eye shadow, and thick black mascara made her look like a raccoon, plump, rich Asian Indian girl, wannabe trendy, all jet-black curls and big hips, gazing jealously at Elvis.

Sure, the time would come when Elvis's good looks and youth would fade, and he would fall to earth, become mortal. In the onslaught of years, he would join everyone else, painted with the same sickly mortal brush. Every faded movie star and fashion model knew the sting of the short and ungrateful human memory, the indignity of being replaced by a younger, prettier face. The long, cold winter was coming. But this night was Elvis's night.

And this night Elvis belonged to Chase.

Despite this, Elvis stood in the nightspot called Gonzalez y Gonzalez, half bar, half dance hall, half restaurant, basking in the glow he saw reflected back in the eyes of women who passed and found him irresistible.

"*Vaya*, Puerto Rico," Elvis said and threw back his shot of whiskey. "After this is over, I wanna treat you to a buff spa at Seabrook's."

"What's a buff spa?"

"A place where they give manicures and pedicures and a mint-cream exfoliation. It will change your life."

"Thanks," I said. "But no."

Chico Santana don't buff spa.

"Maybe we could do a Miami weekend after we find Gabby and this crap is all over?"

"Chase, too?" I said. "Since you don't seem to be able to go anywhere without her."

Elvis laughed. "Sorry. I had to bring her. But I'll make it up to you. Miami is boys only."

He tapped a Newport cigarette out of a crumpled pack and offered me one.

"I got my own," I said and pulled my Djarums.

"Good," Elvis said. "That's better, Chico. You're not just a private investigator looking for the boss's daughter anymore. There's plans being made for you. Me and Chase already talked. You and me, members. And you won't even have to give anything up. You can give up giving things up."

"What do you mean?"

"TSP's gotta change," said Elvis. "Life's too short. Enjoy a good smoke, a stiff drink, a good meal, a good lay. You're not going to live forever, *papá*. Believe me, I looked into it. We got a lot to talk about."

We went outside and lit up.

"Chase and I are getting married tomorrow," said Elvis.

"Congratulations," I said. "Where's Pablo's brother?"

Elvis poked his head back into Gonzalez y Gonzalez and waved at Chase, who signaled the man sitting across from her.

TWENTY-NINE

Pedro Sanchez came outside, and for a moment I could have sworn he was Pablo. Pablo had grown a neat handlebar mustache, and he was many pounds thinner, older, but he was Pablo, walking toward me.

"Pedro," said the man by way of introduction; he had a Spanish accent as thick as guava nectar. "Mi mother es dead. Es no good."

"Yes," I agreed. "Es no good."

I looked at his clothes. His *guyabana* shirt and pants were white and pressed. His alligator shoes were shined. Pedro was not Pablo. He told me he was a former cop and now a private security guard for the wealthy from Santo Domingo and seemed, by the hard look in his eyes and the strength of his rough handshake, like the type who would plug a man without even blinking for shoplifting a green banana.

"So you're a former cop," I said as we walked back inside to the bar, after our smoke, where Chase was sitting. Pedro ordered rum. Straight up.

"*Sí*," said Pedro. He paused. "Many years ago. I also working in the circus."

"What'd you do in the circus?"

"I was *el* midget," Pedro said, laughed, and slammed back some rum.

The four of us went to a corner table already set with four glasses of water and nachos and salsa.

"Have you seen Giovanni?" I asked.

Chase told me that she had not but that she had good news: a deal had been struck, TSP had backed down, Elvis was officially reinstated as a member of The Superman Project, and Hari Lachan was *like* voted the new president of TSP. And a few days ago, Chase had bought Elvis brushes, paints, oils, acrylic, glue, and every other imaginable painter's accoutrements.

"What the hell for?" Pedro wondered aloud, grumpy.

"Well," Chase said, "it's like for his papier-mâché projects."

"*Qué?*" said Pedro.

Chase looked at Pedro as if he were an ignoramus. "Papier-mâché is newspapers mixed with glue, to make things. Andy Warhol had Soup Cans. Elvis will have papier-mâché. Every artist needs like a gimmick. He'll experiment, then when he's real good, we'll sell his pieces at the TSP art gallery."

"Ah," said Pedro. "Money."

"Not only money," said Chase. She looked at Pedro as if he had like fallen off the back of a banana boat. "Elvis will do it because his soul *needs* him to do it. Because he *longs* to create. Elvis needs to *do something* with his hands. He's an artist, not a grocer or a cartoonist. Cartoons are for children. I'm sure you can understand, Chico."

"He's an artist," I repeated. "Not a grocer or a cartoonist. Cartoons are for children. Sure."

"Exactly," she continued. "We're getting married tomorrow. We bought a dog and Elvis has like moved into my condo apartment in Brooklyn. I am really, really happy. The new art will just mean a *rebirth* for Elvis. Part of him has been dead, part of him never, ever came to life. It's like a new and refined beginning for Elvis. Right, sweetie?"

Elvis nodded and winked at me.

The waitress, also dressed in black, came over with more chips and salsa.

"Thank you, beautiful," Elvis said.

When the waitress walked away, Chase said, "That wasn't right, Elvis."

"What?"

"You've been flirting with girls like all night."

"Don't be jealous, *querida*," said Elvis. "My art belongs to the world. My heart belongs to you."

"I don't like it," Chase said, and crossed her chubby arms across her massive bosom. A silence fell over the table; then Pedro asked Elvis to speak at the bar. They got up, and I stayed seated with Chase at the window.

Chase smiled coquettishly and sipped her margarita, sucking on the straw in an obscene manner, her lipstick smearing it red. She reached across the table, grabbed my face, jumped up, and kissed my mouth roughly. She sat back down with a big smile.

"I know about you and Zena," she said.

"There is no me and Zena."

"Not what I heard."

"What do you know about Zena and me?" Now, I'm not used to trading spit without warning but it was a good kiss. I wasn't sure if it said more about her or about me.

"It's okay," said Chase. "I mean, Joey and Zena were in love. You and Joey are from the same place. It makes sense."

"Joey and Zena were in love?"

"Yeah," she said. "I thought you knew?"

No.

"What's so hot about Zena?" she asked.

"I don't kiss and tell," I said.

"C'mon," Chase said. "Are you a man or a wimp?"

"Both," I said. "I like balance."

"It won't last, you know? You and Zena."

"Why not?"

"You're both too ambivalent. You're both afraid of love. You're like my mother and father. I grew up with that. I recognize it when I see it."

"When you see what?" I said.

"Zena. She bats an eyelash and a sucker gets born. Next dope in line is Chico Santana."

"If that's what you see," I said, "I think you need glasses."

"Or maybe you do."

Maybe.

Chase exhaled cigarette smoke and laughed. "Poor Hari doesn't know! My little sister Zena's a whore!"

I sucked the dark burning clove smoke into my lungs.

"Don't call her that," I said.

Zena and Joey.

I sucked the dark burning clove smoke into my lungs.

"You fuckin' Puerto Ricans think you *run* shit!"

I turned and saw a massive young Dominican kid with a shaved head, holding an empty Presidente bottle and staring Elvis down. Pedro was nowhere in sight. I jumped up and ran over.

"Hey," I said, hands up and open. "We don't want any trouble."

"*Manito,*" he said, looking at me. "You Dominican like me, how you gonna stand up for this Puerto Rican punk?"

I didn't want to break the news to him that I was also Puerto Rican in the hopes that he wouldn't break his bottle of Presidente beer over Elvis's head.

"Can't we all just get along?" I said, and smiled. "What's your name?"

"Juan."

241

"I'm Chico, Juan."

Juan looked like he was calming down. But then Elvis took out a dollar bill, threw it at Juan, and said, "Go buy some socks, you fuckin' *platano!*"

"I'm gonna kill you!"

"Problema?"

I turned and saw Pedro. Me and Juan traded stares, and I shrugged. Juan outweighed Pedro by at least a hundred pounds. A handlebar mustache would not be enough.

"Problema?" Pedro repeated. I stepped between them. Juan grabbed my right shoulder, squeezed, and turned me. As I spun around, I swung the palm of my left hand up into his nose, not hard enough to break anything, but enough of a blow to ward off any further physical contact. His head snapped back, his massive body went loose, and he stumbled into some men at the bar, clutching at his nose. And Pedro exaggerated and swung his Presidente beer bottle into the guy's head. *"Cabrón! Pendejo!"*

The bouncers came running over, and Pedro flipped out a badge and said, *"Policia."*

"Call an ambulance," I said and pushed everybody toward the door. We walked briskly out of Gonzalez y Gonzalez, through the doors, and into the warm night. Chase hurried out behind us.

"Where'd you learn to do that?" Elvis asked me.

Chase looked at me suspiciously. "Same place you learned everything you know, right? In da Bronx?"

"St. Mary's in da Bronx," I said.

"Those must've been some tough nuns."

We walked along Broadway in the heat of night. "And where'd you learn your technique, Pedro? The circus?"

"Que vaina," Pedro said. "I no like disrespect me."

Elvis slapped me on the back and unlocked the black Porsche's door. A barking dog, the size of a small black fox, jumped up into Elvis's arms.

"Poros!" yelled Chase.

"Welcome to The Superman Project, Chico," said Elvis and kissed the dog on the mouth.

Disgusting.

I thought about my Chihuahua, Boo, and how mouth kissing was never gonna happen between us. I liked my dog, Boo. But only as a friend.

"I need to find Giovanni," I said.

"You think this man kill my mother and not the boy in jail?"

"I think something's fishy and starting to stink and I got an itch to take out the garbage."

"Yes," said Pedro, pulling back his jacket and revealing a gun almost two times his size. "I, too. I want this Giovanni." He nodded as if he already had Giovanni in his sights.

"I'm not saying that Giovanni is guilty of anything," I said.

Pedro nodded. "What kind of gun, Chico, you have?"

"None," I said.

Pedro Sanchez shook his head, looked around, and slyly pulled a small handgun from his ankle holster.

"Take."

I took the gun from Pedro, wrapped my hand around it, got my finger into it. Checked the chamber, filled with bullets. It was an old pistol.

I shook my head and handed the pistol back to Pedro.

"No guns," I said.

"Okay," Pedro said, nodding his head. "But I need you alive. Stay alive, Chico Santana."

"I'll see what I can do," I said. "And don't tell Pablo about any of this."

"Pablo is a fool," said Pedro, "for no to call me when this happen. But no matter for, nobody, no way, kills the mother of Pedro Sanchez and lives."

And the way Pedro said it, I believed he was, if not a good man, or an innocent man, he was, as Pablo probably feared, at the very least, a man of his word.

THIRTY

A deal had been struck, Mara Gupta had backed down, Elvis was officially reinstated as a member of The Superman Project, and Hari Lachan was *like* voted the new president of TSP. Why? What had changed? Why now? That's what raced through my head on the 6 train to go and finally pick up my 1972 Charger on River Avenue, putting the money I had gotten from Willow so far to good use, and by the time I drove home, it was raining when I found her.

Zena Gupta was sitting cross-legged, dripping wet, in front of my door. Sweet clove smoke drifted from her lush mouth, and an inch of ash rested on the sleeve of her light blue sari. Watching Zena on the floor, smoking, drinking a beer, a box of half-eaten chicken wings in her lap . . . it broke my heart.

I don't know why.

Zena handed me a clipping. It showed a color photo of a café-au-lait-colored woman with strategically messy reddish hair clipped to the top of a long, pretty face. She wore a V-neck blouse, hung low over generous cleavage. Her thick lips formed neither a smile nor a smirk, something in between. Her eyes were auburn and wide open, not cynical, but not innocent either. They were tired but hopeful; beautiful. The name beneath the photo of the writer was Ramona Guzman Balaguer. A caption read: *Balaguer's "The Detective" is a brutally poetic ride filled with the tragic and the absurd.*

"That's your wife," said Zena. "Ramona."

"That's my soon-to-be ex-wife," I said. "What're you doing, Zena?"

"Keeping tabs on you. Snooping."

"I don't like that."

"Too bloody bad."

"I mean it, Zena," I said.

"What?" she said. "You can snoop, but I can't, Mr. Private Investigator?"

"It's my job to snoop," I said, crumpling up the clipping and sitting down.

"So," she said, "Private Investigator, have you done what the police haven't managed? Have you found Gabby?"

"No."

"Joey?"

"No."

"Have you seen him at all?"

"No," I lied.

I watched her face fall a bit and I knew. She was looking for him all along.

"I didn't think so," she said softly.

She told me that she had purchased the British beer from a *very charming and quaint* pub on 36th Street called The Ginger Man, named after a novel by a cat named J. P. Donleavy, very funny, very naughty writer, also from the Bronx, had I read him? Not yet, I said. She made me promise I would. I did.

We could also, she said, smoke my sister's ever-so-lovely

Djarum cigarettes all night long. I told myself that I would smoke a pack with Zena that night, get the information on Giovanni that I needed, and quit again in the morning.

I told myself a lot of things as I sat down there with her smoking and took the eighteen-ounce Fuller's London Porter.

If I said I wasn't glad to see her in that blue sari with her long drooping golden earrings, matching golden choker, and sweet little diamond stud in her sweet little brown nose, I'd be lying.

"So," I said. "You and Joey."

She smirked. "Who told you?"

"Mara. Chase. Aurelio, the mechanic who worked on my car. Everybody knew but me."

"Sisters," Zena said and shook her head. "Chase is a bloody slug. She doesn't do anything but wait for Elvis to come sniffing around. Then he has to drag her everywhere he goes. She tries to use me to break up the boredom. No thank you. Let them stew in their soup and grow up a bit, grow some bloody balls."

"That's cold."

"Cold," Zena said, and laughed. "They bought a dog. They call it Poros. It's like their child. That makes me sick, too. Sorry. I like animals. So I don't eat them. I am not a hypocrite when it comes to that. If someone is a vegetarian and treats animals with great respect and even coddles them, I can accept that. But when carnivores like Chase and Elvis act as if they have a spe-cial bond with an animal, it makes me sick. A tiger doesn't coochy-coo a baby zebra, and say how important it is, and then go out and eat an emu. I can't respect that. I'm ranting. However, I do know this. Chase is a lazy bitch, always has been, and Elvis is a shortcut, get-rich-quick kind of guy, they deserve each other. So be it. I just don't want to watch it."

"What're you doing here?"

Zena Gupta sat there with her bronze face, no makeup, guilty strawberry lips, dark lashes, dark eyebrows, thick mouth, her black hair a mess, and touched me. She whispered, in that smoky voice of hers, "Can you be my Superman?" and before I even had a chance to answer, before her lips were anywhere near my mouth, I wanted to stand, go in and slam the door in her face like a man.

But I'm not a man.

I'm a private investigator.

She took her hand away and looked me in the eye.

"You don't fancy me or something?"

"I do," I said. "I fancy you more than I should."

"Well," she said, "I don't mean to be forward." She checked her watch. "It's almost three in the morning and you haven't even attempted to kiss me."

"I'm trying to be a Superman."

"Well," she said, "knock it off."

"I've dated models who required less maintenance than you," I said.

"You dated models?" said Zena.

"Sure," I said. "Mostly for Walmart and Duane Reade. But the store discounts were great."

"You're a wanker."

"And you're trouble," I said.

I nodded, and noticed a light bruise under her left eye.

"What's that?"

She pushed my hand off.

"Mara and I got into it."

"Why?"

"Listen," she said. "I don't want to be alone, but I didn't come here to talk about Mara or Joey or Hari. It's bloody hot and humid, and I'm emotionally exhausted, and I need some loving. I don't need a Superman. I need a man tonight. Can you manage that? Have I come to the right place?"

Zena fell into my arms and whispered, "When you hold me I feel like saying those three words every man likes to hear from a woman he cares deeply about."

"'It's not your baby'?"

"That's five words."

"'I love bowling'?"

"No."

"'I love White Russians'?"

"Stop joking!" said Zena and whispered, "Do you believe in reincarnation?"

"With my luck, I'd come back as a lobster in a butter factory."

"Do you believe in true love?" she whispered.

"I don't know," I whispered back but I was bothered, in more ways than one.

"I didn't think I did," Zena said as I held her. "But I do. Love? Love is the most difficult thing on the planet, Chico. Faith, faithfulness, honesty, trust, giving, being open. So much work. Never ending. So hard. I am trying so hard to be a better person, a better human being in every way, to make a difference. But it's not easy, it's the most difficult thing. Life, when you look at it, is the most difficult. Death is easy. But that's not the problem. The problem, if I can call it that, is that death is not final. No, no. It would be easy if it was. Death is an in-between phase, the tunnel under the East River, between Manhattan and Queens. Because we all come back. Except for those who reach enlightenment. Father Ravi, my dear, might be close to it, but I in all honesty, I'm not ready for it yet. I love myself, I do, to the extent that I am a sinner. I suffer, make problems, create them, all on my own. But I love my little sins. So how can I become chaste with that attitude? How can I become the Superman? Very difficult, you'll agree, and I can't tell exactly what's happening here, but I can feel the wheels of fate turning in my favor when you hold me."

In her favor? One of her sisters was missing. She was a married woman. She was a liar. She couldn't be trusted but she spoke of fate. Even for me, Zena Gupta was a tango I had yet to dance.

"Here's to happy families," Zena said, downing the last dregs of her beer. "Are you having fun?"

"Interesting so far; and it is beautiful out here in the hallway but maybe we should go inside and talk."

She put out her arms and said, "Carry me."

I lifted her up and carried her in.

I wanted to drop her out into the backyard.

I should have.

But she was lying to me, playing me, and I needed the truth.

I wasn't happy to be holding her in my arms, finally.

That's what I told myself.

THIRTY-ONE

I opened my front door, holding Zena in my arms, and Mimi sent Max to bed laughing and yelling all the way, "Oooh! I'm gonna tell Auntie Willow!"

Mimi smiled, threw on her coat, whispered, "It's about time," and left without another word.

Zena sighed as I put her down on the sofa. She closed her eyes and rested her head on my shoulder.

She asked to see my bedroom and if I had any music that she could borrow. Here we go again, I thought as we went to the bedroom in silence, holding hands, and I told myself that she was probably just curious about Bronx interior design, even while she closed the bedroom door behind her, walked toward me, and started undoing my belt—which made her non-Superman intentions crystal.

"Why did you come here?" I said.

Zena looked away and said, "I'd rather not talk."

"I wanna help you, Zena. You tell me the truth. No matter what you've done, I'll help."

She leaned back against the white wall.

"Did you, Joey, and Giovanni have something to do with Gabby disappearing?"

"Don't be ridiculous," said Zena.

"What about your husband Hari?"

"Hari?"

"Hari was jealous of Joey," I said. "Joey was the favorite. Hari brought Joey into TSP and got forgotten. Hari had the honor of marrying you, but really, Joey was going to take over after Father Ravi. Hari was being promoted to Joey's office boy, while Joey was to be elevated to president. Joey had your father's love. Joey's gone. Hari controls everything now. You could've run for president, too. Don't you want control?"

"I have my share."

"Were you in love with Joey?"

She hesitated.

"It was just an affair with Joey?"

"Does it bloody matter, when the world is run by thugs, bureaucrats, and know-nothings, who makes love to whom?"

"I happen to have an allergy to liars," I said, "but I confess to a weakness for the truth. And you still haven't answered my question."

"With Gabby gone," Zena said, "I have no sisters I can trust. Me and Mara and Chase just grew up in the same fucked-up bloody family, and it wasn't even a family. Just a disconnected bunch of people with no traditions and no love, a bunch of strangers who lived together. I would never hurt Gabby or let anybody hurt Gabby. I've been looking for Gabby, just like you, Chico."

I held her hand and pushed her to talk.

"My father," Zena continued. "He said he loved my mother. He dragged her from England to America. Then he left. He abandoned all of us. For years I didn't see my father. He was too busy building his little Superman Project. He just left. Then my uncle

Edgar, after my cousin Arjuna died and my aunt Anu left him, he abandoned us. You'll abandon me too soon. I know that."

"I won't abandon you."

What the hell are you saying, Santana?

"Promise?"

"I promise," I said.

I blame biology. I blame the fact that when the blood rushes out of a man's head before a night of passion, he is at a loss when it comes to thinking logically or critically. I blame biology. I blame Darwin.

"Would you marry me? I mean, if it came to that? If there was a mishap?"

"Yes," I said. "Of course."

"I wouldn't marry you," she said. "I don't believe in marriage. I don't believe love should be reduced to a state-sponsored contract. But it's nice to know that you would marry me. I mean, if anything happened."

I grabbed her hand, dizzy with desire again, and kissed it and said, "Of course I'd marry you. Tell me more. I want to know everything. Help me help you."

I was working now. I knew I was working. I felt like a rat. Then I thought about the missing girl Gabby Gupta and the murder of Esther Sanchez and that poor sucker Yayo, if he was innocent. "Tell me everything, Zena."

"In my family," Zena said, "achievement was demanded. Everything was results. We were all told to become lawyers, doctors, engineers, businesspeople, computer people, scientists. Or the wives of men who were. Mother was raising four daughters alone. But we didn't attack Father, we attacked Mother and she attacked us. He left us for his TSP. He didn't come to my college graduation at Trinity College in Cambridge because he was probably shacked up with some rich man's wife looking for TSP donations. And then he comes to us, drops out of the blue, like it's some fucking gift that makes up for years of neglect. Father

Ravi is not as fucking bloody great and good and wise as most members think or we pretend he is."

She told me she had always been unpredictable. That, I believed. I could never tell what Zena would do, from one minute to the next. Would she disappear, leave Hari, love me, confess to some terrible act involving Giovanni and Joey?

"If women got together and started thinking less about what they want and more about what the world needed, they could change the world. Instead, women want to finish the job men started of destroying the world. Why? Because most women can't think for themselves. When most women start thinking, they start thinking about what men want and how to please their men, and they call it love and we all go to *shite* along with this whole fake, makeup-wearing, diamond-wanting, diet-pill and beauty-magazine world."

Zena gave me a naughty smile and said, "My father inherited that Utopia Farms property from a wealthy member of TSP when she died. I think they were shagging. Not bad, huh?"

"Kryptonic behavior?"

"My father was all about Kryptonic behavior; that's why he invented the confession circle, where all that toxic gunk gets washed away, and you live another day to perform even more Kryptonic hijinks."

She came close again. Too close. We kissed. Her mouth was sweet and plump. She pressed against me, her lips on mine. We tumbled into one of Willow's spidery dreamcatchers.

She took off her blue sari. The condoms appeared, and the moaning and groaning began. Weak, Santana, your flesh is so weak!

Making love to Zena, Kryptonic Zena, imperfect Zena, the real Zena, was like making love to a summer night, humid, dark, disturbing, and comforting.

I almost coulda forgiven her for anything in that moment.

Almost.

That night, with her warm and naked beside me, her dark body pressed against my stomach, her face buried in my chest, I slept long and deep, the soundest sleep in a long, long time, without nightmares but dreaming that she and I were somewhere in that nude painting of hers, some heaven, where she was sparkling, brown, and naked, not afraid, not wrestling anymore. But dreams must come to an end, right? *Sí*. But why so quickly?

I was making love to Zena.

I opened my eyes.

I stood up.

Dumping used Trojans in a small red wastebasket.

Zena rose from the bed like a beautiful brown statue, rubbed her dark forehead, and lit one of the Djarums.

"I feel so wicked all of a sudden," she said. "I don't know what's wrong with me."

Zena, brown-eyed Zena, lover of contradictions, sweet acrobat, sweet liar. Zena, who wondered out loud if the mad are attracted to one another, if they flock toward each other looking for company and comfort. I told her I didn't think so, and she doused her cigarette and we made love again, and she fell asleep again, wrapped in my arms, naked, her backside pressed into me, breathing lightly and filling the room with her sweet, unmistakable scent.

Ramona was yesterday.

Zena.

No. I wasn't forgetting the case. I was still on the case. But even the devil, I hear, gets a holiday. The case would have to wait a moment. Anyway, there was no telling what I could learn from Zena. Yeah. Lie to yourself, Santana. Keep lying. Lie until the truth comes knocking. And it will knock . . .

I opened my eyes and saw the baseball. The fake baseball allegedly signed by Roberto Clemente sitting on the dresser. Roberto Clemente was never a Yankee. The ball was a phony. Everything I remembered about that ball. Everything I knew

had been a lie. My father had said it was signed by Roberto—
or had he? There were childhood memories associated with that
ball and the memories were as phony as the ball itself. Maybe as
phony as Zena and Joey.

Enough!

I jumped out of bed again.

"What're you doing?" Zena said, stirring.

"Nothing," I said. "Go back to sleep."

Suddenly I had to get up. I felt sticky and hot and completely confused. I headed for the shower, but stopped short at
the bedroom door, haunted.

I rushed to the bathroom, sat on the edge of the bathtub,
and lit another Djarum cigarette. I longed for another drink. I
smoked ten cigarettes in a row, until I was weak and sick from it.

My bloodstream full of nicotine, I was finally starting to relax. I stood and turned on cold water for a shower; then a knock
came.

"Chico," said Zena, and threw open the door. "Are you
okay?"

"Of course. It's hot, and I'm sticky. I'm taking a shower."

"Nothing else?"

"Nothing."

"There's a three-legged cat in the living room."

"Damn," I said. "Thanks. I was lookin' all over for those."

"You don't always have to hide behind jokes with me, Chico."

"I'm not joking," I said. "Of all my three-legged cats, that's
my favorite. I'd really hate to lose him. What's he doing?"

"Snuggling with a sleeping Chihuahua."

She blinked her brown peepers.

"You're mine now," she said, grabbing me. "You belong
to me."

And she bit me. She actually bit me.

I held my hand. "I'm bleeding."

"Don't be a baby," she said. "You're The Superman now."

She smiled and said, "Do you know why I fancy you?"

"Because I'm not fancy?"

"You don't talk much," Zena said. "Most men talk too much. You listen."

"It's my job," I said.

"You make me feel safe," she said.

In the shower, she asked me, "Again . . . please," and we did it again. I believed, for the first time since Ramona, that I was in love again—no longer with Ramona, not anymore. I had evolved, moved on, found a new love. If it gets me nowhere, if it means the end of everything, my case, my office, my childhood friendship with Joey, so be it . . . until I saw a vision of Esther Sanchez with those knife wounds, and I pushed Zena away.

What are you doing, Santana?

Zena sighed deeply. It sounded familiar; Ramona had sighed like that all the time. Maybe it was me? Zena got out of the tub and was in the bathroom doorway, naked, and suddenly I wanted to run. I wanted to go back to a time before I had ever set eyes on her, to be left alone, to sit still, but the world kept coming in. I sank down on the edge of the tub. Again the fear that she was a killer or involved in killing came over me. And for a long while, as she stood there in silence, I was torn between the impulse to run away and the urge to fling myself into her arms. I reached over and shut off the shower and said, "Do you love Joey?"

"No," she said. "You're my Superman."

She touched my face.

"What is Mara planning?" I asked finally. "Why did she back down in her fight against Hari?"

"Who said she was fighting against Hari?"

I got it.

"They're on the same side," I said. "Mara and Hari are working together!"

"You're such a good detective," she cooed as she kissed the palm of my hand.

I kissed the palm of her hand, too. Oh, I would pay for my weakness later. As that old country song says there was a time to fold 'em and a time to hold 'em, and a time to run, and I was still holding when it was time to run. I didn't know that then, or maybe I didn't care, but the dreamer has to waken when the rain falls and the floors beneath his fantasy crumble.

And we kissed and in the bedroom there was chocolate, and cherry, and the faint scent of what I thought was perfume coming from Zena. Her hair across my bare chest, sweaty and breathless on my skin, the heat of her body next to mine, my knees tucked into the back of her naked legs, her scent lingering on my fingertips.

"I've been meaning to ask you," I said. "What's that perfume you wear?"

"Honeysuckle," she said.

A light, pleasant honeysuckle drowsiness came over me. With a sense of comfort that I had not known since I broke up with Ramona, I nestled my head into the dark pillows, Zena at my side, and sank into a deep, sound, refreshing sleep . . .

In the morning she was gone.

Pablo finally called back.

"Pedro?" said Pablo with a frantic tone. "You called Pedro? Please tell me you didn't call Pedro!"

"Not me," I said. "Maybe Elvis. Do you know where Giovanni is?"

"No."

I got a second call. It was Nicky. "Gotta go, Pablo. Hang tight." I hung up.

Nicky next.

"I never did ask you," I said. "How was Atlanta?"

"Hot and sweaty," said Nicky. "How are you?"

"Same."

"Well," said Nicky, "while your ass was relaxing, I did a little investigating of this Superman Project. There's some kind of emergency meeting."

"When?"

"Tonight."

THIRTY-TWO

We parked, jumped out of the Charger, and entered the green doors of TSP, Nicky at my side.

TSP MEETING: Spiritual Healing
Monday 8–9:30 PM
1134 West 47th Street
Suggested Donation: $25

The auditorium was wall-to-wall with members and fellow travelers, ready and willing. Hari and Mara had arranged this emergency meeting.

I strolled with Nicky into the TSP auditorium, decorated with flowers and red, blue, white, and yellow silks. There were no chairs this time. Everyone was standing. TSP wives had baked cakes, and children ran wild past buffet tables set up with huge pots of rice and curried vegetables, green and gold and sweet and salty. Father Ravi's books were on display on a long table in a corner, where a band wearing prayer beads, ponytails, and robes played traditional Asian Indian music on sitars. The aroma of incense was everywhere.

At the head of the auditorium, onstage, was a lavishly upholstered throne and to the side of the throne, a giant shrouded sculpture. I was standing with Nicky at the back, surrounded by a chattering crowd of men, when Hari Lachan rolled in, in his wheelchair, followed by Mara Gupta. Mara wore a golden sari and a long green-crystal necklace, her black hair in two braids that fell beside her maple-brown cheeks. She pushed Hari up the ramp to the stage.

Hari sat in his wheelchair, before the two thrones, silent for a few minutes, smiled, then scowled at the audience. "They want me to be weak. But I will NOT be weak for them."

Nicky gave me a look.

"Father Ravi was sent to earth to save the world."

Mara applauded enthusiastically. The audience followed her cue.

"You all know," Hari said, "that as we move up the ladder of power, we must take a different spiritual name. Well, my brothers and sisters, last night, a voice came to me in the darkness, and this voice told me that my new spiritual name was Father Aziz. Father Aziz? I was confused. There is only eternity, said the voice, and in that eternity is The Superman. You are a gentle warrior, Hari. Father Ravi is your teacher and your master. But you must overcome your master, the voice said. That is what Father Ravi teaches. You must love him and hate him. He taught you that, Hari. Your goal is to one day overcome your master. He taught you that, Hari. Your job is to become The Superman."

This time, Mara didn't have to prod the mob. They applauded without her cue.

"The British," said Hari, "have left India. Father Ravi has returned to both Britain and India to teach them. In India where most books in English sell few, said the voice, Father Ravi's *Wrestling with The Superman* will sell over a million copies. In America and Europe, said the voice, it will sell double that. The Superman Project will be welcomed in Ohio and London, Shanghai and Mumbai and Texas."

More applause.

"India and Britain have concepts but no model, Hari, said the voice. TSP is the concept and the model. TSP speaks the truth. TSP works. TSP has cured and taken more people out of ignorance and spiritual poverty than any other program in the history of man. You are a CEO, you are a college dropout, you are a trust fund child. All you know is self-doubt. You arrive at TSP, upward and onward you go until a spiritual name arrives. A spiritual name arrives only when one has reached a new level of wisdom. You have arrived, Hari Lachan, said the voice. I was confused, my brothers and sisters. I was perplexed. Until—"

Hari Lachan paused and then EXPLODED out of his wheelchair, jumped up and stood, arms outstretched, eyes closed, in ecstasy and pain, like an ant that had just burned all of its strength lugging a giant crumb into its hill. And then he stood up straight, looking strong and tall and healthy. And the place went mad with applause and swooning and tears and OH, MY GOD, OH MY GOD, Hari Lachan was a leader, a power, and a miracle! Hari Lachan was The Superman. Then Mara unveiled the giant sculpture to the side of Hari's throne.

It was a statue of Hari Lachan.

Hari Lachan at the edge of a cliff in robes, a mighty wind blowing, his arms pushed back, his head thrust defiantly forward, fighting against the winds, as if about to take flight.

I recognized the workmanship.

Giovanni Vaninni.

"Good evening, everyone," said Hari, arms still outstretched. "Allow me to introduce myself. I am Father Aziz. I AM THE SUPERMAN!"

"Long live Father Aziz!" yelled Mara and applauded.

"LONG LIVE FATHER AZIZ!!!" everyone repeated and applauded wildly. Some people were crying and holding each other and raising their hands to the sky.

Hari Lachan was now officially the president and spiritual head of TSP, replacing Father Ravi, who, Mara announced, had gone to the mountains of Nepal, to retire and live in prayer and silence, a sacrifice he made for each and every TSP member.

"TSP! TSP! TSP!" Hari chanted.

"TSP! TSP! TSP!" everyone repeated.

My cell rang again. "What's up?" I asked, a finger in my ear to try to block out the screaming and yelling and applauding and pounding of feet.

"Max is missing."

"What?" I said. "Louder!"

"The air conditioner broke down on Parkchester!" Joy shouted. "Mimi let Max play outside in the yard. She turned her head for a minute and before she knew it, the gate to the backyard was open and Max was gone. A few minutes later she got an anonymous call from a woman saying that Max was safe and that Chico knew why this was happening and if Chico ever wanted to see Max alive again he'd back off Joey Valentin until she called back with instructions of where Max could be found safe and sound."

"Did Mimi call the police?" I asked with gritted teeth.

"No!" Joy said. "Not yet. She feels so guilty, she wanted me to call you."

"Tell her I'm coming," I said and slapped my cell shut. I felt my hands tremble, not for me, fuck me, for the kid.

"Chico!" yelled Nicky.

I turned and saw a horde of TSP guards headed right at us. No sign of Big Man. Maybe he retired after Nicky's clothesline. Lieblich was there and Doyle led the charge.

I gave Doyle, coming at me like a wounded beast a loud slap. The blow landed on his left cheek and propelled him past me, almost turning him around 360 degrees. If I hadn't held on

261

to his arm, he would have gone through the window behind me and then to the street outside like falling timber.

Doyle regained his balance and rushed out.

"I guess one serving was enough," said Nicky.

"Some folks fill up easy," I said.

"Who's up for seconds?" said Nicky, stepping back and demonstrating a perfect roundhouse kick.

None of the TSP guards came forward for the Nicky Brown buffet.

Lieblich looked at Nicky and nodded and calmly walked out of the auditorium without a word.

That's when I heard screeching tires and turned to the window behind me and spotted Doyle pushing Mara Gupta and Hari Lachan roughly into a Lincoln Town Car. They took off in a hurry.

It didn't add up. Taking Max was a block to keep me busy. But for what? Why?

We took off.

"I just got a call from Joy," I said, walking fast. "Somebody has Max."

"The kid?" Nicky growled. I knew that growl.

I felt it, too, rage like a rip from my gut to my throat.

"What's going down?" asked Nicky as we walked.

"I put it together like this," I said. "With Hari the new president, Joey's no longer a danger to Mara and Hari's will to power even if Gabby is found and Joey returns. The fight for power between Hari and Mara was a fake, just like Hari's injury. It made for a good show and high emotion and the final 'miracle' of Hari walking and Mara embracing him makes for deep love and forgiveness between all factions of TSP. Mara and Hari must have been planning this move as soon as Joey was cut out of the picture."

So was it Mara and Hari all along? Did they have their goons silence Esther Sanchez and her secrets?

"But why now?" asked Nicky. "Why prematurely launch this plan? Give it to me, brother."

I stopped. "Jeez,' I said.

"Undoubtedly,' said Nicky and nodded.

"Go pay these people in Manhattan a visit," I said, jotting down some names for him as I walked. "Then hit Queens. Tell them that a child named Max is missing. Ask them to tell you everything they know. Ask real nice."

"What if they don't cooperate?"

"Get Nicky Brown on their asses," I said.

THIRTY-THREE

I followed the dark Lincoln Town Car in my Charger, playing Tupac's "Me Against the World." I knew exactly where they were going as soon as the highway sign overhead read MONTAGUE. I thought back to the scuffling I heard up at Utopia Farms, the sound of Wagner, then the crashing noise, then the scuffle.

I sped ahead, past them, to Utopia Farms. I knew that in order to find Max (before we had to call in the boys in blue) I would have to go hard and fast. I didn't have forty-eight hours. I gave myself twenty-four. Beyond that I'd have to pass the ball. And God forbid if you fumble, Santana.

As I approached the dirt road leading to Utopia Farms, I stopped the Charger, got out, gingerly closed the car door, and waded through the humid air.

I jumped a fence, tripped in the dark over a tree stump, regained my balance, and walked through a thick mess of bramble

and forest, and down a curvy, steep dirt-and-gravel hill, and jim-
mied open a basement door. I walked blind through the bowels
of the enormous lodge, not knowing where I was headed, moving
forward, searching for Max or anyone who could lead me to her,
looking into rooms behind endless white doors.

The first room I saw looked like an air-conditioned labo-
ratory and was full of bottles of pills; the second room was a
small, abandoned private zoo. Then I entered a small private
theater with a projector and an enormous library of movies.
The next room was a trophy and billiard room, then came a
gym with fancy exercise equipment and a swimming pool,
then finally a small bowling alley. A bowling alley. This is some
basement, I thought as I walked through another door that led
into a bright white hall and a honeycomb of . . . more white
doors!

"Hey!"

I turned and almost soiled my Fruit Of The Looms when I
saw the giant called Lieblich bulging like an enormous muscle
in his red TSP blazer.

"Hey?" I said, smiling, extending my hand for a friendly
shake. "Howdy, Lieblich. I'm here with Zena and Chase Gupta.
I think I took a wrong turn?"

"I don't think so," said Lieblich. "Nobody's allowed down
here."

"Oh," I said, dropping both my hands to my side. "I'm sorry."

"You'll have to come with me."

Lieblich started going for his walkie-talkie. Luckily, they
did not equip Lieblich with a gun or a Taser or I'd probably be
a dead or a shockingly quiet Chico. I moved toward Lieblich
quickly, both hands still at my side, saying, "You know what?"

A quick jab, another, a throat punch, a snap to the groin,
and then two sudden uppercuts to the jaw and a right to the
temple and the machine called Lieblich went surprisingly flat
as a board and off to see the Wizard. Nobody, except perhaps

Lieblich, was more surprised than I was. I stepped over the mountain and moved quickly along the corridor, opening more doors, doors leading to storage closets and empty guest bedrooms and sparkling white bathrooms and empty lecture halls and meditation rooms, until I hit a target. Father Ravi.

I found Father Ravi, dressed in a simple white robe, barefoot in a large, austere room with a table, a chair, a few books, and a bed.

Father Ravi was sitting at the table, with a spiral notebook, a glass of water, and a tape recorder. He looked emaciated, his skin wrinkled and drooping, his long hair gray and dull. In other words, he looked like an old man, an ordinary old man.

He greeted me with a smile so innocent and sincere and warm, I almost cried out, Santa?

He signaled for me to enter and pointed at the spiral notebook. It was marked *Wrestling with The Superman II*.

Father Ravi stood up and he pulled me close and hugged me. I could feel his strength, and behind that, what felt like genuine love.

"Max," I said. "A little girl. Little black girl. Have you seen her?"

Father Ravi smiled wide like a child. "Walk with me, Arjuna," he said.

Arjuna was Father Ravi's dead nephew, Edgar Gupta's son.

I nodded and we began to stroll along the room in circles.

"Arjuna?"

"Yes?"

"I feel strange as of late."

"What's wrong?" I said, hoping to get some information, anything that pointed one way or another.

"Can I ask you a personal question, Arjuna?"

I nodded.

"Are you dead?"

"Yes," I said. "Your nephew Arjuna is dead."

"Am I dead?"

"No," I said.

"We're all going to die," he said. "No rush." He looked out, past me at the white soundproofed wall, as if looking through a tall window at the marvelous landscape of Utopia Farms lit up by an army of night lights and said, "It's so beautiful."

"Yes," I said, looking at that spot on the wall. "It's beautiful. Where is Max? Do you know Max?"

He looked back at me and said, "When you change your trousers from a dirty pair to a clean pair, do you fear the clean trousers?"

"Only if they're plaid," I said. "Do you know Max?"

"Do not fear death. Death is merely the changing from dirty trousers to clean. Do not fear the plaid, Arjuna."

"I'll try not to," I said. "No promises. Have you seen a little girl? A little black girl?"

I thought maybe he wasn't all gone, a fake like Giovanni and Hari, until he stopped and looked at me, wide-eyed and trembling, and said, "I saw the skeletons, Arjuna. Many skeletons. Humiliated, ridiculed, photographed, taped, recorded, controlled. There are no great ones, Arjuna. There are only sheep and killers. The sheep worship the killers. I have seen the skeletons. They are weak and decaying. They are us. Man does not want to be free. Did you know that?"

"No. I—"

"Your father Edgar thinks you are a fool, Arjuna. You don't know, but he really thinks that. Because you are a poet, sensitive to something he doesn't understand. A poet. Ah, how could Edgar really understand. I remember your first poem, Arjuna: 'When Everything Was God.'"

Father Ravi stopped, then said, "Good," correcting himself.

"'When Everything Was Good.' You dedicated that poem to me. Do you remember, Arjuna?"

"I remember," I said. "Have you seen her, Father?"

"Of course!" Father Ravi said. "Your poem was brilliant. What are you working on now?"

"Something about Mara," I said. "Tell me about Mara. Has she been here to see you? Is she keeping you here? Does she visit you? Have you seen her with a little girl?"

Father Ravi frowned.

"Talk to me," I said. "Talk to Arjuna."

I felt like crap, trying to trick a sick old man who couldn't tell the difference between me, his dead nephew, or a house plant. But those are the breaks.

"Arjuna," Father Ravi said. "I was wrong. You don't have to go to war to be The Superman. Devote yourself to your own path with no thoughts of war. You are not dead, Arjuna. You are home, Arjuna. Love and do your work. Whatever it is. Stop making excuses. Start today."

"I will," I said. "But I need Max. I need Max to finish my work."

"I was wrong about your mother. I was wrong about my daughters. I was wrong to tell you that you should go to that war and become The Superman."

The old man began to cry and said, "I was wrong, I was wrong, I was wrong," over and over.

Father Ravi handed me the spiral notebook marked *Wrestling with The Superman II* he had been working on. "Forgive me?" he said.

I flipped through the notebook and encountered a blizzard of question marks, semicolons, parentheses, exclamation points, and periods that swept across the pages; it made me dizzy. There was one word at the end of hundreds of pages of punctuation marks, and nothing more, that read:

SHUTTLECOCKS

"Yeah," I said. "I forgive you." The old man sat on his bed. I walked over and placed my hand on his shoulder. He held my hand and said, "Thank you, Arjuna. Thank you."

Then his eyes glazed and he chanted. Until his voice faded into a whisper and then total silence.

Then the door slammed open, and Doyle rushed in.

I turned away from Father Ravi and took Doyle out with a run-of-the-mill karate chop when he rushed at me again. To the right side of the room he went, slamming into the table and then the floor.

This spiritual stuff ain't easy, I thought as Lieblich (sporting two black eyes) and two more guards, muscles bursting the seams of their red blazers, rushed in at me like bulls at a Spanish run. I remembered that I had told Nicky to try to find Max in Manhattan. Why the hell does he pick and choose when to listen to me, I thought as I hit Lieblich the bull as hard as I could on the snout, and his nose spurted blood. The other bulls looked bewildered and stopped short. Someone (thank God) entered and yelled, "Stop!"

They stopped, turned aside, not more relieved than I was, and I saw her . . . an Asian Indian woman, older than Zena and Chase, a bit older than Mara, with the same bronze skin, shapely and tall and dark, with a long nose, a thick heart-shaped mouth, no makeup, and coal-black hair. She was wearing a red sari and brown sandals. Her hair was cropped, like a black crown of soft coal. Her long nose and dark lashes and thick eyebrows and round brown eyes were all dipped in cinnamon. And she glowed with a peaceful energy that made night look that much darker. When she smiled, the glow around her was radioactive.

I recognized her from the wedding photo that Pablo Sanchez had given me.

Gabby. Gabby Gupta.

"Are you okay?" Gabby Gupta asked.

"I think I pulled a groin muscle," I said, limping toward her. "Other than that, I'm peachy. Where have you been?"

"In Vermont," said Gabby Gupta. "In the hills. I had no idea what was going on here. Where is Joey?"

"Nice of you to start caring," I said. "But you're a little late, don't you think? Everybody's been looking for you."

"You must lose yourself to be found."

Because Gabby Gupta, like her father, seemed so sincere, I bit my tongue.

"Your sisters actually never knew where you were," I said. "But Mara found out that you had returned and she and Hari decided to make their grab for power before Joey came strolling back. Hari was never crippled in that so-called car accident outside TSP. The whole thing was a con brewed up by Mara and Hari after Father Ravi got sick. I had it checked out. Hari had a little accident, a sprain that maybe required a month of rest. Mara and Hari never came to an understanding, they always had one, they were on each other's side from the get-go."

"Mara and Hari's behavior since I ran away has been horrible," she said gently. "I apologize for that. But my sisters and I will try to make things right again. The board will hold another emergency meeting in the morning. We will deal with Mara and Hari internally. The importance of what my father, despite his shortcomings, was trying to do at TSP for an entire generation, for their morals, views, standards, and health, teaching them that they can do anything, is still invaluable."

Bigger sister Gabby Gupta was back. Mara Gupta's last-minute power grab had failed. TSP was closing ranks. TSP was trying to save itself.

"I hope," Gabby continued in a soothing tone, "if nothing else, that your short time dealing with TSP has been enlightening in some way."

"Oh," I said, hearing the crack of a thunderbolt outside. "It has been."

"None of this was their fault, really," she said. "They actually didn't know where I was, as you say. I told no one. Perhaps, I'm the one to blame."

"We'll start assigning fault in a minute," I said. "Where's my kid?"

Before she could answer I got the call.

THIRTY-FOUR

Midnight. I was on the Staten Island Ferry, smoking, a lead weight in my belly, and the mystical sea below. A humid wind was blowing and the sun had dropped down behind the Statue of Liberty. The water was black as the night as the ferry cut through the Hudson waters toward Staten Island. I was sitting on a stiff bench, looking out across the water at Ellis Island where the immigrants landed, a dream deferred for so many, limitations paid for in blood and suffering, again and again and almost lost, again and again, as he approached.

"Hello, pal," I said.

"What're you doing here, Chico?" he asked as he plopped down beside me, wide-eyed.

"Enjoying the ride," I said. "You?"

"I'm confused," he said and blinked.

"Let me unconfuse you," I said. "They're not coming."

"What's going on, Chico?"

"Gabby turned up alive," I said. "She had run away and was hiding out with an old high school girlfriend in the green hills of Barnet, Vermont, meditating. No TV, no phones, no news about what was happening with Joey or TSP. You know what I think?"

"What?"

"Yayo and then Elvis found Esther dead. Yayo removed the knife from Esther's back, just like he said. Then he panicked, just like he said. Realized what he had done, just like he said. A drug addict's prints were all over the murder weapon. Yayo got out of there and took the knife and his prints with him, just like he said. Then Elvis stumbled in like a dope and you know the rest."

"Okay." He nodded, confused.

I continued. "With Gabby Gupta back, Joey was back, too, it was over, so Esther's killer kidnapped my kid Max to get me to back off Joey until they could get what they wanted from him, to buy time."

"What is this all about?" he said. "Why are you here, Chico?"

I turned my head and was surprised to see Pedro walking toward us, fists clenched like mallets and feet slamming the earth like pile drivers, and Pablo looked at me as if for help and said, "What's happening, Chico?"

Dammit!

Pedro must've followed me from Utopia Farms without me knowing.

"Somebody's taken my kid," I said. "Somebody wants to play rough. They've come to the right place. Can I search you, Pablo?"

"What?"

Pedro came sauntering down the aisle.

"Are you serious?" Pablo said, and then looked at Pedro, as if pleading his case. "I didn't do it!"

"You can tell that bedtime story to the cops, Pablo," I said. "I'm not sleepy."

Pedro grabbed and shook him by the lapels.

"I didn't do it! You gotta believe me!" Pablo turned and looked at me.

I said it again, "Can I search you, Pablo?"

"Please, Chico," said Pablo. "What is this?"

"*Cabrón!*" Pedro shook Pablo violently. He threw up Pablo's shirt and pulled a knife marked *Michael Jordan Steak House* (Zena's missing knife) and a pair of latex gloves out of his pocket.

I bent over and picked up the knife and the latex gloves.

Pablo shook his head. "I don't understand."

"You were hoping that this knife would tie your mother's murder back to Zena. Find a scapegoat. That's what you were hoping the night you left your apartment after killing your mother and dropping Joey's card. Before Yayo and Elvis mucked up your plan. You were going to try and use this knife on Joey tonight. Isn't that why you lifted this knife from Zena's car that day you supposedly just went to see Chase at Utopia Farms? Isn't that why you invited Joey and Zena to meet you here on the Staten Island Ferry? The same spot where Joey and Zena used to go to be alone. You knew that. A lover's quarrel on the ferry. She stabs him, he goes overboard, maybe she goes over, too. Nice."

Pablo just kept shaking his head. "None of this was supposed to happen."

"All this for a comic book, Pablo," I said.

"TSP still helps a lot of people," cried Pablo.

"Joey's first Superman comic book," I said. "That's what you were after all along."

"People feel alone," said Pablo. "They come to TSP. They always find someone there who will care for them."

Pedro grabbed Pablo and shook him like a rattle, "I should throw you into the ocean, *cabrón!*"

"She was going to turn me in. My own mother," said Pablo.

"Joey came to you, Pablo, not knowing that you were in Mara Gupta's pocket."

Pablo ignored me and pleaded with Pedro. "I took responsibility for Mami. Do you know how much her medications alone cost? Emergency-room visits? Hospital stays? I was smart enough to go to college, Pedro. But who could afford college and take care of her at the same time? If I'm guilty, you're guilty, too, Pedro."

Pedro shook him. *"Pendejo!"*

"What happened, Pablo?" I asked and pushed Pedro back. Pedro looked like he wanted to kill me but just went and sat down on a bench on the opposite side of the ferry and stared at Pablo.

"Talk to me, Pablo," I said.

Pablo looked at his brother Pedro.

"Don't look at him," I said. "Look at me."

"I told my mother that Joey was coming," Pablo said, "and that I was calling the police so they could pick him up. I told my mother that I was working for Hari. She lost it. She just lost it. She began destroying my room, my things. Tearing everything up. My stuff. I yelled at her. She wouldn't stop. I grabbed the knife. I . . . I didn't mean it. I told her to stop. That I was working for Hari, that he was going to make me a Superman. And she just went berserk. She called me a traitor, a false friend and all kinds of names, after everything I had done for her. She said that she was ashamed of me. It was Hari. Hari was going to make everything happen for me. If I got that comic book back and called the police. He promised me."

Pablo glanced at Pedro. "Don't look at him, Pablo. Look at me."

Pablo looked back at me. "The bills were breaking my neck, Chico. I was a slave. How many more years could I go on being a slave? I couldn't go on. Mara was promising me everything. A job. A real job at TSP. Membership. Why shouldn't I get a shot? At success? Why not me? All I had to do was get the comic book and call the police when Joey got to my apartment. They'd pick Joey up. That's all Hari wanted. To keep Joey out of the way until he was president. I called Hari and told him that my mother knew and that she wasn't happy and he told me to take care of it. Take care of her. To become The Superman. So I did. I tried to get her to leave the apartment. To go out so that I could get the comic and call the cops and . . . she wouldn't go . . . She was going to call some members of TSP and tell them what Hari and I were up to . . . I had to . . ."

Pablo began to weep. "I was a slave. I wanted to be free."

"It's called a door, bro."

"You think it's that easy, Chico? Look at me." He spread out his flabby arms and slapped his massive belly. "I'm an elephant. Where can I go? Hari promised me, to help me, train me. My boring loser life for The Superman. Even Joey never offered me membership. I could maybe win Chase back from Elvis. I could be happy."

"I understand, Pablo," I said. "I get it. How'd you get Max to come with you? That was pretty good, Pablo. You're a smart guy. You have to have brains to get as far as you did with this."

"She's a nice little girl," Pablo said. "I just wanted you to back off until I could think, Chico. Come up with a plan and fix everything. I just wanted you to back off. I paid a girl that Yayo used to hang around with, a drug addict, to call and leave you a message. I told Max that my dog was missing and asked her to help me find him. I showed her a picture. Then I told her that you found the dog and wanted us to meet in Manhattan. I'm good with kids. She's a nice girl. I wouldn't hurt her."

"I know," I said. "You're not that kind of guy. Things just got out of hand and now that I've met your brother Pedro I understand how you could panic and start making really stupid moves, trying to stop me from figuring you out."

"I was trying to fix everything, Chico, but things just got worse. I was going to return Max unharmed, I swear, as soon as I figured out—"

"How to get that Superman comic book from Joey and frame Zena for Joey's murder, maybe take her out, too?"

"I don't know," Pablo said and shook his head.

"I know, Pablo," I said. "At first, I thought it was Giovanni. Giovanni was getting his sculpture money from Hari in exchange for working *secretly* on a sculpture of him as president of TSP. Giovanni was also getting money from Mara Gupta and Edgar Gupta. It takes all kinds. Mara confessed, *after* Gabby had a word with her, that you and Giovanni were both on her payroll as lookouts for Joey. Then I remembered what your mother had said, 'He's good with kids' and it all came together. An associate of mine tracked Giovanni, who was double-crossing everybody but Joey all along, and Gabby called Kirsten, who called her brother Larry, who called Solange and they all ran around like it was a telethon until they found somebody who could reach Joey and let him know that Gabby was back. And Joey told me about your meeting here with him and Zena. He told me that he had contacted you and you had set up the meeting."

"I knew it," said Pablo, shaking his head. "I knew it."

"Oh," I said. "And here's the kicker: Gabby Gupta destroyed Joey's Superman comic book in her fireplace after a fit of rage in Williamsburg. Joey doesn't even know yet. It's ashes, Pablo."

"I knew it," Pablo repeated and almost smiled.

"You're no killer, Pablo," I said. "You were just making it up as you went along. Making things go from bad to worse. My friend Nicky found Max calm as pie watching cartoons with your two ugly mutts in Washington Heights. We got her. She's safe. It's over, Pablo."

Pedro stood up. When we reached the other side, in Staten Island, Pedro said, "You will come with me, brother."

"We gotta take him back, Pedro," I said.

Pedro shook his head. "Come, brother."

"No," I said.

I felt the ship dock. The few passengers got off.

"Come, Pablo."

Pablo sat down.

"Like a man, Pablo," said Pedro, holding a gun now, low in his left hand. "Stand up. Come."

Seeing how Pedro was the guy with the gun, I couldn't argue much. Pedro, leaving nothing to chance, kept a nice, comfortable distance between us and said, "If you yell out, Chico, it will only make things worse. You can follow or you can go back."

"I'll follow," I said. "You're right."

We walked off the Staten Island Ferry in the darkness. Pedro pointed his gun at Pablo once we got to the street and it was clear that no one was around.

"I'm your brother, Pedro," said Pablo and got down on his knees on the sidewalk. Pedro turned away from him.

"Tell him to stand up, Chico."

"Please, Pedro," Pablo pleaded. "I'm afraid."

"Arriba," Pedro said, trying to pull him up. "Do no get down on your knees, brother. Not for me, not for nobody. Stand up, Pablo. *Arriba!"*

And he choked up, because Pablo touched him and he knew he was telling the truth, that he was scared out of his mind, and he wanted to live, and he wanted to start again, and Pedro knew what that's like. But this little piggy had to go home. Pedro had decided.

"This doesn't have to happen," I said, moving closer to Pedro and his gun.

I saw the barrel.

"It would be unhappy, Chico, if we could not say *adios* as friends," said Pedro.

"You are not the judge, Pedro."

"Stand up, Pablo. Stand up and behave yourself. Mami always called you the good boy. Be a good boy now."

Pablo stood up and wiped his tears. Pedro looked at me and nodded and pointed his gun at his brother.

"Don't!" I said. "No!" I reached out for the gun.

I lunged and tackled Pedro. Pedro fell back and threw a

punch. I ducked and hit Pedro twice in his kidneys. Pedro lunged at me, stumbling, with clenched fists. I bobbed and ducked, and let loose a hard, clean shot. Pedro went down on one knee.

Then I felt an explosion in my shoulder, a hard metal punch that ripped at the flesh and bone and spun me around and down. Most definitely not part of the plan!

Pedro walked over to me, still at a safe distance, still holding his gun. "You should never touch a man's gun."

"I apologize, amigo," I said through gritted teeth. "Come closer, let me make it up to you."

"Pedro, please," I heard Pablo plead.

Pedro shook his head and lowered his gun.

Then I saw Pablo try to run and Pedro move faster than I had ever seen a human being move. Suddenly Pablo's head jerked forward violently. I heard no loud report of Pedro's gun firing. When Pablo slammed against the sidewalk, I saw what hit him, protruding from his bloody head, stabbing through the bone into the soft tissue of his brain. It was a professional throwing knife. And I knew then what Pedro had done with that Dominican circus.

"My plan was to take him alive, Pedro," I whispered as everything started growing fuzzy and sirens became audible but distant.

Pedro looked around and said, "My job is done here."

He shoved a cigar in his mouth, winked down at me, said, "*Vaya con Dios*," and disappeared into Staten Island.

I closed my eyes because my shoulder hurt so much, and I lay there on my back as a trickle of pedestrians walked past me toward the docked ferry without stopping, and someone . . . slowly . . . turned off the lights . . . until I heard: "Chico?"

THIRTY-FIVE

I opened my eyes. I was in a hospital room. Nicky was there and Willow was there and Zena was there, too.

Nicky said, "*Hola*, pal. Sorry I missed the boat."

"How are you, Yankee?" Willow asked.

"Flesh wound," I said. I tried to laugh. "Pablo?"

Zena looked down at me. Nicky and Willow shook their heads.

"I'm sorry," Willow said. "I'm so sorry."

"May I speak with Chico alone a minute?" said Zena.

Willow took Nicky's hand and they left. Then it was me there, in my hospital bed, alone, with Zena.

Honeysuckle.

"I'd kiss you," I said. "Only I just washed my hair."

"Don't be cruel."

"What're you doing here?"

"Hari's waiting outside," she said. "He wants to start over. We're going to India."

"Why me?"

"You looked sad," she said, "and I'm the comforting type. Chico Santana, tough and lonesome. Who can resist that?"

"Many have tried and succeeded."

"You and I could go on a trip instead," she said.

"What do you mean?"

"You know what I mean."

"Did you ever love Hari?"

"Hari did whatever was required of him," she said. "To save TSP. Hari is one of the most noble men I know."

"Do you love him?"

"I respect him."

"Ouch," I said. "You lied to me, Zena. You were just using me to find Joey all along. You were in love with him."

Zena's lower lip began to tremble, and her eyes welled up. "Maybe at first."

"Fool me once," I said, "shame on you. Fool me twice, that's two times."

"I haven't been lying to you," she said. "Just in parts."

"Hari doesn't know about you and Joey or you and me, does he?"

She lowered her head.

"I didn't think so," I said. "All that talk about 'no rules' was just a lot of who shot Juan."

"You think I'm wicked," she said. "Don't you?"

"Look, baby—"

"I was protecting TSP," she said.

"From me?"

"From enemies, real, imagined, or . . ."

"You were protecting yourself," I said. "And your inheritance."

"Do you think we still stand a chance?"

"We have a better chance of dying on a train."

"It wasn't just business," she said. "Hari loves me. I don't love him. I'm married to a man who cares about me and if you ask me, I won't go back. It'll be over, Chico."

"What about Joey?"

"Joey was yesterday."

"What was I?"

"Love?"

I laughed until it hurt, so I stopped laughing. "There's a guy in the Philippines," I said, "who sells smoked fish and has nails driven through his hands and feet annually for the tourists to gawk at. I'm not that guy."

"I'm not asking you to be that guy."

"What do you want me to do, Zena? Bust out crying and put my head on your shoulder? We kiss and the pretty music comes up?"

"It wouldn't hurt."

"You're wrong about that."

"Maybe I shouldn't have come."

"Maybe you shouldn't have."

"Do you want me to go back to Hari, Chico?"

"Let me think it over," I said. "Yes."

"I'm crazy about you, Santana, aren't you listening?"

"Take a walk around the block. It'll wear off. It always does."

She went for the door and started crying softly and then she turned. "I hope someone hurts you, Chico Santana. I hope someone hurts you the way you're hurting me right now."

"Too late, baby," I said. "Goodbye, Zena Gupta." I pointed at the door. "It turns to the left."

"You're wrong about me," she said.

"Maybe," I said.

Nicky came back in and saw me watching Zena go, shook his head and I said, "It beez that way sometimes, *papá*."

"Yeah," he said. "Nothing you can do."

I was shot. Pablo was dead. Gabby and Joey were in love again. Ramona and Chris were in love.

Zena . . .

It beez that way, sometimes, *papá*.

"You should go see your mother," Nicky said.

That was the last thing I heard, before I felt a shooting pain in my shoulder and I pressed down on the morphine drip . . . pain . . . pain . . . pain . . . then nothing . . . nothing at all . . . tissue paper . . . and yellow ribbons . . . and . . . honeysuckle . . .

September. Yayo was released from jail and got clean. He even took me out for a little Flaco's Pizza. Extra cheese. The end. Morning again. Mimi's Cuchifrito. I was toying, my busted arm in a blue sling, with that phony baseball and a brand-new pack of Djarum cigarettes. I thought about my mother and father as Mimi went past and sucked her teeth and shook her red head at my cigs.

Adjusting my blue arm sling, I pocketed my cancer sticks.

"Sir?"

I turned and faced two tall, barrel-chested men in suits, one white, one black, flashing badges marked FBI. "We're looking for Pedro Sanchez."

I eyeballed their FBI badges. The real deal.

"He's wanted for multiple murders," said the black agent.

"Whose?"

"Twelve men," said the white agent.

"Kidnappers, killers," said the black agent.

"Seems Officer Sanchez took the law into his own hands after one of these men murdered a husband and wife and their kid. The husband owed their group some money."

"They killed a child?"

"The law is the law," said one agent. "Officer Pedro Sanchez is an illegal in the U.S. and a wanted man in the Dominican Republic."

"We know you've been in contact with Pedro Sanchez."

"I was," I said. "He disappeared. I don't really know the guy.

I only knew his brother Pablo from a case I was working on. Pablo's dead. Pedro killed him."

"We also know," said the white agent, "you were involved with that TSP group that was caught in the steroids scandal."

It's true. The Superman Project was charged with illegally providing members with steroids and growth hormone. It turns out that two hundred members were on steroids. TSP was indicted on reckless endangerment and violation of public health laws. It was also revealed that they were one million dollars in debt. Their assets were frozen. The Superman Project doors were closed and a theater school took over their building. Then Father Ravi died about noon on August 25. Joey, who was co-operating with investigators, gave his funeral oration.

"Do you know the whereabouts of Joseph Valentin and Giovanni Vaninni?"

"I last saw them at a funeral," I said.

It was true. Giovanni had been playing everybody for a sucker, including me, everybody but Joey. The last thing Joey had said to me at Father Ravi's funeral was that he was finally heading to Tahiti with Gabby and Giovanni. "I apologize if I caused you any trouble, Chico. I'm still learning. Goodbye, pal."

I didn't like that goodbye. There was something final in it.

"Are you familiar with a gang that specializes in Goya forgeries?"

"I'm no art historian," I said. "But it's impossible to imagine a Goya painting coming out of the woodwork and someone getting away with selling it."

"Not in New Delhi. Not in Uganda."

"A New York dealer," said the white FBI agent, "was visiting Uganda and was called to appraise a work, supposedly by Goya."

"He bought the Goya," said the black FBI agent, "suspecting that the Africans had no idea what they were selling, and then, when he got back to New York, found it was an almost perfect forgery."

"That's where Joey Valentin comes in. The Africans were arrested and charged, and they named Joey Valentin and his associates Gabby Gupta and Giovanni Vaninni as the people who originally sold them the work."

"Listen, fellas," I said. "I'm just a Bronx boy trying to stay off drugs, outta jail, and outta the statistics. I don't know nothin' about Pedro Sanchez except that he killed his brother. He disappeared after that. As for Joey and Gabby and Giovanni, I haven't seen them or had contact with them since that funeral."

One of the agents handed me a card and said, "Call us if you remember something you forgot."

I nodded.

The two agents left as Nicky and Willow entered with Max. Nicky was holding a brown box full of old comic books that I had given to Max. Hundreds of pages of legends, gods, mutants, freaks, heroes. My world before Ramona, after the Bible stories, after Moses and Pharaoh, David and Goliath, Samson and Delilah.

Willow stopped to talk with Mimi at the counter. Nicky and Max came toward me. Max seemed taller. She was wearing the new glasses with wire rims and the Yankee baseball cap I bought her.

"We're off to Detroit, Uncle Chico!"

"You gonna miss me?" I said.

"Naw," said Max. "You'll come visit. That's what Uncle Nicky said."

"Well," I said, "I've never been to the city of Detroit. Maybe it's time."

"It's easy," said Max. "You just drive past 8 Mile, past 7 Mile, until you see a green sign called Exit 13 by the Southfield Freeway. Then you'll see a sign that says McNichols Road. That's 6 Mile. That's where I live, off 6 Mile. If you get into any trouble there, tell them you know my uncle Dean. That's what I do."

"Your *Black Falcon* comics?" I said and tapped the brown box.

Max looked at me with sad eyes, and Nicky shook his head and I realized that the box was not full of my old comic books.

"Gizmo," said Max.

Max held open the box's lid. Gizmo the cat was dead in Max's box.

"He had a good life," Nicky said. "You treated him real good. You cared. Don't forget that."

I kissed Max on both cheeks and she ran off before she started to cry, excusing herself with, "I'll go show Gizmo to Yolanda so she can say good-bye."

"Sweet kid," I said, watching Max go. I pointed across the room to where Mimi was trying to convince Willow to eat some of her roasted pork. Nicky looked over at Willow and said, "I think I'm in love again."

"I've heard that before," I said.

"Willow says you were playing kissy-face with her when I was in Atlanta."

"It was one kiss."

"I know you can do better than that," said Nicky.

"Next time," I said.

"After Detroit," said Nicky, "Willow and me are going on a trip. You going to see your mother, right?"

"I'm not sure."

"Why not?"

"I don't wanna rock her world."

"Maybe you don't want her to rock yours?"

"Your car is waiting, Mr. Brown," I said and stood up.

Mimi came over, kissed Nicky, and kissed my cheek.

She caressed my arm and my blue sling.

"Are you okay?"

"I'll live," I said.

"Can you believe it?" said Willow, tugging on Nicky. "I can't get rid of him."

"Let's go, brother," said Nicky.

And as we left for the airport, Willow whispered in my ear, "Failure is when you stop trying."

That evening, I went to see my mother at the Gloria's Taza de Oro Beauty Parlor on Bronx River. As I walked into the joint, a little bell went off, and my heart skipped three beats.

There were no customers. A dyed blonde, fifty-three years old, in a white blouse and skirt and white tennis shoes, was sweeping hair off the checkerboard tiles. I recognized her right away. Over one of the three barber's chairs, on a mirror, was a poem by Julia de Burgos, "*Soy una amencida del amor* . . . I am a sunrise of love . . ."

That poem was the only evidence that my mother was once in love with my father. It was their poem. He read it to her the day they got married. It was taped on our blue refrigerator on Brook Avenue. I'll never forget that poem.

"*Hola,*" said my mother. "How are you?"

"Fine," I said. "You?"

"My feet hurt," she said and laughed. "*Pero no es tu culpa.*"

"I'm glad something's not my fault."

"Where are you from, *papito*?" said my mother.

"Here," I said. "The Bronx."

"I have never seen you around here," she said.

"Just passing through."

"*Hablas Español?*"

"Nah," I said. "I never really learned."

"*Que pena.*"

"Do you have time for one more haircut?" I asked.

"*Sí, amor,*" she said. "Sit!"

My mother signaled for me to sit in the reclining chair by the sink for a wash. I sank into the black leather chair, worn-out, dropped my head back into the cool white sink, and closed my eyes. When I opened my eyes, my mother was there, smiling down on me, tears in her eyes, holding a slick black plastic sheet. She tied the sheet around my neck. I felt in her trembling fingers her compassion, and as I looked up at her Caribbean face, she smiled wide, eager to console me.

She knew.

I knew.

But no one said.

She told me to excuse her tears that she was just thinking about her son. Freddy. She and her husband had two sons. Freddy was a soldier stationed in Afghanistan. She cried for him not to join, she prayed for him not to die.

"I am so sorry," she said, wiping her eyes. "I don't know what is wrong with me tonight. How was your day, *papito?*"

I could have told her that TSP and Father Ravi were indicted for fraud but that Father Ravi would never be tried on this side of heaven since he was dead.

I could have told my mother about Joey Valentin, Gabby, Gupta, and Giovanni Vaninni disappearing again after Father Ravi's funeral. Together. Destination Tahiti. How with a sweep of my good arm I had flung a brand-new pack of Djarum cigarettes and the phony baseball into the Atlantic Ocean after kissing Zena a final goodbye in my mind at JFK airport where I had dropped off Nicky and Willow and Max. How Max didn't cry, but left for Detroit like a champ. How life beez that way sometimes. Instead, I said, "I'm trying to quit cigarettes for the millionth time. It's hard. I'm sorry I ever started."

"*Sí,*" she said. "When you quit smoking, it's like losing a best friend. People who have never smoked don't understand. I tell my husband, think of giving up watching soccer forever because they discover it causes cancer. *La vida.*"

"Yeah," I said. "Life."

She dried my hair and guided me to a barber's chair, grabbing her clippers and scissors. Then my mother began to rhapsodize on one of her favorite subjects: cooking.

As my mother buzzed through my nappy locks she let loose

a culinary rat-a-tat-tat of ginger, coriander, paprika, oregano, *sofrito, achiote, arroz con pollo, plátanos, pasteles, gandules, garbanzos, sopa de pescado, sopón de garbanzos, patas de cerdo, chorizos, tostones, flan y tembleque*, cooked in sugar and cinnamon, *arróz con dulce*, coconut cream and coffee, real strong, real black, *café con leche*, rum and Coke, Don Q, always Don Q, and Pina Colada, and always Don Q. She ended my haircut with a square cut at the back, and told me her *mofongo* recipe:

> *3 green plantains*
> *4 cups of water*
> *1 spoon of salt*
> *3 garlic gloves*
> *1 teaspoon of olive oil*
> *½ pound of pork*
> *1 teaspoon of vegetable oil*

Jay Z came on over the radio rapping:

> *Half of Ya'll won't make It*

And then it was over, just like that. I paid my bill, gave her a good tip. She smiled and kissed me on the cheek and said, "Goodnight, *amor*."

"Goodnight," I said.

She knew I wouldn't be back. I knew I wouldn't be back. I don't know why my mother didn't acknowledge me or why I said nothing. Maybe I was, for her, something she didn't want to be reminded of, a sad past best left in the past. I could never come back. She had buried me. She had no use for ghosts.

Maybe I didn't either.

My mother was married again, had kids, a new husband, a business. She seemed alright. Me? I had four limbs and good eyes, a full belly, an office, and a roof over my head now in

Parkchester. There were real tragedies in the world. This wasn't one of them, I kept telling that lump in my throat, as I paid for my cut and went for the door.

It just felt like it.

No matter. Move along, Santana. There's nothing to see here.

Outside, a summer rain was coming down like a waterfall. The water beat on the Bronx in streams. I walked in the warm rain to the elevated 6 platform. I thought about visiting my father's grave. Adam Santana had taken his final ride in a white limo too many years ago. After the funeral mass, the mourners had met at Woodlawn Cemetery in the Bronx, where my father was buried, joining musical greats Duke Ellington and Miles Davis and some folks I knew personally. No. I would not make the trip to the 140-year-old cemetery. I had had enough of graveside visits. I'd be there myself, as the guest of honor, soon enough. I was both afraid and not afraid. There was loss, but there was something else too, something sweet and heavy, like forgiveness. And as someone once said, death would win in the end, but for today, no matter how I felt or didn't feel . . . For now, Woodlawn could wait.

That night I went to an old movie at the Film Forum downtown. Alone in the dark, in the shadow of the flickering light I could still see Max's wet brown eyes. I could still see her waving sadly as I walked out the sliding doors of JFK airport.

Max sucking on a candy ring in the shape of a diamond.

A college girl in a gray Hunter College sweatshirt with purple lettering chanted in the darkness, two seats behind me before the picture started, "Merrily, merrily, merrily, merrily . . ."

I worried about Max back in Detroit with a murdered father.

"It'll all be over in forty-five minutes," said the movie screen.

Later, I returned to Parkchester to a Chihuahua named Boo and an empty co-op apartment.

I never saw Joey Valentin or Pedro Sanchez again.

I never saw Zena Gupta, either.

It was over. Dust and faded kisses. We met with a crash and we ended with a crash. I remember Joey. *"I apologize if I caused you any trouble, Chico. I'm still learning."*

I remember Zena.

I can still taste her kiss and on certain nights when the air is wet and thick and hot enough I am overcome by memory and the scent of honeysuckle.

Better not to think about it . . .

"Goodnight, Chico."

Goodnight . . .

ACKNOWLEDGMENTS

Every book is a wrestling match against silence and the blank page. This book had four corner people: Caren Johnson, my agent; Carol Mangis, always my first; Emily Adler, my partner; and Toni Plummer, my editor at Thomas Dunne Books.

Thank you for being on my side . . .